Never Say Chai

BOOK FOUR IN THE TEA AND TAROT COZY MYSTERY SERIES

KIRSTEN WEISS

This book is a work of fiction. Names, characters and incidents are either the product of the author's imagination or are used factiously. Any resemblance to actual persons, living or dead, is entirely coincidental and not intended by the author.

Copyright ©2021 Kirsten Weiss. All rights reserved, including the right to reproduce this book, or portions thereof, in any form. No part of this text may be reproduced, transmitted, downloaded, decompiled, reverse engineered, or stored in or introduced into any information storage and retrieval system, in any form or by any means, whether electronic or mechanical without the express written permission of the author. The scanning, uploading, and distribution of this book via the Internet or via any other means without permission of the publisher is illegal and punishable by law. Please purchase only authorized electronic editions, and do not participate in or encourage electronic piracy of copyrighted materials.

Cover artist:

Visit the author website: www.kirstenweiss.com

Misterio Press mass market paperback edition / August, 2021
http://Misteriopress.com

ISBN-13: 978-1-944767-73-0

CHAPTER 1

Never panic-shop.

Also, never drink and shop. And *especially* never panic, drink, and shop.

I'd done all of the above.

The tearoom's oven had broken last month while I was baking quiches. The estimate for its repair had been nearly as much as a new oven. In a fit of panic and piña coladas, I'd bought a new one.

The thought still made my insides curdle like over-whipped cream. Industrial ovens ain't cheap.

I hated budget pandemonium, especially when I was its cause. There was a certain joy in watching numbers fall into place, especially on the profit side of the ledger. And I'd just messed with my carefully balanced tearoom universe.

So I was more than a little anxious as I studied the room. Miniature pumpkins lined its broad windows. Paper bats dangled from hanging lamps and sprouted from tiered tea trays.

Even the costumed Tarot readers had gotten into the Halloween groove. The scent of baking sugar and pumpkin hung in the air. Women chatted at their tables, teacups clinking.

It was October first, day one of the Halloween season, and San Borromeo (saint of heartburn) was becoming a Halloween town. This was a good thing for those of us dependent on tourism. Tourists don't flock to the Pacific beach quite as often in October, despite the occasional day of spectacular weather. The Halloween festivities meant more customers.

Beanblossom's Tea and Tarot needed those customers, especially after that new oven.

It was a really awesome oven, though.

A waitress hurried to the counter. "One pot of apple-blossom green."

I poured a pot of tea and handed it across the counter to her. She bustled to a table.

My business partner, Hyperion, slouched into the tearoom. In his black turtleneck and slacks, he looked like a depressed Dracula – the modern, sexy kind.

I tensed. Though he ran the Tarot side of the tearoom and left the rest to me, I hadn't actually told him how much I'd paid for the new oven yet. Or that I'd used my share of this month's marketing budget, and I was *still* in the hole.

Hyperion set an enormous plastic tube-like thing on the white-quartz counter.

"What's that?" I adjusted the monkey hanging from my belt. I'd dressed like a zookeeper, in a pith helmet and khakis. Little had I known the costume would be prophetic.

"A t-shirt cannon."

I puzzled over why a Tarot reader would need a t-shirt cannon. "Okay," I said slowly. "And the—"

My partner groaned. "I hate October." Hyperion rested his elbows on the counter and scraped his hands through his thick, dark hair. His handsome face twisted with despair, and he buried his head in his hands.

"Just because we can't serve Death tea for the season—"

"It's not the tea that's the problem."

"Then what?" We'd been creating a new Tarot-themed tea every month. For October, I'd gone with the Justice card, because it corresponded to Libra, an October sign. So did Scorpio, associated with the Death card. But Death tea was a no-go. I didn't want people to think we were poisoning them.

"October is cursed." Hyperion motioned vaguely around the tearoom. "It's even worse than Mercury retrograde. My readings are always off around Halloween. Nothing goes right." He cocked his dark head. "Though the costumes *are* amazing."

"What's your beef with October? Did something happen?"

"Something always happens," he said. "That's the point of a Halloween curse."

"I meant recently."

"No." His shoulders caved inward, and he dropped his chin, a picture of misery.

An elderly lady rose from her table. Leaning heavily on her walker, she made her way toward the door.

"Hold that thought." I hurried to open the door for her.

"Thank you," she said. "There's my ride share." She nodded toward a blue Hyundai.

"Let me get that." I opened the passenger door and glanced at the driver.

"Mrs. Sterling?" the driver asked.

"She'll be just a minute." I helped Mrs. Sterling inside the car and folded her walker. The driver stepped out and put it in the trunk.

"Getting old is chaos," the old lady said. "Everything you expect to work, doesn't. Take my advice, it's best to lower expectations." She chuckled.

I smiled and waved and watched them drive away, then returned inside the tearoom.

Hyperion was still drooping over the counter and bringing down the tearoom's cheerful Halloween tone.

"Okay," I said. "What's up?"

He sighed. "Nothing."

"Then there's something I need to tell you. About the new oven—"

"Forget your prize oven." He flicked the idea away with one hand. "Everyone knows what a spectacular oven it is. It's the prince of darkness of ovens, okay? What do I care about ovens when my humiliation is probably all over town by now?"

With a supreme effort of will, I did not roll my eyes. "Humiliation?"

He straightened and met my gaze. "Tony. He stood me up last night."

Oh. Ow. "I'm sure he had a good reason."

Hyperion glared.

"Like a police emergency," I said hastily. Detective Tony Chase was nothing if not dedicated to his job.

"Well if he did, he didn't tell *me.*"

"You mean, not even a phone call?" I asked. Tony was also reliable. He'd never leave Hyperion hanging.

"Not a peep. And yes, I tried calling him, even if it did make me look like a desperate tween. And no, he hasn't returned my calls—my call," he amended.

Hyperion really had it bad if he'd phoned more than once. "That doesn't sound like Tony."

"I didn't think so either." He kicked the base of the bar the way a child would, aimlessly and repetitively. A teacup atop it rattled. "Seems we were both wrong."

I rested my hand on the empty cup, stilling it. "Maybe—"

The front door swung open hard enough to bang against the wall behind it, and we jumped.

Tony Chase strode into the tearoom, his navy suit jacket and jeans wrinkled, as if he'd slept in them. Beneath his cowboy hat, his hair looked more rumpled than usual. His normally smooth face was unshaven.

"There." I motioned toward Tony. "He's come to explain."

Hyperion grabbed the t-shirt cannon and aimed it at the detective.

Ignoring the hostess and Hyperion, Tony hurried to the counter and loomed. That's actually not much of a feat. He's well over six-feet-tall. I'm only five-four, with long, curling blond hair. When people call me a doll, it isn't a compliment. Years ago I cut my hair short. People started calling me a pixie. I let my hair grow back out.

"What happened at the tearoom yesterday?" he asked in his Texas drawl.

Hyperion raised the cannon higher. "I have no idea what you're talking about."

I edged farther behind the counter, blinking. The detective's eyes were so red my own itched in a sympathy response.

"Not now, Hyperion." The detective's tone took on a sharp edge. "I was talking to Abigail."

I started. "Me?"

"I bought a cup of chai." Tony pressed his hands on the white quartz, leaning closer. "Like I do every Saturday."

I nodded. The detective was a creature of habit. Even the Tarot readers joked about his Saturday chai. They mainly did it to try to get Hyperion to blush. It never worked. My partner was blush proof.

"Then what happened?" the detective demanded.

"Seriously?" Hyperion's finger twitched on the trigger. "This is what we're talking about? Chai?"

"Um." My gaze darted between the two men. "Next I... gave you the chai." Chai had always seemed like an odd choice for a man like Tony. I'd figured him for black coffee. But I guess the Texan liked things spicy.

"And then what?" Tony asked.

"And then you left," I said.

"How did I leave?"

"The usual way," I said. "On foot, out the back." I pointed to the hallway that led to the rear parking lot.

"Did I drink the chai?"

"I... guess?" I said, baffled. "Why? What's going on?"

He turned toward Hyperion. "Did you see me leave?"

"Forget yesterday afternoon," my partner said. "Where were you last night?"

"I don't know," Tony said.

Hyperion's skin turned a darker hue. "You didn't answer my calls. I got worried and went to your house."

"Was I there?" Tony asked.

My partner's brown eyes bulged. "Don't you know?"

Tony fisted his hands. He closed his eyes, sighed, and dropped his hands to his sides. "No. That's what I'm trying to tell you. I don't remember anything since buying a cup of chai from Abigail."

Hyperion's brows slashed downward. "So you're telling me that the reason you stood me up last night was… amnesia? I've never heard *that* one before."

"I'm telling you that I don't remember anything since I was here, in this tearoom." The detective's voice rose. "And when I woke up, I was in a ditch beside a dead man."

The tearoom fell silent. Heads turned toward the counter.

Hyperion lowered the cannon.

I swallowed. "Maybe we should have this conversation in Hyperion's office," I said in a low voice.

"I told you, there's no time." Tony reached across the white counter and gripped my shoulders. "What the hell happened to me? Was there anyone unusual in the tearoom? Did anything strange happen while I was here?"

"N-no," I stammered.

"Nothing?" He released me, and I staggered back a little.

"No, nothing." *Had* there been? I wracked my brain. "Well, there was this witch, I mean a woman in a witch costume. It seemed a little early for costumes, but only by a day."

"What did she look like? Did she come near me?"

"She did come to the counter," I said. "She was wearing a mask. You know, green face, hooked nose, warts. A witch," I finished weakly. "She was about my height."

Tony looked down at his cowboy boots. "So it could have been anyone. What did she say?"

"Nothing." And that *had* been a little weird. "She just pointed to the menu to order."

"How'd she eat through the mask?" Tony asked.

I grimaced. "She didn't. She took her order to go." I should have *known* something was off.

"How'd she pay?" Tony demanded.

"Cash," I said. "She left a twenty on the bar." And who pays cash in Silicon Valley? Why hadn't I been more suspicious?

"Did you see her leave?"

"No."

"Dammit." He turned, scanning the tearoom. "Who else was working that day?"

"Sierra, Janet, Maricel—"

The front door opened, and three men walked inside. Two were in police uniforms. One beefy man wore a business suit that screamed *underpaid detective.*

My shoulders caved inward. Paper bats aside, the tearoom was supposed to be calm and genteel. Police interrogations were neither, and this seemed like a lot of cops to grill my staff.

"I need to talk to the staff who were here yesterday," Tony said to me.

"Sure," I said. "Maricel and Janet are here now."

"Sierra's not working today," Hyperion said.

"Detective Chase," the man in the brown suit said. "You need to come with us."

"I'm a little busy," Tony said, terse.

"Not anymore," the big man said. "You're under arrest."

CHAPTER 2

"Arrest?" I blurted. "But *he's* the police."

The detective in the brown suit glanced at me. "You're under arrest," he repeated. "For the murder of Cassius Santori."

There was a collective gasp and a whomp. The t-shirt cannon jerked in Hyperion's arms. A t-shirt bulleted into the air, hit a chandelier, and dropped onto the beefy detective's shoulder.

Paper bats fluttered to the floor. The chandelier swayed, tinkling. Hyperion turned three shades paler.

The detective pulled the t-shirt free and let it drop to the laminate floor. From the chandelier, bats jerked spastically, hanged men in their death throes.

Tony gripped Hyperion's shoulder. "Sorry about last night." He nodded to the three cops. "Let's go."

I stared. *This isn't happening.* But it was happening. Tony walked toward the other policemen, his movements sure and inevitable.

Helpless anger sparked inside me, and my jaw tightened. This wasn't *right*. "But—"

The men strode from the tearoom. The blue door closed behind them, its bell jingling.

An elderly customer in a pearl necklace adjusted her cardigan. "And my husband thinks tearooms are staid and stuffy. You can never say *this* place is dull."

Hyperion swayed, still clutching the t-shirt cannon.

"Come on." I gripped his arm and steered Hyperion down the hallway and to his private office. Orange and purple twinkle lights flashed erratically around the door. I led him inside and shut the door behind us.

Bastet, Hyperion's cat, looked up from the makeshift altar against the wall. Hyperion had littered it with crystals, candles, and driftwood, so it was a squeeze for the massive tabby. The cat's golden eyes narrowed, its tail coiling around a length of driftwood.

Hyperion dropped into a high-backed, red velvet chair. He wasn't a small man, a good five-eleven, thin, but muscled. But today, in that tall chair, he appeared shrunken. "Murder?" he whispered.

"It's a mistake," I said, brisk. It had to be, because the alternative was unthinkable. Tony was one of the white hats.

But what if he wasn't? A wave of guilt buffeted me. Tony had saved my life. Twice. He'd saved us all. How could I doubt him?

Short answer: I couldn't. He deserved my faith.

Hyperion gripped his forehead with one slender hand. "How could I have been so stupid?"

Bastet sneezed and dropped lightly from the altar and prowled to his master. He rubbed against Hyperion's leg, depositing orange and white hairs on his elegant black slacks.

"You're not," I said. "Because Tony didn't kill anyone."

His head dropped back against the thronelike chair. His gaze lifted to the ceiling. "Of *course* he wouldn't have stood me up."

I pressed my lips together. *That* was what Hyperion was worried about?

"Or murder anyone," he added hastily. He sunk, unspeaking, in his chair.

Since I'd known Hyperion, his relationship with Tony was the first I'd classify as serious. No wonder this was hitting him hard.

Finally, Hyperion straightened in the chair. "Yes," he said, as if to himself, and met my gaze. "Yes. I'm going to help him."

I nodded. And I would help Hyperion. And yes, I know that's a weird thing for a tearoom owner to decide. But Hyperion and I had done this sort of thing before. More importantly, Tony was a friend, and I owed him.

I owed Hyperion too. I couldn't imagine a better business partner. Even if last Independence Day he had "accidentally" shot off a firework in the back hallway. And last Columbus Day he'd volunteered me as a prize in one of those bid-on-a-date charity events. (He'd told me they'd be bidding on one of our Royal Teas, not on *me*.)

But in this moment, he was the serious, thoughtful, best-person-to-have-at-your-side Hyperion. I loved the devil-may-care Hyperion, but it was *this* Hyperion that suddenly made my vision blur.

"They didn't handcuff him," I said. "Even the police must have doubts. He's one of their own. They'll be careful."

He shook his head, a brief, sharp motion. "It doesn't matter what the police think. Whether he's charged or not will come down to the new DA. And he hates cops."

The new district attorney had been elected by the simple expedients of running unopposed and public indifference. Now he was refusing to prosecute a raft of crimes that he deemed petty, although I doubted the victims would agree.

And I'd heard grumbling that maybe the new guy might be anti-police. While I don't think cops are perfect—they're human—Tony was on the job to protect and serve. "It… does seem that he's not always on their side," I admitted, troubled.

Bastet's striped tail swished.

My partner dragged his hands down his face. "In spite of my cool demeanor, I confess I'm having a hard time concentrating on what to do next."

"Then why don't we start by keeping it simple—for now—and assume everything Tony told us was true."

"Of course it's true," he said sharply.

"Right. He doesn't remember anything since I handed him a cup of chai yesterday. How does that happen?"

"He didn't say anything about having a headache." Hyperion drummed his fingers on the arm of the chair. "So he probably wasn't bashed over the skull. If he'd gotten hit that hard, he'd still be feeling it."

I thought about those reddened eyes. "Could Tony have been drugged?"

Hyperion nodded slowly. "That seems to be what Tony thinks, or he wouldn't have been going on about that chai."

"The police will have to do a drug test. That will give us a better idea of what happened."

"I suppose that witch you mentioned could have done it, slipped something into his tea?"

"We can't be sure the chai was tampered with. But if something was slipped into his chai, then either she did it or I did it. And I didn't do it. Though I guess the police will have to consider me a suspect too." But I wasn't worried. I had no motive. They'd look at me, make things uncomfortable, and move on. I'd survive.

"Don't be absurd. *You* don't have any connection to Cassius Santori." He shifted in his high-backed chair.

"Does Tony?"

Hyperion drew his dark brows downward. "Not that I know of. And if he had, he would have mentioned something to us, right?"

"Maybe. He didn't have much time to say anything."

"It doesn't matter if Tony had a connection to—" He shook his head.

"Okay. Logic. Tony was drugged, and then what?"

"We'll have to learn more about the actual crime. But what are we saying?" I scooted my chair closer to the round table, catching the tablecloth and dragging it closer. "That Tony was framed? That the killer had a grudge against him?"

"He must have been. Tony was drugged—obvs. A man was killed and his body was put beside Tony's. We both know Tony didn't kill anyone. Lately. So it's got to be a frameup."

"Okay, but the killer would have to be a total psycho to kill an innocent person just to frame Tony. So—"

"So the killer had a grudge against Tony *and* Cassius." Hyperion nodded and rubbed his long hands together. "All we have to do is find out what that connection is, who hated them both. Easy peasy."

Sure, it was so easy, the cops had to be on that track. But that didn't mean that we couldn't be on it too.

"Let's start with the victim." I nodded toward the laptop on the table. "Has the news reported on the murder?"

Hyperion opened the computer and tapped the keyboard. He squinted at the screen, reading, and nodded. "Here's something, but it's not very informative." He turned the computer to face me and shoved it toward me, rumpling the tablecloth.

I pulled the laptop closer and read.

Local businessman, Cassius Santori, was found dead last night on Avila Road in what appears to have been a road rage incident. Anyone with information should contact the San Borromeo Police Department.

I grunted, disappointed. The article was so brief it was nearly useless. But road rage? Where had they gotten that idea?

"It's probably too soon for much of an article about the death," I said. "The papers will have more tomorrow." I returned to the search results. "Here's Santori's website. He's a financial consultant, whatever that is."

Hyperion sank back in his chair.

I opened the site. "Retirement, wealth management, holistic planning, insurance... He's got a partner, Johnson Warszowski." And from his smiling photo, Johnson was a devastatingly handsome guy. But this wasn't the time to mention that to Hyperion.

"Excellent," Hyperion said. "We have our first suspect. I'm thinking, business relationship gone south? Someone cheating on someone else's spouse? If they work with money, there have got to be all sorts of motives for murder."

I studied the site. "Cool, there's an address..." I lifted my head and studied Hyperion.

He examined his nails.

"It's in your old office building," I said.

"That will give us an excuse to pay our condolences." He sucked in his breath. "What if Tony doesn't have a lawyer?"

"There's a police union. I'm sure he's got representation. And Cassius worked in your *old office building*."

"So we shared a building. It's not *that* big of a coincidence. This is a small town. Everyone knows everyone. And what if Tony's union lawyer is no good? I need to talk to Tomas." Lifting his hip, Hyperion pulled his cellphone from the rear pocket of his slacks. He dialed, waited, and blew out his breath. "He's not answering."

"I know where he is." Tomas Salazar was a semi-retired lawyer and my grandfather's best friend. I'd grown up calling him uncle and attending raucous picnics with his ginormous family.

"Don't keep me in suspense," he said. "Where is he?"

"At my grandfather's. It's October first. They're putting up the Halloween decorations today."

Hyperion leapt from the chair. It wobbled, nearly falling. "Let's go." Ignoring the cat's irate meows, he hurried from his office.

I made a quick stop in the kitchen. I'd planned to take a frozen lasagna over to my grandfather tonight anyway, and had kept it in the tearoom freezer. I grabbed the lasagna then followed him down the hallway and out into Beanblossom's rear parking lot.

We climbed into his green Jeep, and Hyperion and I blasted onto the narrow street.

I clutched the door arm and squeezed shut my eyes. At the best of times, Hyperion's driving is enthusiastic. His speed today made me crave valium. And I've never had valium in my life.

But we made it to my grandfather's cul-de-sac intact. Hyperion screeched to a halt in front of the driveway to the storybook house. I pried my hand from the grab bar.

Tomas sat in a lawn chair in the front yard, my grandfather's mallard, Peking, nestled in his lap. A familiar blond-haired figure stood on a ladder and strung orange lights beneath the turret's sloping eaves, covered in the wavy shingles so typical of the style.

I pointed. "What's Brik doing here?" My grandfather's house was supposed to be a protected, happy space, with ducks and lasagna. Now I was as tense as the cables on the Golden Gate Bridge.

"Do the math. It looks like Brik's helping with the decorating." Hyperion opened the Jeep door and hopped out. "Tomas!" He trotted toward the elderly man in the lawn chair.

The arched front door to my grandfather's house opened. Gramps toddled out carrying a plastic box.

I hurried to help before my grandfather tripped over one of the pumpkins lining the steps. "Let me take that." Casserole dish braced on my hip, I reached for the box with my free hand.

"I've got it, but thanks, Abigail." Gramps set the box down on the flagstone pathway, and we hugged, his cheek scratchy against mine. "This is a nice surprise. Is that lasagna? And shouldn't you be at the tearoom?"

I glanced at Brik, still on the ladder, his back to me like that night he'd walked away. *Whatever's between us has to end.*

And it *had* ended. Though it would *feel* a lot more ended if he wasn't always popping into my life.

But maybe that wasn't the issue. Maybe I was hanging on. Maybe I just didn't want to be alone anymore. The thought flooded me with shame.

"It *is* lasagna," I said. "Um, what's my neighbor doing here?"

"I was at Brik's party the other night—"

"What?" My grandfather had gone to a party next door and hadn't stopped by? Hurt, I tugged down my zookeeper's vest.

"You weren't home, or I would have come in."

"Wait, aren't you still on medication for that infection? Can you drink?"

"Not alcohol, no. So I had a beer."

My mouth puckered. "That's—" *Never mind.* Gramps was an adult. He made his own choices. I wouldn't insult him by scolding him like a child.

"Anyway," he continued, "I was complaining to Brik about the decorating. Ladders aren't so easy to manage when you're getting up in years. He offered to help. You know how the kids love to visit this house on Halloween."

"Yeah, because you give out full-sized candy bars."

But it *was* a cool Halloween house, like something out of the Brothers Grimm. San Borromeo had many of these storybook homes, and even some businesses in the style. And I was sure Brik was only helping out of the goodness of his heart and not to get under my skin.

But Brik was totally getting under my skin. Also, my hands were starting to freeze.

"Tony Chase has been arrested for murder," I said.

My grandfather blinked. "Detective Chase? Who'd he kill?"

"He didn't. I mean, he couldn't." I set the lasagna on the edge of a raised stone bed and rubbed my hands together to warm them.

Gramps sighed. "We all have the potential for violence. Though Detective Chase doesn't seem the type to lose his cool. What happened?"

Brik clambered down from the ladder. Squinting up at the peaked roof, my neighbor brushed off his broad hands.

I told my grandfather about the scene in the tearoom. "Hyperion wanted to ask Tomas's advice." I angled my head toward the two men in their lawn chairs.

Gramps shook his head. "Not sure it will do much good. Tomas doesn't know that new DA like he did the last one."

I lowered my head and studied the flagstones. "Oh." I hadn't even thought of that.

"What's going on?" Brik asked.

I pasted on a smile and turned toward my neighbor/contractor/pain in my backside. Then I realized smiling was inappropriate under the murdery circumstances and smoothed my expression. "Tony Chase has been arrested for murder," I said stiffly. Because I was over Brik.

Completely over.

Done.

But it bugged me that he was having a grand old time with my relatives. And yes, I knew that was unreasonable.

But still.

Brik's face spasmed. "Oh."

That was all he had to say? *Oh?* "He didn't do it," I said, annoyed. Because Tony had once saved Brik too.

"Huh."

How could Brik be so... casual? I grabbed the lasagna and took it into my grandfather's kitchen. Then I returned to the front yard and stomped across the lawn to Tomas, Peking, and Hyperion.

The duck's feathers stood up in angry tufts. The mallard glared at Hyperion.

I know. *Weird.*

Tomas petted the duck, smoothing his feathers. "Bastet will come to see you next time."

"Honestly," Hyperion told the duck. "Bastet has a cold. I couldn't bring a sneezing cat. He needs his rest. That's why I left him at the tearoom."

I'd have preferred Hyperion didn't leave his cat in the tearoom under any circumstances. But that was a battle I'd long ago given up on winning.

"So?" I asked Tomas. "What do you think?"

"I think your grandfather's duck has a very strange relationship with Hyperion's cat."

"Not about Peking," I said, "about Tony."

"As I told Hyperion, he'll have a union rep and a union lawyer, if he wants one. The police will be looking for a personal connection between Tony and the victim, for a motive."

"The paper said it may have been road rage," I said doubtfully.

Tomas snorted. "Road rage? Detective Chase? He's one of the coolest customers I've met. That's just speculation by reporters. Like I said, they'll be looking for connections, and I'm sure Chase doesn't have one."

Hyperion gulped. "The thing is... *I* sort of do."

"Just because you were once tenants in the same building doesn't mean you're connected," I said.

"It's, ah, more than that," my partner said.

My eyes narrowed. "More than that, how?"

"Cassius and I might have... dated."

CHAPTER 3

I paced outside the doors of the squat, concrete building. Fog had turned the sky mercury, swaddling Hyperion's old office building like a cold, damp blanket and chilling my skin. I adjusted the soft, olive-colored scarf around my neck.

It was Monday, my day off, and the tearoom was closed. I'd been too wired to sleep in, automatically awakening to greet the stupid sunrise. I wanted to be the kind of person who could lounge in bed. Instead, I was the kind of person who loitered in front of buildings at odd hours. We all have our crosses to bear.

A woman pushed a stroller past me and shot me a wary look. I leapt to open the glass doors for her, and she walked inside.

Insides jittering, I checked the clock on my phone.

Hyperion was late. And he usually wasn't.

I pulled my bomber jacket tighter and inhaled to calm myself. The air still smelled like Pacific morning, though the sun had risen hours ago. The building stood in a depression, a swell of hill blocking the ocean view. I caught a whiff of what smelled like pizza.

Mm. Pizza.

I shifted my weight, and a sense of claustrophobia—which I don't usually have—settled on my chest.

A man exiting the building glanced at me and got into a sports car, backed out.

I tapped the screen to call my partner.

Hyperion's green Jeep whipped into the spot the sports car had just vacated. The parking gods really did favor my partner.

The jerks.

He jogged toward me carrying a bouquet of flowers, the tails of his charcoal blazer flapping. He looked professional and somber in his matching turtleneck and slacks.

"Everything okay?" I asked.

"Fine," he said shortly. "Let's do this." He held open the door.

I walked inside the low-ceilinged seventies-style entry. It had been updated since Hyperion had moved out. Its seventies vibe had turned chic. Along one wall stood aqua sofas accented with striped, white-and-gray pillows. An open stairway with a gardenlike area beneath it rose to the second floor.

I walked to a corrugated signboard and scanned the listings. "Warszowski and Santori are on the fourth floor." I turned to Hyperion.

He was already jogging up the stairs. "Never trusted that elevator," he called.

I followed Hyperion upstairs and inside a cheerful office in turquoises, greens, and yellows. A couch pressed against the wall opposite the reception desk. Its cushions were thin, rectangular, and uncomfortable looking.

A voluptuous redhead in her early thirties looked up from a modular, blond-wood desk and smiled wanly. She wore a black-and-white checked business suit and made it look like high fashion. "Hello, Hyperion." She also had the high cheekbones of a supermodel.

And yes, I *was* a little jealous. I bet she was tall, too.

He handed her the flowers. "Verena, I'm so sorry for your loss. Please accept my condolences."

"You two know each other?" I asked. Hyperion hadn't mentioned if other people in Santori's office had known about their relationship.

"We *did* share a building." Hyperion motioned toward me. "This is my new business partner, Abigail Beanblossom."

"Hello," Verena said to me. "I've been meaning to stop by your tearoom, but we've been so busy." She motioned toward a closed office door, the thick, gold bangle on her wrist catching the light.

"It's nice to meet you," I said, "though the circumstances are terrible. I'm so sorry for your loss. It's hard to believe something like this could happen in San Borromeo."

"I know." Verena sniffled and grabbed a tissue from a box on the desk. "I moved here because it was *safe*."

"Have the police talked to you yet?" Hyperion asked.

"No." Verena blotted the corners of her eyes. "And I doubt they will. Why would they? I don't know anything. And Johnson told me they had someone in custody."

I frowned, my insides tightening. Were the police so certain they had the right guy that they weren't bothering to interview her? Or would the interviews come later?

"They talked to Johnson?" Hyperion asked.

"Yes." She glanced again at the closed door. "He told me they came by last night, after I'd left."

I shifted my weight. At least they'd talked to his business partner. That sounded like they considered the murder something more than road rage. Or that they were trying to find a connection between Tony and the victim.

"I suppose they wanted to know if there was any personal connection between the suspect and Mr. Santori. To determine motive," I said. "I wonder if they'll be looking at other people who had a grudge against Mr. Santori? Maybe clients?" I hinted.

"We didn't get many of those." Verena pushed a section of wayward red hair behind her ear. "Unhappy clients, I mean. And we *never* had any with Johnson. He's excellent with people."

"But it *has* happened with Cassius?" Hyperion asked.

She grimaced. "Once or twice."

Hyperion sat against the edge of the blond-wood desk. "Tell me *all* the gory details."

"I shouldn't," she said uncertainly.

"Cassius is dead," Hyperion said in a gossipy tone. There was no one better at getting someone to dish than Hyperion.

"This is murder," he continued. "Of course you should talk. The police may not be asking you about angry clients yet, but they will." He lowered his voice. "We've heard they've got the wrong man."

"But that's terrible." She flushed and pressed one hand to her cheek. "And it's terrible that I thought it was terrible because the killer might still be running around, putting us in danger, not because of a poor man who's been wrongly accused."

"You're only human," Hyperion said. "At least you're self-aware. Most people aren't. Now what about those angry clients?"

She glanced toward a glass-walled meeting room. "Only last week, one of his clients, Mr. Grief, got a little shouty."

"About what?" Hyperion asked, breathless.

She leaned closer. "I couldn't hear the details. The glass is insulated."

"Talk about inconvenient," Hyperion said.

"Cassius was angry, too, though. After Mr. Grief left, Cassius stormed from the office. That was always his problem. Cassius had no patience. People get nervous about money. But it's their *money*. You have to project confidence and be patient, like Johnson."

"And the other client?" I prompted.

She blinked. "What?"

"You said it happened once or twice," I said. "Who was the other person? Or people?"

"Just one other." She bit her bottom lip.

"Do tell." On the edge of the desk, Hyperion bent closer.

"You can't blame Johnson," she whispered. "He was supposed to be in the meeting, but he couldn't, there was an emergency, and he had to leave Cassius on his own."

"No way that was Johnson's fault." Hyperion folded his arms.

"Exactly," she said. "Cassius should be able to handle client meetings on his own. He's a partner in the business, but like I said, he had no patience. And Dr. Tarrach is a big client."

"This Dr. Tarrach was upset about his, er, financial management?" I asked.

She shrugged. "I couldn't hear the details, only the raised voices. But then Johnson called him later. He must have smoothed things over, because we're still managing the funds. I haven't heard of any problems since."

"What kind of doctor is he?" I asked.

"A dentist."

"When was this?" Hyperion asked.

"About a month ago," she said, "or maybe six weeks."

"Any other clients who lost their minds?" Hyperion asked.

"Not that I know of," she said. "Are you sure the police have the wrong man?"

Hyperion drew breath to speak.

"Is Johnson in?" I asked quickly. "We'd like to give him our condolences."

Her brows lowered. "I'm sorry. He's not available."

"We can wait," Hyperion said, grim.

"But he's not in right now." She shook her head, her cheeks pinking.

"When will he be back?" he asked.

She lowered her chin. "I can leave a message for him, if you like," she said firmly.

"When would be a good time for us to return?" I asked.

"He has a very busy schedule." She laid her hand atop a leather planner. "Would you like me to leave a message?"

"No thanks," I said. "We'll catch up with him later."

I drew Hyperion from the office and we stopped outside a closed door opposite. "I don't think she knows when he's coming in today."

"That must be killing her," he muttered. "What are you thinking?"

"I could really go for some pizza."

"At this hour?"

"I know. Inappropriate. You wanted to talk about—"

The door opened beside us, and a man with the face of an Adonis and body of an Olympian swimmer looked blandly out. His hair was curling and thick and nearly as dark as his eyes.

I stared back, my heart thudding. He had to be gay. This was California, and men that good looking had to be gay. Also, I'd forgotten how much I'd liked the look of a man in a business suit. Brik never wore suits.

"Do you mind?" the man asked.

With a start, I realized I was staring—and probably drooling. I stepped aside.

The man strode past us and jogged down the stairs.

"Now there's a tall drink of water," Hyperion said.

I swallowed. "Yeah."

He sighed. "Too bad he's not my type."

"Right," I said, watching the empty stairs. "Because you're taken."

"That, and he's straight as an arrow."

"And likely married."

"No, he's single. Odds are he's got a girlfriend though. Or dozens."

"Yeah. Right." This was dumb. A man that attractive couldn't possibly be trustworthy. Plus, he'd looked at me like I was a bug.

I cleared my throat. "But since his office is so close to the victim's, maybe he heard or saw something useful."

Hyperion gave me a long look.

My face warmed.

Hyperion nodded, his expression calculating. "Perhaps we should find out. But you know what that means."

"I'm guessing it doesn't mean free pizza."

"It's going to be a long, pizza-free day."

CHAPTER 4

"It's not as if we have anything better to do right now. Monday's our day off." Hyperion pushed a mug of coffee toward me across the rickety table. Behind his head was a bulletin board covered in flyers. They advertised everything from energy healing to a school play.

We sat in a blink-and-you-miss-it café across the street from Hyperion's old building. The bear claws were spectacular, so I forgave the "nothing-better-to-do" comment.

Also, he'd been acting snarkier than normal, and it wasn't hard to guess why.

I squinted at my phone. "I'm just saying, Johnson may not come back until this afternoon. Or he may not return today at all."

"Verena was expecting him. I could tell."

I typed in Lafayette Grief's name. "Have you heard from Tony?"

Hyperion's expression shuttered. "He's in jail. There isn't a whole lot to hear."

I caught on and shut up. Even I could take a hint when it bludgeoned me over the head.

"Hey," I said. "It says here that Lafayette—"

"Has an office in my old building too. I know."

I pocketed the phone. "You could have told me that before I gave myself eyestrain. What about that dentist, Dr. Tarrach?"

"No idea. There aren't any medical offices in that building."

I cleared my throat. "So you dated Cassius."

"We went out twice. If you want my impressions of the man, I only learned the fake stuff."

"By which you mean...?"

"The best-foot-forward stuff. The first and second date phoniness." His expression shifted to regret. "That's what made everything with Tony so... right. We knew each other before we went out. No one had to put on an act."

I pretended I hadn't noticed the past tense. "I hate dating. It's so much easier when you just get to know someone, no pressure, and realize you'd be good for each other."

I thought of Brik, hanging out on my back porch with Gramps and Tomas. We'd been friends then. But that hadn't ended well. I scrubbed a hand over my face. Maybe I *should* give dating another try. But dating was so… awkward.

"I find that hard to believe," he said.

I blinked. "What?"

"That you hate dating. Because you were eyeing Gino like he was a juicy cut of steak."

"I *do* like a good steak." Gramps could barbecue them like nobody's business. And with his horseradish on top…? Perfection. "Who's Gino?"

"Gino Redmond. The sexy estate attorney in office four-oh-six."

"Oh. I couldn't possibly date a Gino," I said loftily. "Too mobster-y."

He rolled his eyes. "Sure you couldn't."

"Anyway," I said, "you went out with Cassius twice…?"

"And still have no idea what the connection could be between Cassius and Tony. They aren't his financial advisor. He uses some guy with the police union. The only connection is… me." His shoulders caved inward. "It's ironic—" His mouth clamped shut.

"What?"

"Life."

That hadn't been what he'd started to say, but I let it lie. "You're not responsible for what happened," I said.

"How do we know that?" he asked, his voice bitter.

"*I* know." As a child, I'd been abandoned by two narcissistic parents. I knew what responsibility-dodging looked like. This wasn't it.

They'd left me at an airport. I'd been small enough that my legs had stuck straight out over the end of the chair. I'd sat and studied the tiny white, decorative holes punched into my shoes' white leather for what had felt like forever, scared and—

A hot wave of fury swelled inside me, and I slowly, carefully exhaled it away. My parents still refused to take responsibility for anything, including themselves. Every time I thought I was over it…

I swallowed. "There's only one person responsible," I continued, "and that's the killer. Unless he has an accomplice, and then there are two people responsible. And you're not either of them."

"I adore your moral clarity, Abs, but it's not that simple."

"Why can't it be simple? Why does it have to be morally confusing? The whole point of morals is to lessen the confusion."

"I don't like—" He shook his head.

I picked at the remains of a bear claw. "Don't like what?"

"Never mind."

"Fine," I said. "What do the cards say?"

"I told you, they're useless the closer we get to Halloween."

"Try."

He shrugged and drew a small pack of Tarot cards from the pocket of his charcoal blazer. "Fine, but mark my words, there will be tears." He shuffled them roughly, laid three on the wobbly table, and turned them over.

The first card depicted a woman sitting up in bed, her head in her hands, nine swords surrounding her. It was the card of nightmare, but one mainly caused by one's own roiling thoughts.

Next, a man with ten swords plunged into his back. Disaster, but something that looks worse than it is. And it was a ten, so it was an ending.

Finally, the Ten of Wands, a man slogging down a road, ten rods on his back. The card meant a heavy burden, but as a ten it also represented the end of one phase and the beginning of a new one.

"Well?" I asked. Sure, I could read the cards. But Hyperion was the pro, and I didn't want to step on my partner's toes.

"It's like I told you." Hyperion motioned to the cards. "They make zero sense."

The cards told *me* that Hyperion needed to get out of his head to see things clearly. He had a rough road ahead, but there was light at the end of the tunnel. We just didn't know what that light was yet — freedom for Tony or... moving on.

"Yeah." I nodded. "*Zero* sense."

A silver Mercedes pulled into the lot across the street, and Hyperion straightened, watching.

A handsome blond man in a navy business suit stepped from the car.

Johnson. The photo from their website hadn't done him justice. He was even better looking in person.

"That's Cassius's partner," Hyperion said. "Come on."

We rose and hurried to the coffeeshop's exit.

Snick. One end of the garland of bats strung across the door sprang loose. Paper spiders fluttered downward and tangled in Hyperion's hair.

"Even the décor is out to get me this month." Roughly, he brushed the bats aside. "Stupid thinning of the veil."

He stumbled onto the sidewalk.

A blue sports car screeched into the parking lot opposite and parked across two spaces. A silvery-haired woman leapt from the car and stalked inside.

"That sort of careless parking is why it's so hard to find a spot in San Borromeo." I thrust my finger toward the sports car.

"I never have a problem."

"Yeah, yeah, yeah." It was true. He never did.

We returned inside the building and climbed the steps to the fourth floor.

I tried not to breathe loudly when we reached the top. Okay, so maybe I was a little out of shape. But who has time for aerobics when you're running a tearoom?

Hyperion opened the office door, and ushered me inside.

Verena, behind the desk, didn't seem to notice us. Her blue-eyed gaze was glued to a closed door at the other end of the reception room.

"What do you MEAN he changed the policy?" a woman shouted from behind the door.

Verena winced.

"Is Johnson back?" Hyperion asked brightly.

The receptionist tore her gaze from the office door. "What? Oh. Yes. But he's in a, er, meeting."

"He can't DO that," the woman yelled.

Hyperion sidled to the desk. "Problem?"

"It's Cassius's wife," Verena whispered. "I mean his widow."

Wife? But he'd dated Hyperion. I glanced at Hyperion, and my partner's face turned scarlet. He looked away. So I guess he wasn't blush-proof after all.

"Poor Carla," Verena continued. "She's really upset."

"No one's at their best when they've lost a loved one," I said.

The receptionist shot me a doubtful look.

Someone flung the door open, rattling a painting of a sailboat. One corner of the frame canted downward.

A tanned woman in a *Caffeine Queen* t-shirt and clingy gray skirt stormed from the office. The skirt rounded over her gentle curves. Her hair skimmed her shoulders in soft, mercury kinks.

She whirled to face the open office door. "This isn't over, Johnson." Carla glanced at us. "Ha. You think you're in good hands? Get out while you can."

"Oh, they're not clients," Verena said. "They're just here to give condolences."

The wife gave me a longer, sharp-eyed look. She brushed past us and out the door, slamming that as well.

"So," Hyperion said brightly. "Is Johnson free now?"

"I'll just..." Verena leapt up and scuttled toward the office. She nearly careened into Johnson, on his way out, and dammit, Verena really *was* tall. Some people had all the luck.

Johnson's chiseled face wore a stunned expression. "Verena, get the insurance paperwork for Cassius, will you?" He frowned at us. "Who—?"

Hyperion leapt forward and grasped his hand. "We came to extend our condolences. I don't know if you remember me, I'm Hyperion Night, third floor. Tarot consultant."

Johnson blinked rapidly. He was a white man – the stereotypical California blond. Fit. Tanned. Blue-eyed. And dressed to kill in a designer suit.

"Oh," he said. "Right. Sorry. I remember you. Come in." He turned and walked into his office.

I shrugged and followed Hyperion inside, Verena hot on my heels.

"Johnson," she said. "Can I get you anything?"

"I'll have coffee, thanks." He sat behind his desk and glanced at Hyperion and me. "Would you like anything?"

Framed ancient Egyptian-style papyrus paintings hung behind him. Actual papyrus plants in a gray, narrow and rectangular container lined one wall.

"Tea would be great," I said. Because if we were sipping something hot, it would be harder for Johnson to hustle us out. And knowing how our investigations went, he'd probably try.

"I'm too upset to drink," Hyperion said.

Uncertainly, Verena edged from the room. She didn't close the door.

"This is Abigail Beanblossom," Hyperion said. "My new business partner."

"You're a Tarot reader too?" Johnson asked.

"No, we own Beanblossom's Tea and Tarot, downtown." I sat in one of the leather chairs in front of the desk.

"We became partners after I moved out," Hyperion explained, taking the chair beside me. He shook his head. "That's when I lost touch with Cassius. You know how it is with start-ups. It took up all our time. Friendships fell by the wayside. I couldn't believe it when I heard he'd been killed. You must be in shock."

He studied his hands, splayed on the desk. "I guess... I guess I am. Sudden death is always shocking, but murder..." He shook his head. "It doesn't seem real."

"Do the police have any idea who was responsible?" I asked.

"It seems to have been a road rage incident."

"That's not the only rage around here." Hyperion angled his head toward the door. "We couldn't help but overhear."

"Carla." He grimaced. "Yes. She—"

Verena bustled inside carrying a tray. "Your coffee." She set it on the desk. "And I hope black tea is okay?"

"It's perfect." I sipped the bitter brew and tried not to wince. This wasn't England. How long had she steeped the stuff? Overnight? I mean, what good's a revolution if you can't brew tea the way you like?

Verena dropped the tray to her side. "Is there anything else I can get you?"

"No, thanks," Johnson said.

She hesitated then left, making a pretense of closing the door while leaving it open a good inch.

"I can't imagine losing a husband to sudden violence like that." I picked up the ivory-colored pyramid on his desk and turned it over. The paperweight was heavier than it looked.

He glanced at it. "Er, yes."

"How's a person supposed to deal with such a loss?" I prompted, returning the pyramid to its place.

"I'm not sure," he said, "but they *were* getting divorced."

Hyperion's eyes widened. "Really? But they seemed so happy together."

"I'm afraid Cassius was not. But the divorce was a blow for Carla. She was—" Johnson shook my head. "Not my client. Sorry, I don't gossip. Cassius's death has..." He blinked rapidly. "It's like the world is off kilter, none of the rules apply anymore." He coughed and took a deep breath. "And I'm babbling to kind strangers."

"Murder isn't natural," I said quietly. "It's outside the order of things. And without justice, it's hard to move on."

Johnson shot me an odd look, and no wonder. Now *I* was babbling. "Um, yes," he said.

The door behind me sprang open, and Verena bustled in. She laid a stack of pink message slips on his desk. "Sorry, I forgot to give you these."

She smiled insincerely at me and strolled out.

"I see you're a fan of Egypt," I said, nodding to the paperweight.

"It's my dream to see the pyramids, the great temples," Johnson said. "I never seem to have the time though." He checked his watch. "Thank you for stopping by. I appreciate the thought. But with my partner's death, I'm afraid I've got a lot to do."

"I can only imagine." Hyperion stood. He pulled his wallet from his hip pocket and whipped out a business card, laid it on the desk. "If you need anything, please let us know."

"I will," he said in a tone that said the opposite. "Thanks."

We walked out, Verena's gaze burning a hole in my back.

"Cassius was married?" I hissed. "To a woman?"

"I didn't know, okay? That's why I stopped seeing him. There was no way I was going to be the other man."

"Did they have kids?"

His skin darkened. "Well, at that age, they're not exactly children." He didn't meet my gaze. "The youngest was just starting college."

I groaned. No wonder Hyperion hadn't wanted to talk about their relationship. "Do you think Carla knew he was cheating?"

"I doubt she knew about me." He gnawed his bottom lip. "Like I said, it was only two dates. But they were getting divorced for a reason. I guess she could have found out... something."

My insides writhed. What a mess. And what had that bit been about the *policy*? Carla had to have been talking about an insurance policy. Had it been changed? Been canceled?

"Well," I said. "We're here. Should we talk to Lafayette Grief?"

But when we knocked on his door, no one answered. I tried the knob. Locked.

I studied the black placard beside the door. "Lafayette, Inc. That doesn't say much."

"It's better than Grief, Inc."

"Any idea what he does?" I asked.

"None."

I sighed. Back to cyber stalking.

CHAPTER 5

There are some things that should go without saying. For example, don't leave a coffin in your business partner's driveway. It's just not done.

But there *was* a coffin in my driveway. And it had wheels. I looked from the black coffin to the yellow bungalow. Yep, it was my house. Just above the peaked roofline, fog blurred a watery sun.

"Do you have any idea why there's a coffin in my driveway?" Because there was really only one person who would have put it there. I dragged my gaze from the wooden coffin to Hyperion. "And why is it on wheels?"

He shifted his weight. "Didn't I mention the coffin race?"

"No."

"Why'd you think I had a t-shirt cannon?"

"I still have no idea why you've got one."

"For the coffin race." He patted the coffin's hood.

I waited.

"I entered Beanblossom's in the race," he said patiently. "We're going as the Death card. I've got a scythe and everything."

"A scythe at high speeds. What could go wrong?"

"It'll be like one of those Italian medieval morality parades. Did you know those parades most likely spawned the Tarot's major arcana cards?"

"Oh, boy."

"Or was it the Renaissance?" He shook his head. "They were in Italy. I know that much."

I blew out my breath. "Why is a racing coffin in my driveway?"

"I live in a condo. I only get one parking space. I couldn't put the coffin in mine. Where would my Jeep go?"

I rubbed the bridge of my nose. "Yes, of course. Condo. Driveway. Coffin racer. It all seems so clear and logical. *Not.* Why didn't you tell me about the race?"

"What are you talking about?" he said. "I just did."

"And if you hate all things Halloween, why on earth would you enter us in a *coffin race*? Right before Halloween?"

"A prodigious madness overcame me."

"Prodigious," I said flatly. Hyperion was working his way through a Lovecraft word-of-the-day calendar. I wasn't going to admit it, but I needed to look that one up.

"I was there, and the coffin was there, and I was telling that man all about the morality parades called Triumphs, which historians think is the origin of the trump suit in the Tarot deck. And he told me I should sign up, so I did."

I studied the coffin. It was still parked in my driveway.

"So," I said. "Just to clarify. You entered us in a coffin race. You plan to carry a scythe in the coffin, while in the race. Even though for you, October's the most dangerous month of the year."

"There might have been tequila involved."

"Is there anything else I need to know?" I asked. "Any other Halloween promotions you've gotten us into?"

"You'll *love* this one."

"Seriously?" I sagged against the coffin, and it shifted slightly. "There's another?"

"I made a deal with a costume rental place. They're going to send you and me new get-ups every day leading up until Halloween."

"How much is that going to cost?" I asked and grimaced. I was a fine one to talk about surprises. I *still* hadn't told him about that oven.

"I told you, I got a deal. And you can't wear that manky zookeeper's costume all month."

Since I'd borrowed and already returned it to a writer friend of mine, that much was true. "You think Halloween's cursed, and you want to get into a rolling coffin to celebrate?"

"First, not to celebrate it, to promote Beanblossom's Tea and Tarot. Second, I believe in facing my fears. I'm not going to let a curse keep me down, even if the wheels fall off, we're plunged into moving traffic, and I cut my own head off with the scythe."

"Oh, boy."

"You've been saying that a lot."

"I'm hungry. Hunger makes me repetitive." It was past lunchtime. My well-trained stomach starts grumbling at noon. And I still had pizza on my mind.

"Don't worry." He patted my shoulder. "I'll be driving."

My stomach bottomed.

The phone rang in my purse, and I dug it free. "It's Tomas." I put the phone on speaker and set it on the coffin racer. "Hi, Tomas. I'm here with Hyperion. You're on speaker."

"Your friend is being arraigned this afternoon. Want to come with me?"

"You're going to the courthouse?" Hyperion shouted into the phone.

"Aren't you?" he asked.

"Yes," Hyperion said. "Yes, of course."

"I'm headed there now. I'll meet you out front." Tomas hung up.

Hyperion looked at me. "We're going to have to table the coffin racer question. I'm—"

I dropped the phone in my purse. "I'm coming too." Maybe the courthouse had vending machines. I could go for some barbecue chips.

The county courthouse had been modern in the sixties. Now, it was just minimalist and depressing. The low, flat building was surrounded by a sloping lawn. Its high windows were narrow enough to prevent escape. Or to shoot arrows from, should the need arise.

Tomas stood at the top of the wide, concrete steps. He wore a dress shirt and tie beneath his Giants baseball windbreaker. The two men gripped hands.

"The arraignment itself won't take long," Tomas said. "Waiting for Tony's name to be called is another story though."

We made our way through security, past a promising vending machine, and into a faded courtroom. Frayed chairs for the audience were screwed in rows into the floor.

We found three seats together in the middle of the rows. Shifting impatiently, we sat and watched while attorneys buzzed about the courtroom.

My stomach growled.

Tomas shot me an alarmed look.

"I haven't had lunch yet," I whispered.

An elderly woman in a Jackie Kennedy-style suit took a chair in front of us. She brushed the fur collar on her suit and adjusted her matching hat.

Tomas straightened his tie.

The judge banged his gavel, and the court came to life.

A parade of misfits and miscreants were led through the courtroom. The process was quick. The judge called the case, and the suspect trudged to the podium. The judge read the charges and asked how the suspect pleaded. Then the judge scheduled a court date and the suspect left—sometimes led out by deputies.

"That's because he couldn't make bail," Tomas said in a low voice. He pointed to a miserable-looking man with a jigsaw tattooed on his bald head.

Led by a deputy, the tattooed man shuffled out a side door.

"Your detective will be out soon," Tomas said.

Hyperion bounced his heel.

My stomach whined. I should have stopped at that vending machine in the hallway.

More people came and went. My stomach growled more loudly.

"Is there a cat in here?" a woman whispered behind me.

I sunk lower in my chair.

"I swear I heard a cat," she said.

"Raccoons," a man hissed. "The court had an infestation last year."

The elderly woman in front of us turned to glare at the speakers.

Tomas grinned. "Nice hat," he whispered.

She smiled and touched it, pushing it slightly askew on her silver hair.

The judge banged his gavel. "Quiet in the court."

The audience tried to make itself smaller.

More suspects came and went.

My stomach made a sort of squeaky wail.

The woman behind me gasped. "Something brushed my foot."

The fur hat wobbled atop the older lady in front of us.

The bailiff stood and read a case number. "Anthony Chase vs. The State of California."

Tony Chase entered through a door in the wooden wall and walked to the podium. He wore a business suit, a full business suit instead of his trademark blazer and jeans. My heart fell. You *do* have to dress up in court, I just hated seeing him this way.

Hyperion jerked forward and grasped the old woman's seat back.

"You are charged with felony murder," the judge said. "Detective Chase, how do you plead?"

"Not guilty, your Honor," Tony said in his Texas drawl.

Hyperion stared intently.

"Your honor." A district attorney rose. "We believe Detective Chase is a flight risk and ask to increase the bail to five million dollars."

Tomas sucked in his breath. Hyperion's knuckles whitened on the chair in front of him.

My hands clenched. "That's not fair," I hissed. "Where's he supposed to get that kind of money?"

A man in a blue suit rose. "Your honor, I'm the attorney for Detective Chase. Detective Chase is a respected member of the community and poses no flight risk."

"But this isn't his first time before a court." The DA strode to the judge's bench and laid a manila file folder on top of it. "At his last position in Austin, Texas, Detective Chase was brought up on charges—"

"And acquitted," his attorney blurted. "It didn't even go to trial."

"Nevertheless," the DA said, "there seems to be a pattern, and murder by a police officer—"

"Alleged," the defender yelped.

"—is something the community is reacting to strongly. This is a high-profile crime."

"High profile?" I hissed. "What's that got to do with anything?"

Tomas shushed me.

The judge adjusted his glasses and perused the file.

"That's ridiculous," Tony's attorney said. "Detective Chase is not a flight risk. He didn't run in Texas, and he's not going to run here."

The judge closed the file. "We'll raise the bail to two million dollars."

My stomach let out a blood-curdling screechy growl. The woman in front of me started. Her fur hat slipped off her head, dropped onto the linoleum between our chairs, and rolled behind me.

A woman screamed. "Vermin!"

The crowd lurched, shouting, to its feet. People stormed toward the doors.

Tomas grabbed me, pulling me close. Hyperion grasped Tomas's shoulder. My partner straight-armed a man shoving past and threatening to knock us all to the ground.

The judge banged his gavel, but his shouts were lost beneath the clatter and roar of the stampede. At the podium, Tony hung his head and pressed one hand over his eyes.

The crowd streamed through the doors, leaving the three of us and the silver-haired woman, who sat ramrod straight in her chair.

When the crowd had filtered out, Tomas bent and retrieved the fur hat.

He handed it to the pink-faced woman. "Your hat, madam."

She nodded stiffly and rose. "Thank you." The woman paced from the courtroom.

"Now *that's* class," Tomas said admiringly.

A deputy led Tony Chase from the court.

Hyperion glared at me.

"What are you blaming me for?" I pressed my hand to the front of my blouse. "It's October."

CHAPTER 6

There are days when some people might mistake me for a lady of leisure and not a busy tearoom owner. Today seemed to be one of those days.

It was a busy Tuesday afternoon. The tearoom was full. But instead of serving scones, I was standing beside Hyperion on a sunny street corner.

"Maricel can handle the tearoom." Hyperion nudged me.

I stared at the little red man on the pedestrian signal and willed the light to turn green. "I know she can handle a normal tearoom. But let's face it. Nothing's been normal at Beanblossom's lately."

"That's why all the *interesting* people come to Beanblossom's Tea and Tarot. It's because of the Tarot," he added modestly.

People in bathing suits and board shorts pressed behind me. It was a balmy October day. No one who had a chance to was passing up this beach weather.

"I wouldn't mind some boring customers." I smoothed the front of my burnt-orange blouse. Since I was without a costume, I'd settled for Halloween colors. White slacks and on-your-feet-all-day brown tennis shoes.

"Yes," he said, "you'd mind. You love the customers, quirks and all."

He was right. Chatting with customers, learning about their lives, was one of the great joys of my work. I got to shoot the breeze with people for a living. And bake and make teas, but a lot of talking went into the job too.

"And FYI," he continued, "I've been debating whether I should say anything or not, but you look like a candy corn."

"Candy corns have a yellow stripe. I don't." The light turned green, and I stepped into the street. "And I can't help it if I feel guilty when—"

Hyperion grabbed me by the waist and yanked me backward, onto the sidewalk. A city bus roared past, belching exhaust.

"See?" he said. "A boring person would have just stood there and let you be flattened."

I gulped and tried to slow my speeding heart. I don't know who the city hired for bus drivers. But their attitude seemed to be, "if you can't see me, that's your problem."

"Thanks," I squeaked.

We crossed the street toward Dr. Tarrach's dental office, a low, fifties-era building with a Japanese garden in the front.

Hyperion slowed to a halt and stared vacantly at the building. He shook his head, as if snapping out of something unpleasant.

I touched his arm. "You okay?"

"I'm fine." His jaw firmed.

We walked past a koi pond.

"Have you spoken to Tony since the arraignment?" I asked.

"It was only an arraignment," he said quickly, "right? It's not a trial. It doesn't mean anything."

"Of course, but it must have been a disappointment for Tony." And he hadn't answered my question.

"I wouldn't know," he said, voice brittle. "He doesn't want to talk to me."

Oh. I waited a beat for Hyperion to tell me how he felt about that.

He didn't.

Hyperion opened the office's door for me, and we walked into a reception area. People sat in squarish chairs and thumbed through magazines.

"We're on a deadline," he continued. "The longer Tony's in jail, the worse his chances. Tony's a cop. He'll never last in the pen."

"He's not in the pen. He's at the county jail. There's a big difference." But a cop in any sort of jail… I gnawed the inside of my cheek. Any kind of jail wasn't going to be easy for Tony. We needed to find answers, fast.

We stopped in front of an unmanned reception desk, and Hyperion pinged the bell.

After a moment, a plump, redhaired woman in a neat blouse and slacks emerged from a back office. "Hello. Have you got an appointment?"

"No," Hyperion said loudly. "We're here about the murder of Cassius Santori."

I winced. We might be on a deadline, but I wasn't so sure about the direct approach here. Still, I hadn't come up with any better ideas for getting to the dentist short of getting my teeth cleaned. And appointments were three months out. (I'd tried.)

The receptionist blinked. "Murder?"

"We'd like to see Dr. Tarrach, please," I said more quietly and glanced at the name tag on her chest. "Esther."

"About a murder?" She leaned closer. "Who did you say died?" She asked in an eager undertone.

"Dr. Tarrach's financial advisor," I whispered.

Her eyes widened. "Oh God. That means I'm going to have to manage the insurance payments now."

"Yes," Hyperion said. "Is he available?"

"I'll... Just a moment." She vanished through the open doorway.

I turned from the reception desk. Patients stared.

"The dentist is a witness," I said, "not a suspect." But who knew? Maybe we'd get lucky and he'd break under our interrogation.

No, I didn't think that was really going to happen either.

The receptionist emerged a few minutes later. "This way, please."

"I don't suppose Dr. Tarrach's wife is around?" I asked.

"No," Esther said. "She doesn't stop by the office often, and she's in Hawaii with her sister."

"Oh?" I said. "When did she leave?"

"A week ago," the receptionist said. "She's been posting photos. I wish *I* was on vacation."

She showed us into a dentist's operatory and motioned to two blue chairs against the wall. "Please wait here." She retreated with a reluctant air.

We sidled around the examination chair. Hyperion grabbed the swivel light, flipped it on, and aimed it at me. "We have ways of making you talk," he said in a German accent.

"Watch it." I shielded my eyes.

"Oooh, free mouthwash." He pushed the light down and strode to the sink. "Hm... I'm not sure about the whitening stuff." He plucked a massive swab from a jar. "Do I look medical?"

"Are you thinking of playing dentist for Halloween?"

"Dentists *are* lightyears more terrifying than doctors. But I told you, I've got a guy. Our costumes for tomorrow will be waiting at the tearoom, and they won't be boring."

A man who qualified as tall, dark, and handsome strode into the room in a doctor's white coat. His close-cropped hair was brown and curling. His face was chiseled, with a roman nose and deep-set, brown eyes. A bandage swathed his wrist.

Hyperion and I both straightened. My partner jammed the swab in his back pocket.

"What's this about a murder?" the dentist asked briskly. "Are you with the police?"

"No," Hyperion said. "We're private."

I had a pretty good idea it was illegal to pretend we were PIs. But Hyperion hadn't actually *said* we were PIs. It was more implied. Good thing I'd never been obsessed with rules.

"We're investigating the murder of Cassius Santori," Hyperion continued.

Again, my partner hadn't actually put the words "private" and "investigation" together. But it was awfully close.

Also, I kind of wanted to be a PI.

"I understood that was a road rage incident," the dentist said. "Didn't they arrest some local detective?"

Hyperion bared his teeth. "The evidence points in another direction."

"It does?" Tarrach asked. "What direction?"

"Another," Hyperion repeated. "What happened to your wrist?"

The dentist grimaced. "Poison oak. I got it pulling weeds last weekend. The bandage itches like crazy, but I don't want to pass it on to anyone else." He tugged at the bandage, exposing blistered, reddened skin.

Hyperion shuddered and edged away.

"We understand you were a client of Mr. Santori's," I said. "We hoped you might be able to give us some insight into the workings and personalities in that office."

Doctor Tarrach checked his dive watch. "I've got five minutes until my next patient. What do you want to know?"

"Was Cassius managing your investments?" I asked.

"They were managing parts of the business side of the office as well as my personal investments." The dentist's cadence was slow and cautious.

"Oh?" I smiled politely.

Dr. Tarrach motioned around the room. "I became a dentist to fix people's teeth, not to be a businessman. But running an office takes both management and financial skills. I've got a terrific office manager. You met her, Esther. But I decided the smart thing to do would be to outsource the finance side."

Hyperion cocked his head. "Such as...?"

"Medi-Cal billings, insurance for the staff, that sort of thing."

"And were you working directly with Mr. Santori or with others in his consulting office?" I asked.

"My account was with both Johnson and Cassius."

"Is that usual?" I asked.

"I don't know," the dentist said. "But there are a lot of moving pieces. My own finances. The office's insurance. You have no idea what a tangled knot dealing with Medi-Cal is. My understanding was each man played to his strengths when it came to my account."

"In your opinion, did they work well together?" I leaned against the exam chair, and it swiveled sideways. Contrite, I jerked away.

"There did seem to be a strain between Johnson and Cassius. I overheard them arguing a month or so ago." He readjusted the chair.

"Over what?" Hyperion leaned closer.

"I couldn't make it out," the dentist said, "but I heard raised voices. Sorry."

"And Verena?" I asked.

"Ah. Verena." He grimaced.

"Something wrong?" I said.

"No." The dentist slipped his hands into the pockets of his white lab coat. "I suppose it's natural in a small office like that for feelings to, er, blossom."

"You mean she had a thing for Cassius?" Hyperion asked.

"For Johnson." Tarrach grimaced. "At least it looked that way to me."

"And were you satisfied with the services their company provided?" I asked.

"My practice is flourishing, so, yes."

"But we understand that you had a conflict with them roughly a month ago," I said.

His olive skin turned a shade darker, and he grimaced. "I was getting a spanking."

Hyperion's eyebrows lifted. "A what now?"

The dentist rubbed a broad hand across his cheek. "I bought a condo near the beach a couple months back, and it was not in the annual plan we'd devised. Cassius, quite rightly, told me off. But the condo seemed like a good investment, and it *is* my money."

"So what was the problem?" Hyperion asked.

"As Cassius correctly pointed out, we'd made an investment plan. He couldn't be expected to execute on it if the money wasn't there. I should have talked to him first. Not that I regret the purchase. I can earn a rental income from the property. Keeping everything in stocks and bonds is lunacy."

"Tell me about it." Hyperion rolled his eyes.

I resisted the urge to elbow my partner in the side. "Do you know of any enemies Cassius might have had?" I asked Tarrach.

The dentist's gaze flicked to the tile ceiling, and his forehead wrinkled. "No. Cassius was well liked. So is Johnson. They have to be personable in the business they're in. They call themselves financial consultants, and they are. But let's face it, there's a lot of sales involved. Rough personalities don't make it in that business."

"No," I said, "I guess they wouldn't."

Doctor Tarrach checked his watch again. "Is that all?"

"Yes," I said. "Thank you."

He nodded and took a step toward the door.

"Wait," I said. "Have the police been by to ask you about any of this yet?"

"No." The dentist arched a brow. "Should they?"

I rubbed my cheek. "No, I'm only..." This was bad news for all sorts of reasons. "I'm sure they have their own process."

The dentist strode from the examining room.

"I guess we can find our own way out," Hyperion muttered.

I followed my partner to the sidewalk.

"I can't believe the police haven't interrogated that dentist." Hyperion fumed. "Have they decided Tony's guilty and stopped investigating?"

"It does seem... lazy." I slipped my hands into my pockets. Were we just that good at finding suspects and witnesses? Or was something else going on?

Because Tony was one of theirs. You'd think the police department would be doing everything they could to clear his name. So why *hadn't* they talked to the dentist? Because he had no connection to Tony, and therefore no motive to frame him for murder?

Though if the police did follow up with the dentist and learn about us, we could be in trouble.

I glanced back at the dental office. A woman exited, one hand to her jaw, and wobbled toward the koi pond. A man hurriedly put one arm around her shoulders and guided her to a car.

"Wisdom teeth. I know that dazed look." Hyperion jabbed the button for the walk light with his thumb. "What do you think?"

"I think you shouldn't have implied we were private investigators." I also thought Tony was in real trouble.

"It's a madcap adventure, Abigail." His expression turned serious. "Or it would be if so much wasn't at stake."

He pushed the *walk* button again.

"I read those walk buttons are fakes," I said.

"What do you mean they're fakes?"

Tourists gathered behind us, waiting to cross.

"I mean they don't do anything to change the walk light from red to green," I said. "They just pacify pedestrians."

"Have you become a conspiracy theorist while I wasn't looking?"

"I read it on the internet." I folded my arms. "So it *has* to be true."

He laughed. "What do you think about Tarrach's story?"

"I think he's right about Verena having a thing for her boss," I said. "But I don't see how that gives her a motive to kill Cassius and frame your boyfriend."

"I thought that bit about Johnson and Cassius having a strained relationship was interesting."

"Yeah." I watched the pedestrian light. "We should have asked the dentist for more details. What did you think about Tarrach?"

"The jury's still out." His fists clenched and loosened. "I know it's early days. I know we're just at the beginning. But the stakes this time…"

"We've got an advantage over the police. We know Tony's no killer. And we can focus on proving it."

"Yeah." His voice cracked, and he cleared his throat. "We will."

I glowered at the little red man on the pedestrian signal. "Oh, come *on*."

"At the arraignment…" Hyperion shifted his weight. He stared hard at a flower shop across the street. "You must have noticed—"

A hand thudded into my mid-back, shoving me forward, knocking the wind from my lungs. A shout. A blaring horn.

I was falling. I couldn't stop myself. And I couldn't stop the grill of the SUV bulleting toward me.

CHAPTER 7

Time really does slow when you're about to die. I had time to think about the nature of time. I had time to notice the sunlight twinkling off the SUV's bumper, the bug smashed on its right headlight. I had time to see a gum wrapper flutter on the pavement, and the pavement rushing toward my outstretched hands. And I had time to feel a burst of unfairness at it all. The tearoom was just finding its feet. I didn't have *time* to die.

Hyperion grabbed my wrist in an iron grip. He slung me sideways, using my momentum to fling me out of the car's way.

I slammed into a mailbox, and the air exploded from my lungs.

The SUV sped past, horn blaring.

I crumpled over the mailbox. Pain blossomed in my chest and elbow, and I gasped. "Ow."

"Are you okay?" he asked.

"Ow." I push-upped off the mailbox.

"You're okay." Hyperion helped me onto the edge of a brick planter on the sidewalk. "What the hell? Do you have a death wish?"

"I didn't—" I exhaled, sharp and loud.

A breeze flitted the gum wrapper into a sewer grate, and a tide of heat rose in my body. I had nearly been killed. Someone had pushed me into the street, and they'd done it intentionally. And it would not have been a good death. It would have been messy and ugly and painful. And even if I'd survived...

The heat reached the top of my head. My nostrils flared. "Someone shoved me."

Hyperion straightened and looked around. "Who? Who shoved you?"

"I didn't see who did it. He or she was behind me." I scanned the street. "I didn't recognize—"

"Really, Abigail," a woman said. "Can you *try* not to be such a drama queen?"

Beatrice Carlson and the handsome man from Hyperion's office building stood on the sidewalk. The PR maven wore a vintage suit the color of a molting cobra. She was also sneering.

I wheezed at my nemesis and rubbed my chest. I'd hoped Beatrice and I were past such petty taunts after her PR firm had sent a flash mob to disrupt the tearoom. Though in fairness, we *had* once or twice accused her of murder.

Okay, twice. We'd accused her twice.

"I saw everything," Beatrice said. She was slim and taut. And though her smooth brown hair held gray streaks, she made them look good.

I stood. "You saw who pushed me?" *Yes.* If it was one of our suspects, we could consider this case closed. That was one of the great things about small towns. You got to know people, even people who might not like you much because of two measly murder accusations. And those people talked.

"Pushed you?" Beatrice shook her head. "Sure. *That's* what happened." She turned to Gino. "Like I told you. Drama queen." She spun one finger around her ear.

"It *is* what happened," I said hotly.

"I always suspected you had a death wish," she said. "Or was this a pathetic attempt to get out of the coffin race?"

"Why would we do that?" Hyperion asked.

She arched a brow. "Because the competition's too hot?"

"You're in the coffin race?" I scanned the road for trained killers, but all I saw were tourists on their way to the beach.

"It's a marvelous PR opportunity and a beloved San Borromeo event." Beatrice crossed her arms, her reptilian smile broadening. "Of course we're in the race."

Good. Beating her like a rug would give me a chance to get back at her for that flash mob stunt. I smiled, showing teeth.

"I'm not in the race," Gino said hastily. "Not my thing."

I focused on him, because he was easier on the eyes than his companion. "How do you two know each other?"

"Gino's a client," she said.

"Gino...?" I asked.

"Redmond," he finished for me.

"Nice to meet you," I said, by which I meant nice for investigative purposes. I wasn't looking for love after my near-death experience. "Did you know Cassius Santori well?"

"Not really," he said. "Why do you ask?"

Someone brushed past me on the sidewalk, and I stepped closer to the planter box. "Because I noticed your office is—"

"They fancy themselves amateur detectives." Beatrice's venom-green eyes glinted. "It's all fun and games until you accuse someone of murder."

She was *never* going to let that go. "You sure you didn't see anyone after I fell?" I asked him. "Maybe someone who ran away?"

Beatrice rolled her eyes. "You fell. Stop trying to make it a thing. Today's victimhood mentality is so boring." She strode down the sidewalk.

Gino gave me a long look. "It was nice meeting you too." He followed her into a café.

"Everyone's so *nice*," Hyperion said, tone caustic. "Come on. Let's get out of here."

We returned to the tearoom, which was not on fire or in the midst of a riot. Yes. Both those things had happened. Blessedly, not at the same time.

I tied on my apron and strode into the kitchen. The new oven gleamed at me maliciously.

I held my palm above its warmth and sighed. It was the kind of oven I'd always wanted—big and gleaming and modern. Now we could actually bake our scones in-house instead of outsourcing.

But if I'd had more time, if it hadn't been an emergency, I would have bought something less expensive and more practical. Instead, I'd let panic take over and had been seduced by a sexy oven. But the temperature control—

The phone rang in my purse, and I hurriedly excavated it from its depths. It was a number I didn't recognize, the type I'd usually ignore. But with all that was going on, I answered. "Hello?"

"Hello, Abigail. Susan Wilkinson here. I heard Detective Chase was arrested in your tearoom, and I'd like to get a statement."

"No comment." Susan was a rising local journalism star, largely because she never said anything nice.

"Did he resist arrest?" she asked.

"No, of course not."

"You've encountered Detective Chase before. Did he ever display any violent tendencies?"

"No," I said angrily, "and he didn't kill Cassius Santori either."

"Really? Do you have any evidence to support that?"

"I just can't believe he—"

Hyperion slouched into the kitchen carrying a garment bag in each hand. "Our costumes are here."

I jumped and hung up the phone. "Thanks." Dropping the phone into my apron pocket, I took the bag from his outstretched hand and tugged at the zipper. It was stuck.

"I keep thinking about your raccoon riot yesterday," he said. "It made the paper."

I nodded. We'd been lucky Susan Wilkinson didn't know we'd been there. There was no way I could explain that and look good.

Hyperion shook his head. "Normally, Tony would have been right in the thick of it, helping people get out safely. Instead, he just stood there."

"It was all he could do. The bailiffs would have—"

"Yes, the bailiffs *would* have. He's a cop, Abigail." He frowned at my perfect oven, and my heartbeat jolted into a guilty sprint.

I really needed to break the bad news, and sooner rather than later. "Listen, about the new oven—"

"Forget the oven," he said. "What happened in that courtroom is important."

"I'm sure it was hard for Tony not to act, but he's a professional, and—"

"You don't get it. I'm not worried about any feelings of inadequacy he may have. He'll get over them. I'm worried because no one in the department seems to be supporting him. And he's their only detective capable of figuring this out."

If Hyperion left me twisting in the wind, in real trouble, it would be a gut punch. But being a cop, on the street, facing potentially dangerous situations every day… I couldn't imagine how the police could function without trust between officers. And now, Tony had lost that trust. How would he get past that?

I hooked the garment bag on one of the coat hooks beside the kitchen door and smoothed its black folds. Getting derailed by worries about what *could* happen wouldn't help Tony.

"If he's the *only* detective," I said, "then who's investigating his accident?"

"I hear they brought someone in from Santa Cruz."

"Well," I said, "that's good, right? He should be more impartial."

"Then why hasn't he interviewed that dentist? Or Verena?" He paced the kitchen, his long fingers twitching. "It seems to me we're the only ones who really care about getting to the truth, and Tony doesn't want our help."

"How do you know that?"

His jaw tightened. "He told me."

Oh, no. "I thought he wouldn't see you?"

"He called."

Judging from Hyperion's expression, it hadn't been a good call.

He shook himself. "And that's not the point. The point is, if I respect Tony, and I do, I can't ignore his wishes."

That... *was* a good point. But it might not be the right one. "All right. Come on." I steered him out the tearoom's back door. We crossed the parking lot and walked through the wine bar's rear, outdoor patio.

Hyperion and I walked inside the cool interior. Winding through the tables, we bellied up to the smooth, black bar. Wine racks lined the wall behind it.

I ordered the best tequila they had for Hyperion, a glass of Zinfandel for me.

"Alcohol isn't the answer," Hyperion said, expression hangdog. "At least not before noon."

I hung my purse on a hook beneath the bar. "And we'll have two prosciutto paninis with salads on the side," I told the bartender. He nodded and vanished around the corner of the bar and into the kitchen.

I swiveled the barstool to get a better look at Hyperion. "It's okay to drink before noon if we're eating too." I'm sure I heard that somewhere.

He grunted.

"Okay," I said. "If his department isn't backing him, like you say, I get that he wants to keep us out of it and out of trouble."

"Obvs." The skin bunched around his brown eyes. "Tony likes to take care of his own problems. It's one of his better qualities."

"And what about your better qualities?"

"Meaning?"

"Meaning you've successfully investigated several murders. It's kind of our thing."

His brown eyes narrowed. "And?"

"I'm just saying, if Tony doesn't want us investigating, I'm still going to ask around. He may have been drugged in our tearoom—"

"Tea and Tarot room."

"Or assaulted in our parking lot," I continued. "Even if I didn't know him personally, I'd want to know what happened." Okay, maybe I was self-justifying. But I wasn't lying.

His mouth pursed. "Meekly following Tony's orders *would* go against my lovable Puckish nature."

"I know. Right? When have we ever done what we're told?"

"Like, never." He brightened. "And Tony knows that too. You're right. We can't pretend to be obedient. We both have to be the people we are."

"So he still hasn't made bail?" I asked, changing the subject.

"Not yet," he said. "He doesn't want my help with that either. Not that I *could* help on that score."

The bartender returned and poured our drinks.

I turned my wine glass on its cocktail napkin. "So we're agreed. We've got another lead, Lafayette Grief, to follow up on. And there's still the wife."

Hyperion drummed his fingers on the bar. "The spouse *is* always the most likely suspect."

"And she seemed pretty bent out of shape at the financial consulting office yesterday."

"True," he said. "But would she have pushed you in front of a car?"

"I don't know." And why hadn't Beatrice and Gino seen anything? *Could* I have imagined that shove? I shifted on my barstool and remembered the feel of the hand at my back, the forceful shove. "All I know is someone shoved me. Hard."

"Why would Santori's wife do that? She doesn't know we're investigating."

Lightly, I bit the inside of my lower lip. "She might know. We're assuming none of the suspects are talking to each other. Maybe they are. And she saw us in that consulting office."

"And Lafayette Grief?"

"I have no idea, but we should still check him out."

"Oh, we'll check him out all right," Hyperion said darkly.

Our food arrived, and we fell silent, polishing off the paninis.

"Abigail?" A round-faced, older man who ran the local Ombudsman office clapped my shoulder. "Good to see you." Strands of wispy gray hair covered his balding head.

"Hi, Mr. Henderson. Do you know my business partner, Hyperion Night?" I motioned toward him. "Mr. Henderson is the president of that charity Gramps has been working with," I told Hyperion. "The one that advocates for senior citizens in long-term care homes."

"Not just seniors," Mr. Henderson said. "Any adult in care. I just wanted to thank you for your potentially generous donation."

Um, what? I'd donated fifty bucks for their casino night six months ago, and I'd already gotten a nice thank you card. "Erm, you're welcome."

"Beatrice told me all about your bet," he said. "It's wonderful. You deserve all the press you can get."

Bet? My hand jerked, knocking into my wine glass. It tilted, and I made a wild grab for it, catching it before it could fall. "Press?" I asked.

"I think she said the press release is going out tomorrow," the older man said.

"Press release?" Hyperion asked blankly.

"Take all the credit you want," Mr. Henderson said. "I have no trouble with donors getting publicity for their good works. You're helping a good cause and getting us more publicity too. Thank you again for your support." He winked and walked away.

"Donation?" Hyperion asked.

"Beatrice," I snarled. I yanked my phone from my purse and called the PR consultant.

"What now?" she snapped. "I told you, we didn't see any psychos pushing you into traffic."

"I just ran into Mr. Henderson. He said you told him we were making some sort of donation."

Her voice smoothed. "Oh, didn't I mention that? The loser of the coffin race will be matching the proceeds from their rival's sponsorships and donating it to Ombudsman."

I sputtered. *Sponsors? What sponsors?* "I don't have any sponsors. I didn't even know about the race until yesterday."

"Then you'd better get some. I've already raised five thousand dollars. That means if I win—"

"I have to chip in five grand?" I asked, aghast. I didn't have that kind of money.

"You can count. How clever."

"Beatrice, look, I thought the flash mob ended our rivalry. You win, okay? I don't have five grand to donate to anyone."

"That's embarrassing. The press release has already gone out to the local media. It would be humiliating for Beanblossom's if you backed out now. What would people think?"

Hyperion grabbed the phone from my hand. "You dead-eyed, ichor-infested *consultant*. We're not paying a cent, because we're going to win that race. Get ready to suck it up, you bilious hybrid." He cut the connection.

More Lovecraft. "So," I said weakly. "How are we going to win this race?"

"We need a ringer," Hyperion said.

"A ringer in a coffin race? Who?"

"You know who."

"Honestly, I don't." But I was starting to get an idea, and I rocked on my barstool.

He tossed back his shot of tequila. "We need Razzzor."

CHAPTER 8

A glass crashed, and my shoulders jumped to my ears. A rowdy lunch gang at the back of the wine bar cheered.

My ex-boss messing with the coffin car? "No," I said, panicked. "No, we don't."

"Razzzor's a tech genius." Hyperion swiveled his barstool to face me. "He'll know how to make our entry the fastest coffin on wheels."

"First, there's a big difference between tech and mechanical." I paused. The Silicon Valley tycoon, Razzzor, had the mechanical side down too. And that was terrifying. No one should have that much knowledge.

I gulped. "Second, if you invite him in, he'll take over. I've seen it before. He'll get obsessive and soon the coffin will be flying. I mean literally flying. Like airborne."

"Now I'm definitely calling him." He pulled his phone from the inside pocket of his charcoal blazer.

"In the name of all that's unholy, don't."

"I'm being tortured by a Halloween curse. My boyfriend is in the slammer. Who *knows* who he's meeting there?"

"What?"

"The point is, I may as well get *some* fun out of this rotten month," he said, dialing.

"I'm telling you, don't," I said rapidly. "It won't go the way you expect. It never does when Razzzor's involved."

"Sounds perfect. Anything's better than leaving our fate in the hands of Halloween."

Oh, forget it. In the grand schemes of this month's disasters, Razzzor couldn't possibly make things worse. I swallowed the last of my Zinfandel. "I'm going back to the tearoom."

"Tea and *Tarot* room." Hyperion put the phone to his ear. "And don't forget your costume."

"Whatever." I set some bills on the counter and stomped across the parking lot to Beanblossom's.

Maybe it wouldn't be a total disaster. Maybe Razzzor would even sponsor our coffin? I hated to ask my ex-boss for favors, but if Hyperion asked, well, that was between them.

I hustled past the kitchen and poked my head into the tearoom proper. Cups clinked genteelly, and women murmured in soft voices. Costumed waitstaff poured tea and whisked away plates. Tarot readers mingled among the guests, laying out cards and making predictions.

Returning to the kitchen, I unzipped the garment bag, hanging from its wall peg. A frothy black and white confection popped free. I opened the bag wider.

A French maid's costume.

My gaze flicked to the white ceiling and back to the costume. Hyperion had got me a freaking French maid's costume? I couldn't wear this in the tearoom. I'd look ridiculous.

The rear door slammed. "Razzzor's in," Hyperion caroled.

I stepped into the hallway. "A French maid? Seriously?"

Hyperion pocketed his phone. "What's this about a French maid?"

"Your costume guy. I'm not prancing around the tearoom in a French maid costume."

"I told him to get you Marie Antoinette."

"Well, he didn't. What did he get you?" I followed him inside his office.

Bastet meowed loudly from his perch on the table, covered in a garnet-colored cloth. The cat growled, his tail whisking. He sneezed, leaping to the carpeted floor. The cat hopped onto Hyperion's makeshift altar, covered in driftwood and crystals.

"Sorry," Hyperion ruffled the cat's fur. "The doctor said you needed to stay here and rest, or I totally would have brought you to lunch." He unzipped a matching garment bag, revealing a French courtier's outfit with gold embroidery and a ruffled collar. "He got mine right."

At least we were in the same country, if different eras. But how was *this* fair? *I* wasn't the cursed one.

I was the one who'd bought an overpriced oven. I'd be using my share of the marketing budget for the next year to help pay for it.

"Look, ah, don't worry about it." I took a step away from him and bumped into the altar, rattling the crystals. "I'll take care of my own costume from now on."

Hyperion snapped his fingers. "I know, I'll ask for the unicorn costume tomorrow. It takes two people, so he can't get it wrong. And that way, I can stab people with my head."

"Yeah no."

"Well, you can't go into the tearoom dressed like a civilian. What will the staff think? Besides, I've already paid for the month. Well, Beanblossom's has."

"What?"

"It's the rest of October's share of the marketing budget."

"The rest?" I asked, shrill.

"The part you didn't use."

Oh… No. We split the marketing budget fifty-fifty each month. And I'd used the rest of my meager share to help pay for the oven. He couldn't mean he'd used my share of the marketing budget. Could he?

Sweat beaded my brow. "The rest? All of it?"

"You used so little this month on the Halloween décor, which by the way, is an amazing testament to frugality, because the decorations are great. Anyway, there was a bunch of money left."

I sucked in a deep breath.

He raised his hands in a pacifying gesture. "I know, I know. Technically it was your part of the budget, but it was going to waste."

He'd done it. He'd used my share. Which no longer existed, because I'd put it toward the oven. "You can't just use my share without telling me," I ground out.

"Oh…" He dropped into his high-backed velvet chair. "You used the rest of your share. Didn't you?"

"*Yes.*" For the rest of the year and several months beyond. Which meant less promotions for the tearoom, and that hurt his side of the business too. The Tarot readers needed customers in the tearoom to sell their readings to. My anger evaporated, replaced by shame.

"Okay," he said, "don't worry, I'll put the money back. I shouldn't be so spontaneous. I know how you feel about the budget, and you're right. It's not any good if we don't at least try to stick to it. Though I do think…" He canted his head.

"What?"

"I think you'd enjoy yourself more with a little less planning and order in your life. I'm not talking about the costumes," he said quickly. "Only a *little* more going with the flow."

"I just think we need rules and budgets and order to create a space where we *can* have fun."

"Ah." He nodded wisely. "The Emperor card. You always were one to believe in the logic of the world. Not me. I hope for logic but expect chaos."

"I don't believe in it... Okay, I guess I do believe in a logical world. There's always a reason people do things." Now if only we could figure out why someone had framed Tony. "Alternate idea," I said. "I check in with Maricel, and we talk to Lafayette Grief." I'd already lost half the day to investigating. I may as well blow the rest.

"Now that's what I call going with the flow."

"Great." I bustled from his office. Behind the tearoom's white granite counter, I held a whispered confab with Maricel. For better or worse, all the staff knew about the Hyperion/Tony situation. So instead of the annoyance I deserved, she was sympathetic.

"No problem." Maricel smoothed the front of her witch's costume. "Do what you need to do."

"Thanks." I tugged at the collar of my orange blouse. "Do you need me to call in any more staff?"

"No," she said. "We've got this." Maricel smiled. "It turns out I'm pretty good at managing."

And as soon as I could afford to, she was getting a raise. "Yeah, you are."

I studied her outfit. The costume looked a lot like the witch who'd been in the tearoom when Tony'd experienced his lost time. "Where did you get that costume?"

"From the Halloween store on Fifth."

I nodded. Every year, a temporary Halloween store set up in August and shut down just after Halloween. It was big, impersonal, and affordable. And it was unlikely anyone who worked there knew who they'd sold witch costumes to.

If that little witch had had anything to do with Tony's memory loss.

"Maybe I'll go there for my costume," I said.

"I thought Hyperion had arranged for a costume a day for you?"

"It didn't work out." I checked my watch. The next seating would be at one-thirty. "I should be back before the four o'clock seating."

She poured boiling water into a teapot. "No worries. We'll see you when we see you."

"Soon," I assured her. "You'll see me soon."

When I returned to Hyperion, he was in his French courtier's costume.

He smoothed his white wig and struck a pose. "What do you think?"

"You look great," I said honestly.

"I know." He plucked a gentleman's walking stick off the round table and twirled it. "Too bad I can't enjoy it, not with Tony... Let's go."

We drove in his Jeep to his old building. No one gave Hyperion a second glance as we crossed the parking lot. It just went to show how normalized Halloween had become.

We climbed the wide stairs to the fourth floor. Hyperion's walking stick sounded hollowly on the concrete steps.

"I'm spending more time here now than I did when I had an office in this building," Hyperion grumbled.

"Having our suspects in one spot *is* convenient," I said. "Think of all the travel time we're saving."

"Abigail, ever thrifty," he murmured.

We passed Gino's office. I forced myself not to glance at his wooden door.

Hyperion stopped in front of the office next door.

"Lafayette Grief is nearly right across the hall from the financial consulting firm." I pointed. I glanced at the consulting office door.

The *Santori and Warszowski* door stood ajar, so it probably didn't close automatically. And I didn't remember closing it behind us when we'd walked inside yesterday. Could Grief have overheard us interrogating Verena? She'd dropped the dime on him. Had the financial company's office door been closed when we'd been speaking?

Hyperion pressed a doorbell beneath a small sign that read: *Lafayette, Inc.* "As brand names go, his isn't internet friendly. How is anyone supposed to find him or know what he even does?"

"He runs a tent rental company," I said.

"Aren't *we* well informed."

"I looked him up online last night." And I was a little surprised Hyperion hadn't done the same.

My partner rubbed his chin. "I suppose we could pretend to need a tent."

"No way. We'll just end up renting one, and we can't afford it." The oven, that stupid bet I hadn't even made with Beatrice... My insides knotted. "We have to win that coffin race. Or at least beat Beatrice."

"Ah." He looked down the hallway, his chin dipping. "About that."

"What? What's wrong?"

"The thing is, our odds are dropping."

"Why? How?"

"You're going to have to drive the racer," he said.

"What?" How was I supposed to drive a coffin? "I thought you were driving."

"I know." He adjusted his white wig. "It's not ideal, since you drive like an old lady."

"I do not."

"But I've thought it over, and I can't do it. Not only will I have no time to practice—not with what's happening with Tony. But this is also the worst October curse in my history of Octobers. We'd probably end up flying off the pier."

"But..." I sputtered. "This race was *your* idea."

"And I'll be manning the t-shirt cannon, spreading joy and shooting Tea and Tarot t-shirts into the crowd as we whiz to victory."

"Unbelievable," I huffed. But it was mainly for form's sake. The race would be a lot more fun in the driver's seat. And I actually am a good driver. It would also give me greater satisfaction when I beat Beatrice's time. So okay, I'm a little petty.

The office door opened, and a round face smiled out at us. "Can I help you?" He looked Hyperion up and down. "Great costume. French courtier?"

Hyperion planted his walking stick on the thin carpet with a flourish.

"Mr. Grief?" I asked.

"That's me." He opened the door wider. He was a white man in his late thirties or early forties, and he was only a little taller than me. A broad gut strained his short-sleeved button-down shirt. But there was a sense of power and energy about the man.

"I'm Abigail Beanblossom, and the French courtier is Hyperion Night." I motioned toward my partner. "We—"

"We're amateur detectives investigating the murder of Cassius Santori," Hyperion said.

"And you came in costume?"

"The costume's for my day job," Hyperion said. "Like I said, we're whimsical amateurs. And—"

"Maybe I should dress up this month," Lafayette said. "It's a good marketing gimmick. I can install tents in costume. What's your day job?"

"We own Beanblossom's," Hyperion said, "and we're desperate. Can we talk to you about..." He motioned toward the door across the hall. "Them?"

"Cool. I love amateur detective novels. Come in." Lafayette stepped away from the door and ushered us into a waiting room. Its walls were covered with photos of tents. Big tents, small tents, striped tents, plain tents. Tents without sides. Double-decker tents.

"Wow," I said. "That's a lot of tents."

"I know," Lafayette said, rapid-fire. "Right? Who would have thought there were so many varieties?" He lifted a stack of blue binders off a chair and nodded toward it. "Sit down, sit down."

We arranged ourselves in uncomfortable gray chairs against the wall.

Lafayette set the binders on the coffee table. The little man pulled up a third chair and sat across from us. He bounced one knee, the impact of his heel jolting the floor and vibrating through my chair. "Amateur detectives, huh?" he asked. "The cops must love you."

"You have no idea," Hyperion said wearily.

Lafayette pulled a tissue from a box on the low table between us. He blew his nose. "I heard about the murder. Road rage, they're saying."

Hyperion flushed.

"We think they have the wrong guy," I said.

"Why?" Lafayette asked.

"The evidence doesn't add up," I said. "So we're looking for alternate explanations. Like something that might be connected to his business?"

"Crazy." Lafayette shook his head. "But miscarriages of justice happen all the time. It's why I prefer mystery novels, where the good guys win. How can I help?"

"What can you tell us about Santori's consulting firm?" Hyperion jerked his head toward the door to the hallway.

Lafayette edged his chair closer, his knees bumping the table. He glanced at the closed door. "You know, you may have something. Because something funny *was* going on there," he said in a low voice. "Probably still is."

"What do you mean?" I asked, my pulse accelerating.

"Look, I'm not just their neighbor," he said rapidly, "I'm a client. I mean, it seemed like fate, having a financial consulting firm right across the hall, right? And they had good reviews. So it only made sense I made nice with the neighbors. You never know who's going to need a tent."

"It's just smart business," Hyperion agreed.

"Right, right. Right? So, I made some investments with them, and they did okay. Santori had put me in a lower-risk investment tier, but lower risk means lower reward, right?"

I nodded.

"The thing is, I'm not a low-risk guy. I *like* to take risks. Not crazy risks, but calculated risks. I mean, I know what I can lose. So I asked to be put in a higher-risk investment tier. I signed the paperwork and everything." He rolled his eyes. "You wouldn't believe how many signatures they needed."

"And then what?" Hyperion asked.

"They didn't do it. Nothing changed. They kept my money in the low-risk tier. The returns were, *meh*." The little man shrugged.

A binder slid off the top of the stack. Lafayette made a grab for it, missed. It thunked to the gray carpet.

"You couldn't have been happy." I picked up the binder and handed it to him.

"No, I gave 'em hell." His nostrils flared. "After all the stinking papers I'd signed, you'd think they'd have made *some* changes. I thought my hand was going to fall off from all the signatures. Cassius swore he'd changed my risk tier, and the market was just down. But it wasn't down. It was up."

"Weird," Hyperion said.

Lafayette folded his arms and thumped backward in his chair. "It seemed fishy to me."

"Have you noticed anything else, er, fishy about that office?" I nodded toward the closed door.

"The secretary's got a thing for Johnson." He smirked. "You should have seen her tearing into the conference room when I blew a gasket. I thought she was going to rip my head off."

"Wait, so Johnson and Cassius were *both* there for that meeting?" I asked.

"Oh, yeah. That was a little weird, now that I think about it. Cassius was the guy handling my account. I think Johnson came in because he wanted to sell me some insurance. *That* didn't happen."

"Do you have any idea who might have wanted to kill Cassius Santori?" Hyperion asked.

"Nope. But he handles a lot of people's money, right? And people get tense over money. I didn't lose anything, and *I* was tense. If I had lost, well, I'm just saying…"

We talked more and learned less. Frustrated, my partner and I returned to the tearoom.

"Don't worry," Hyperion said. "Tomorrow, you'll have a fresh, new, and non-French maid costume."

Since he looked fantastic in his costume, I pretended to believe him. Hyperion vanished into his office, shutting the door.

I stared at the twinkle lights, then shrugged and walked into the kitchen. I didn't want to bring down the Halloween tone in the tearoom with my streetwear.

Maricel streaked into the kitchen and plated a scone. "Hey, we're running low on tins of Justice tea. It's flying off the shelves. I think it's because—" She bit her bottom lip.

"What?"

"There's been a lot of talk about the arrest. A cop arrested in a tearoom selling Justice tea…"

"Let's not market it that way," I said.

"I wouldn't. Not with…" She glanced toward the kitchen's open door. The reflected glow of orange and purple twinkle lights blinked dully. "When are we going to start baking our own scones now that we've got the new oven?"

"Next week, I think. I just need to make some practice runs." And tell the bakery I'd need to change our standing order.

She set a pot of jam on the plate. "Cool. I think the customers will like that." She whirled from the kitchen.

Grimacing, I pulled out my phone and called the bakery to give them the bad news we'd no longer need them for scones. I had to do it. Now that we had the new oven, we couldn't afford to outsource. I had to save every penny.

At least the bakery was still making our desserts, so I hadn't cut them out completely. And they were cool about the order change. But I couldn't shake the sense I'd betrayed a fellow businessowner.

The day meandered on. I nearly sent a devoted vegan a Quiche Lorraine, but caught my mistake before the plate went out the door.

"Get your head in the game," I muttered to myself. I watched a waitress bustle out with the correct meal. But it was hard to concentrate when all I could think about were Hyperion and Tony.

Finally, my staff and I cleaned up, and I drove home, feeling exhausted and out of sorts.

I dropped into a chair at my dining table and booted up my laptop. There had to be something in our suspects' backgrounds that connected them to both Tony and Cassius.

I typed Cassius's name into the search engine and clicked on the first article.

—*By Susan Wilkinson*

At a press conference on Monday, Police Chief Nathaniel Daniels stated the investigation into the alleged murder of Mr. Cassius Santori by Detective Anthony Chase is ongoing, "and that's all I can say at this time."

Detective Chase was discovered standing over the dead body of Mr. Santori after a minor traffic accident and claimed amnesia. "While amnesia is a popular device in detective fiction," said District Attorney Robert Falucci, "it is rare in the real world."

The San Benedetto mayor's office released a statement that it will hold an emergency meeting this evening to discuss the response by the SBPD.

Discuss the response? A sour taste spread in the back of my mouth. The San Borromeo police department had handed the investigation off to a detective from another department. What more did anyone want? And how political had this investigation become?

Roughly pushing back my chair, I stood. I wavered there for a moment, then strode to the kitchen, where I reheated a burrito in the microwave. I'd no appetite, but there's something to be said for comfort food.

I returned to the living area and plopped onto my blue couch. Adjusting my virtual reality headset, I entered Razzzor's new first-person shooter game—*Zombie Nazis in Space*, ZNS for short.

I sat in the captain's chair on a gleaming spaceship, leaned back, and bit into my cheesy burrito. The ship's deck was my favorite part of the game. I loved hanging out and staring at the stars through the viewscreen. Relaxing tech sounds beeped and booped and swished in the background.

The viewscreen went to static, and Razzzor's pale face appeared. (Tech geniuses don't get a lot of sun.)

He adjusted his glasses. "I thought we were supposed to meet on Planet AB-532. We need to eradicate the Nazi base there before they colonize that quadrant. And why didn't you tell me about your coffin race?"

Here we go. I sunk deeper into the captain's chair. "Because it's Hyperion's coffin race. I just got roped into it."

He ruffled his brown hair. "I'm totally sponsoring you. It's a great fit with the VR game's theme."

Yes! Stay cool, Abigail. You don't want to sound desperate. "We can't turn the coffin into a spaceship," I warned. "It's a coffin race."

"I'm talking about zombies. Lots of zombies. We're going to have a zombie band in the pre-parade."

I'd forgotten about the pre-parade. Every year, a gaggle of Halloween creatures drew the coffins down the street to the start of the race.

"My team can pull your coffin," he continued. "We'll add ZNS stickers to the coffin, like on a racing car, and voila."

I relaxed deeper into my captain's chair. If that was all Razzzor had planned, we were probably in the clear. "Thanks," I said. "I hadn't gotten around to getting any sponsors yet, so you've saved my bacon."

"No problem. I can spare five-hundred bucks."

I winced. Beatrice had raised five-thousand. If we lost, I'd need a lot more than Razzzor's sponsorship. "That's great," I choked out. "Very generous."

"And I've got a schematic for the engine."

"Engine?" My fingers twitched, and one of my laser cannons accidentally fired. A green blast ricocheted off the forcefield surrounding Razzzor's ship. "It's supposed to be person powered," I said. "We push and let gravity do the rest."

"Right. Right. Don't worry, I've got you covered."

I sat up. An alarm blared on the ship's deck, and I punched it off. "Covered how?"

"Whoa. Incoming suspicious spaceship, twelve o'clock."

My insides did that unpleasant, wriggly thing. "Covered how?"

An explosion rocked my port side.

"Incoming!"

Warm burrito insides dripped down my hand. "Covered *how?*"

CHAPTER 9

Dealing with undead space invaders was a cakewalk compared to getting Razzzor to promise he'd keep his hands off my coffin. I signed off, licked the remains of burrito off my hand, and dropped the headset on the couch.

I looked out the French windows on my left. The solar lights in my back garden were blurry reflections in the darkened glass.

Rising, I trudged to my dining table and returned to my laptop. I was afraid to see how other reporters had covered Tony. But I couldn't ignore possible intel just because I didn't like the way it was presented.

Once again, I typed Cassius Santori's name into the search engine.

Police Officer Charged in Death of Local Businessman
— Susan Wilkinson

Accused murderer Detective Anthony Chase was arraigned yesterday in the shooting death of financial consultant, Cassius Santori. The evening of November 30th, Santori's body was found beside his car, which had been damaged in an accident on Pine Ridge Road in what officers believe was a fit of road rage.

A member of the District Attorney's office reported that evidence from the scene suggests Santori struck Chase's vehicle. Santori was killed by a bullet from Chase's police-issued gun.

"Unfortunately, while the police department attracts many fine officers who join to help people," District Attorney Robert Falucci said, "it also attracts people who want to have power over others. Society cannot tolerate extrajudicial killings and blatant violence toward the public."

The owner at the tearoom where accused murderer, Detective Chase, was arrested, expressed shock that a member of the police department could shoot an unarmed man.

Mr. Santori, a prominent local philanthropist, is survived by his wife, Carla, and his two children, Charles and Caroline.

Anyone with information about the death should contact the San

Borromeo Police Department.

My hands fisted. *Susan.* I hadn't told her that. Okay, I *had* expressed shock—well, disbelief Tony could have killed anyone. But her article implied I thought Tony *was* a killer. And I hadn't said anything about Cassius being unarmed. How was *I* supposed to know if he was unarmed?

I cursed and tried to think positive. At least now I knew where the murder had occurred.

Pine Ridge Road ran up above my grandfather's house. The land was owned by the county, and the trees blocked any ocean view. In short, there wasn't much up there.

Motorcyclists loved the road's twisty turns, but what had Tony been doing there? What had *Cassius* been doing there?

I typed in Carla Santori's name. She worked at... I groaned. The Ombudsman office. How was I supposed to show my face there with that bet in play? I did a frantic search for Carla's home phone number. She was unlisted.

I sagged in my dining chair. Ombudsman it was. I'd go there with Hyperion tomorrow.

And then, since I was online and he *did* work near the victim's office, I typed in Gino Redmond's name. His social media account was private. "Phooey."

Gino had a website though. He was an estate attorney, a sole practitioner by the looks of it.

Why would an estate attorney need Beatrice's PR firm? Was that even allowed? There were strict rules against advertising in California, but PR and advertising weren't the same things. Not exactly.

I drummed my fingers on the dining room table. When Gramps had been a CPA, he'd done a lot of work with estate attorneys. He'd worked with financial planners as well. Had Gino done any work with Cassius and Johnson? They were right across the hall from each other, after all.

A song by Twisted Sister blared from next door. My French windows rattled, and I jerked in my chair.

I twisted to glare at the wall behind me, imagining I could see clear through to Brik's house next door. It was only Tuesday night. Did he *have* to have another stupid party now?

Putting aside my revenge fantasies, I shut the laptop, got out my earplugs, and went to bed.

*****

Hyperion wasn't at the tearoom when I arrived at eight Thursday morning. He hadn't shown up on Wednesday either. This had a) derailed my plan to visit Ombudsman, and b) worried me, since he hadn't returned my calls.

A new garment bag *had* turned up, however.

I unzipped the bag.

It jingled.

I parted its dark-gray covering.

A belly dancer outfit, complete with coin bra, hung from the thick hangers. "Are you kidding me?" It would work for one of Brik's parties, but not the tearoom.

I should have been irritated, but a heavy sadness sunk deep into my chest. Hyperion had tried to do something fun for us both. And the costumes *would* have been fun, if things hadn't gone so wrong.

Maricel bustled into the kitchen dressed like the Bride of Frankenstein. "What's wrong?"

"Nothing." I zipped up the garment bag and turned to an oversized bin on wheels where we kept our flour. We wouldn't need scones baked by me today, so this would be a test run. I wanted to make sure I could time everything correctly. "Cool costume."

"Thanks." She touched the streak of gray in her oversized wig. "What are you dressing as today?"

I measured flour into an oversized mixing bowl. "Um... My costume got sort of mixed up again. I think I'm stuck in the kitchen."

She laughed. "It can't be that bad." She opened the garment bag and stepped backward. "Oh."

"Yeah. I mean, nothing against belly dancers. But the outfit's not exactly tearoom appropriate."

"Our Moroccan mint tea *is* popular though."

I shot her a look, and she laughed again. "Hey, I took a belly dancing class once. It was great exercise. So what are you going to do?"

"I don't know." I studied the costume's cropped purple vest, peeking from the black bag. "Maybe I can make a pirate costume out of the top part?" Because I was getting tired of hiding in the kitchen.

I shrugged the vest on over my white blouse and wrapped one of the silky scarves around my head, pirate style. It jingled, but it worked.

We prepped for our first seating, and I tried not to worry about Hyperion. Ignoring my calls wasn't unusual, and neither was him going AWOL. Besides, the Tarot day usually didn't get started until later.

I worried anyway.

And I really needed to track down Carla Santori. But maybe the interview would be better on my own. Maybe Hyperion's absence was a blessing in disguise. After all, Hyperion *had* dated her husband.

The eleven-thirty seating came and went. I helped clean up, loading dishes into our industrial washer.

Hyperion strode into the kitchen dressed like Ali Baba. "Lunch break. You're free to help me investigate." He stopped short, his dark brows slashing downward. "What are you supposed to be?"

"Pirate." I closed the washer with my hip. "And I was planning on tracking down Carla Santori today."

"Pirates don't jingle. Is that what they sent?"

"Mostly." I found a plate I'd missed and put that in the dishwasher too.

"I'm coming with you to interview Carla."

Because that wouldn't be awkward. Not at all. "Are you sure you want to do that?" I asked carefully.

"I didn't know Cassius was married when we went out. And I didn't know he had children. When I did, it was over. Done."

"I know, and it's not your fault he lied to you. But won't it feel a little weird?"

"I've got plenty of sins to feel guilty about. Being lied to isn't one of them."

I blew out my breath. "Okay then."

"You drive."

I narrowed my eyes. He *hated* it when I drove. "Why?"

"You'll be piloting the coffin. You're going to have to learn some time."

"I know how to drive. My driving's just fine."

"For an eighty-three-year-old."

We argued all the way to the Ombudsman office. I think we both felt uncomfortable about the donation we'd sort of pledged and didn't yet have.

Autumn leaves scuttled through the parking lot, driven by a light breeze. Kids played baseball in the park next door. A fit-looking woman jogged around a track. I looked up at the two-story, dark-wood structure built sometime in the seventies and swallowed.

Keeping an eye out for Mr. Henderson, we checked the signboard by the front door. Hyperion and I climbed the carpeted steps to a cramped, gray reception area off a long hallway.

A woman I guessed was in her sixties looked up from her desk. "Can

I help you?" She blinked at us through cat-eye glasses on a plastic pumpkin chain.

"We're looking for Carla," I said in a low voice. The sign on a nearby door read: *PRESIDENT.* But the door was closed. If we could get in and out without running into Mr. Henderson, we were safe from being asked about sponsors we didn't have.

"Are you volunteers for the haunted house?" the receptionist asked.

Hyperion started.

She eyed his costume. "Because I don't think they're ready for the dress rehearsals yet," the woman finished.

A sound between a groan and a whimper emerged from behind my partner's gritted teeth.

The woman shot him an uncertain look. "But Carla should be there by now. Are you all right, young man?"

"He will be," I said. "What's the address for the haunted house?"

She gave it to us, and we stepped into the hallway.

Mr. Henderson waddled through a doorway and stopped short. "Abigail? Hyperion? What are you two doing here?" His round face beamed.

"Just um, some questions about the coffin race," I chirped. "It's our first race. I want to make sure we do everything right."

He blotted his damp head with a handkerchief. "And did you get what you needed?"

"Yes," I said, "thanks."

Mr. Henderson snapped his fingers. "You'll be wanting stickers, since you're one of our donors now."

"Ah..." I shuffled my feet on the thin, gray carpet. "Yes."

"Excellent," the older man said. "Come into my office. We've got t-shirts for you too."

"Um..." *T-shirts?* I was only donating our sponsorship money because I'd been railroaded into it. I was an imposter. A fake. "I think we're wearing—"

"Costumes," Hyperion said. "I'm Death. But not today."

"These t-shirts and stickers aren't for the race," he said. "They're for you, because you're helping our cause. There are a lot of good people volunteering in long-term care facilities. But they're overworked, and sometimes it's the residents who suffer. Your donation will help us train more volunteers."

"That's great," I said weakly.

"Fortunately, most of the problems that arise are easily remedied, rather than outright abuse." His face darkened. "But I could tell you stories... How's your grandfather, by the way?"

"Good. He's still getting around." And I'd do everything in my power not to send him into a care home. He'd hate leaving his house. But there were too many people who didn't have that option.

"So what sort of things do you work out?" Hyperion asked.

"Oh, things like residents being woken up at two AM to be weighed. Why wake them up? Why not weigh them when they're already awake? Sleep is important."

"And if there's abuse?" Hyperion asked.

"We work with the police on those cases."

Cases, plural. My heart sank. At least we had a sponsor now, so we could donate whether we lost the race or not.

I didn't want to lose the race though. And five hundred dollars didn't seem like much.

He gave us t-shirts, brochures, and stickers for our coffin, and saw us to the door. "Thank you for your support," he said. "We're a small organization, but I like to think we have a big impact thanks to our volunteers and people like you."

"You're welcome," I choked out.

Hyperion and I returned to my hatchback.

"We need more sponsors," I said grimly.

Hyperion buckled up in the passenger seat. "The wine bar behind us is pitching in a hundred bucks. So don't worry about it."

"That's six hundred dollars to Beatrice's five large."

"Forget the sponsors. Didn't you hear? Carla's at a *haunted house.* It's twenty-thirteen all over again." He gripped the door arm, his knuckles whitening.

"What happened in twenty-thirteen?"

Hyperion's lips tightened. "October 2013. The curse began dogpiling me, starting October one. I couldn't escape. Everywhere I turned I was embroiled in all things haunted, and everything went wrong. And now Tony's been arrested. I tell you, it's happening again."

"Hold on. You can't think Tony was arrested because of a Halloween curse?"

"I know you think it's ridiculous. *I* think it's ridiculous. And I understand the reverse placebo effect. When you believe you're cursed, everything seems cursed. But the reverse placebo effect doesn't explain Tony getting arrested. Maybe it's all in my head, but look at what's happened to him."

"And I guess telling you it's just reverse placebo doesn't fix anything."

"And now we're being sent to a *haunted house*. They're distilled Halloween, where the curse has its greatest power." He gulped.

"The haunted house isn't even finished yet. I'm sure it's got no real Halloween mojo."

"Just you wait," he said darkly. "Just you wait."

CHAPTER 10

We stared up at the ramshackle Victorian. Weeds filled the front yard. Paint peeled off the old home's gray siding. The Ombudsman team had no doubt posted the WARNING, CONDEMNED signs for effect. But they were eerily believable.

Clouds blotted out the lowering sun and framed the two-story house in gloom. The whir of an electric saw screeched from inside the house.

Hyperion swallowed. "Tell me you can't feel evil emanating from that house." His red harem pants billowed in the breeze.

"I can't. Let's get this over with." I wanted to get back to the tearoom before it closed.

"Wait, you can't tell me, or you really can't feel it?"

I strode down the overgrown path and up the porch steps. Hyperion trailed behind me, his head on a swivel.

The door stood halfway open. I pushed it wider, and its hinges squealed.

"Are you sure this is the right place?" Hyperion whispered. "I mean, shouldn't there be a—"

I stepped inside, and there was a loud ping. Motion blurred on my left. I gasped and jumped backward, landing on Hyperion's sandaled foot.

He grunted. "Ow."

A monstrously sized jack-in-the-box grinned, its painted head bobbing and weaving. The walls were draped with crimson fabric. Its folds puddled on the dusty floor like spilled blood. A clown face with a door in its gaping mouth covered one wall. The overall effect was... horrifying.

"Cool. That works." A clown with a grin full of razors and fluffy orange hair lumbered toward us.

Hyperion shoved me off his foot. "Get back!"

The clown stopped, swaying on his oversized, red shoes. He frowned at Hyperion. "Are you looking for the Fortune Telling room? Because we already have our Mystic Mystic."

"We're looking for Carla Santori," I said.

"Are you two volunteers?" the clown asked.

"Oh, hell no," Hyperion said.

"I'm assuming *you* are though," I said to the clown.

He plucked at his floppy outfit. "Yeah. We're doing a dress rehearsal tonight. The house opens this weekend. This is the creepy clown room."

"And Carla's in the...?" I prompted.

"Mystic fortuneteller room."

Hyperion shuddered. Slowly, he stretched a quivering finger to the jack-in-the-box. It loosed a shriek of malevolent laughter.

"Haunted circus theme?" I asked brightly.

"Yeah," the clown said. "What do you think?"

"Nailed it," I said. "I've got to say, it's impressive that Carla is working today, all things considered."

The clown's shoulders sagged. "Yeah. What that woman's been through." He shook his head.

"She's a tough lady," I agreed, hoping he'd elaborate.

"You have no idea." He studied Hyperion. "Are you here to take over for her?"

"I'm Ali Baba, not a fortuneteller. Though I do read—" Hyperion shook his turbaned head. "Never mind."

I paused. How could I dig for more gossip on Carla without looking like I was digging for more gossip on Carla? "Did you know her husband?"

"I saw him at a few parties." He shook his head. "Never trusted the guy."

"Yeah," Hyperion said. "I guess it wasn't such a surprise when he was killed. Not that I'm excusing it," he added quickly.

"Tell me about it." The clown scratched his orange wig, pushing it off-kilter. "Carla's a saint."

Never trusted the guy? A saint? Had Carla known her husband was cheating on her? Because it sounded like she might have. But there was no way I could ask. "I had to say though, I was surprised to hear death by road rage."

"Me too," the clown agreed. "Cassius knew how to shine you on when you first met him. He could talk his way out of anything. I'd have thought an angry driver would be no problem."

I nodded sagely. "But after you got to know him, you learned he had enemies."

"I wouldn't exactly say enemies," the clown said. "I mean, I guess he did because someone killed him. But I don't know about *enemies*."

Okay, now I was totally confused. "And the mystic fortuneteller room is...?" I pointed toward the door between the wall clown's teeth.

"Through there. Second floor."

"Great," Hyperion said, teeth clenched. "Just great. The irony of maiming me in a haunted fortuneteller's room will be too good for the curse to pass up. You know something's going to go haywire and collapse on top of us."

"It shouldn't," the clown said uncertainly. "The haunted house is pretty much done."

"*Pretty much* isn't done," Hyperion said. "It's not-quite-done. It means there are still things that are undone."

"Second floor," I said to the clown and steered Hyperion toward the door. "Gotcha. Thanks."

We emerged into a dimly lit passage of crimson fabric. The door slammed behind us, and the room went dark. Fabric brushed my arm, and my skin twitched.

"This looks like one of those mazes where monsters jump out at you to make you scream," Hyperion said. "You first."

"Thanks a lot," I hissed, my eyes adjusting to the lack of light.

"It's for your own protection. I'm cursed. Remember?"

The fabric billowed eerily, the labyrinth seeming to shift. I crept forward, waiting for the jump scare, Hyperion treading on my heels.

"Hurry, hurry, hurry." He pressed me forward.

"I'm going as fast as I—"

A shadow shifted, and I yelped.

"What?" Hyperion whirled. "What is it?"

I deepened my breathing. "Nothing."

"Why are you yelling about nothing?"

"Because I thought it was something. Okay?"

Scaly arms and legs bulleted toward us. We shrieked, and I tried to climb on top of Hyperion. The lizard man faded back into the folds of fabric. I released my partner and dropped to the floor.

"Enough. I'm done." Wild-eyed, Hyperion grabbed my wrist and hauled me through the rest of the maze. We exited into another tented room filled with mannequins of circus freaks.

"This is so not good," Hyperion said. "One of these is real, and they're going to jump out at us, and one of us is going to wet her pants."

"Her? Why do you assume I'm the pant-wetter?"

"Everyone knows women have smaller bladders."

"That's a fallacy."

"Really?" He shrugged. "Learn something new every day."

Huddling together, we edged through the mannequins. A bearded lady slowly turned her head, tracking our movements.

"Bearded lady," I whispered, "three o'clock."

"We see you." Hyperion pointed at her. "So there's absolutely no point to—"

"Raugh!" Someone shouted behind us.

I tried to jump out of my tennis shoes.

Hyperion shrieked, bolting forward. He stumbled over a plastic skull and plowed into a pair of Siamese twins.

Both heads tumbled from their conjoined bodies and clunked to the wooden floor. A smiling mannequin head rolled to a stop, swaying, at Hyperion's feet.

A clown in black jangled toward us. "That's going to have to—"

"I'm outta here." My partner raced to the door.

"Hyperion," I said, "wait."

He vanished into the next room.

Nodding apologetically to the clown, I followed, and walked inside a maze of mirrors.

My partner was gone.

"Hyperion?" I whispered.

No answer.

I pivoted slowly. My reflection splintered and turned. I tugged down my purple pirate vest. "Hyperion?" I said more loudly.

Something creaked behind me. I whipped around and stared at my own reflection. And I'm sure I only looked pale because of the bad lighting.

I gulped. Where could he have gone? This was a maze of mirrors. I should be able to catch a glimpse of him somewhere.

I edged deeper into the hanging mirrors. "Hyperion?"

"Here," he said.

My back muscles unknotted. "Here where?"

In the mirror in front of me, his disembodied head appeared over my shoulder. "Here."

I gasped and pivoted.

The rest of Hyperion's body emerged. "I found a way out."

I pointed. "Yeah, through the maze." We had to be near the stairway to the second floor by now. The house wasn't *that* big.

"There's another way out." He motioned me toward him. "This way."

I shifted my weight. "Shouldn't we just go the, um, regular way?"

"And risk seven years bad luck?" He returned to the door we'd come in through and edged along the wall, squeezing behind a mirror.

"That's not— That's cheating," I sputtered.

"I told you, there's a door here." His voice was muffled.

I sucked in my gut and edged past the mirror too. Behind it, Hyperion opened a door and revealed a staircase. "Come on."

I glanced behind me. "I don't think we're supposed to—" I said to his departing back. "Go that way," I finished. Leave it to Hyperion to find an escape hatch in a haunted house.

We climbed the stairs, which were just ordinary wooden stairs, to a second floor.

Hyperion opened a door to a swathe of red fabric. He shoved the drapery aside and stuck his head through. "Helloooo? Is there a haunted fortuneteller here?"

My partner looked at me over his shoulder. "Ugh, this is stereotype central. I'd be offended on behalf of all professional readers and psychics, but who needs the stress?" Hyperion stepped inside, and I followed.

A parachute hung from the center of the ceiling, simulating a tent. Giant Tarot cards decorated the walls. Creepy clown mannequins slouched in the corners. A table with a red cloth and an enormous crystal ball stood in the center of the room.

Hyperion edged closer to study an enormous Death card. The grim reaper had gone to town, leaving a bloody trail of severed heads and entrails behind his scythe.

There are all sorts of styles of Tarot cards. Steampunk. Vampire. Fluffy Bunny. These cards were beyond disturbing. "That's, uh... Wow."

My partner stopped in front of the Strength card. It wasn't the usual maiden holding open a lion's mouth. Instead, a female zombie in circus-acrobat gear swung a whip over a decaying lion.

"That just ain't right," Hyperion said.

"It's a haunted house. They're not going for historical accuracy."

"The Strength card represents—" He shook himself. "Whatevs. Carla's not here. Let's go."

"Hold on." I lifted the tablecloth. A chic blue purse sat hidden beneath the round table. "She'll be back."

"Unless she's dead."

I adjusted my head scarf, and it jingled lightly. "Stop it. You're freaking yourself out." And he wasn't doing my nerves any good either.

Hyperion swallowed. He edged along the wall to the next Tarot card, a bloody bride and groom representing The Lovers.

I stuck close to the table in the middle of the room. If anything was going to jump out at me—and I had my eyes on that clown—I'd be ready.

A woman cleared her throat behind me. I did one of those graceful high jumps that I can only manage when someone's snuck up on me.

"You looking for me?" Carla, in a gold lamé turban, oversized earrings, and a blouse and skirt stood with her fists on her hips.

"Gagh." I cleared my throat. I stuck out my hand then dropped it to my side. "I'm Abigail Beanblossom, and this is—"

"I know who you are," Carla said. "What are you doing here?"

"You know who we are?" I glanced at Hyperion. Had she tracked us down after we'd visited her husband's office? Because that seemed a little... weird.

"You run the tearoom downtown," she said. "I saw you in the paper."

"Right," I said, relieved. My insides tensed. Wait. Most of the times I'd been in the paper it had been because I'd been involved in a murder. Beanblossom's didn't get a lot of love from the local press.

"So?" she prompted.

"We don't think your husband was killed in a road rage accident," Hyperion said.

I sucked in a breath. Laying it all out there might not be the best way to gather intel. But it had worked before.

Carla's jaw jutted forward, then retreated. She exhaled slowly. "Neither do I."

CHAPTER 11

The Devil, dressed like a magician in top hat and tails, leered from the fabric-covered wall. A phantom breeze stirred the draperies of the red tent, and the Devil card swayed, serpentine.

Carla leaned one hip against the table. The crystal ball in its center wobbled, and she rested her manicured hand on the globe to steady it.

"Why don't you believe it?" I asked.

"Cassius could talk his way out of—and into—anything," she said. "He wasn't the sort to get into an argument with a stranger. To kill him, that cop would have had to have been insane, or guns blazing when he stepped from his car."

"And you don't think he was," Hyperion said slowly.

"I guess anyone could be unstable," Carla said, "including cops. But... I don't know. Something's off."

"But the detective was caught red handed," I said.

Hyperion glared in my direction. For a moment, in his red vest, he looked a lot like that Devil card.

Carla nodded. "Yeah. I get it. The odds are the detective is guilty. But it doesn't smell right, you know? Or maybe I'm just in denial."

Hyperion clasped her hands. "Believe me, we know. We think the cop was framed. Someone drugged him, used his gun to shoot your husband, and left Detective Chase at the crime scene."

"That sounds... complicated," she said.

"It is," I agreed.

"So the question," Hyperion said, "is who would want your husband dead?"

Carla lifted the crimson tablecloth and glanced beneath the table at her purse. "Johnson Warszowski." She dropped the tablecloth.

"His business partner?" I said. "Why?"

"Something was going on between those two, some strange conflict Cassius didn't want to tell me about. I think Johnson was up to something criminal, and Cassius found out."

"Why do you think that?" I asked.

"Because Cassius was acting strange. He was tense, nervous. And he was working longer hours, including weekends, like he was searching for something."

Or cheating on his wife. I narrowed my eyes. "Did he say anything to you about what was bothering him?" I asked her.

"All he told me was he was under pressure at work."

The lament of the cheating husband. Okay, I'd never had a husband, cheating or otherwise. But from what I'd read, *busy at work* was the classic cheater's cover story.

"I'm sorry to bring this up," I began, and I *was* sorry. But Hyperion was right. We didn't have time to be delicate, not with Tony in jail. "But I heard you two were getting a divorce."

Carla shifted, and her skirt jingled faintly. "Yes."

I waited.

"But the long hours and weird moods were going on before we separated," she continued.

"Do you think his stressed-out behavior could have been connected to him asking for a divorce?" I asked.

Carla's mouth compressed again. "That's what I thought, at first. But then someone killed him." She swallowed jerkily. "We have two children. They're both away at college, but—"

Carla looked away and pressed a hand to her mouth. "This hasn't been easy. They loved their father."

I looked away too, and pretended to study the zombie lovers. My parents had let me down in the worst way. I'm not sure what hurt more—their betrayal, or the knowledge that my childhood gods were more broken than most.

And now things would come out about Cassius and his secret life. The ugly truths rarely stayed hidden. And two more children would have to come to grips with the knowledge that their parents were flawed, and maybe more than most.

Hyperion's shoulders bowed. "I'm sorry," he said quietly, and I knew he was offering more than condolences.

"How'd you find me?" she asked.

I cleared my throat. "We heard you were volunteering at the haunted house. The clown downstairs told us you were up here."

"Frank's a good friend."

But was he *only* a friend? Because he'd seemed awfully admiring, and Cassius might not be the only cheater.

"Is there anyone else you can think of who might have done this?"

Hyperion asked. "Anyone in your husband's personal life?"

"No," Carla said. "No one."

Dread wrung my stomach. What I needed to ask next was the sort of direct question that the police were a lot better at getting answers to. "I have one more question. Where were you last Saturday afternoon at three o'clock?"

She blanched. "Here. Decorating the haunted house. You think *I* killed Cassius? He was my husband, the father of my children."

"Sorry," I muttered. "I had to ask."

"I think you should go now," she said, voice taut.

Hyperion and I shuffled from the room and downstairs. We made our way to the front door, and no one made us scream. I kind of wished someone would have though.

I paused in the foyer. The clown in black lounged beside the jack-in-the-box.

"Hi," I said, "there was another clown here, Frank. Is he still around?"

The new clown shook his head, the bells on his collar clanging. "Nope. His wife just went into labor. It's their first kid. He took off out of here like a..."

"Clown out of hell?" Hyperion suggested.

"Yeah," the clown said. "Like that."

"Well, thanks," I said. "Hey, were you working here last Saturday?"

"Nope."

"Was Frank?"

"No idea," the clown said.

Hyperion and I left the haunted house. We paused on the cracked sidewalk.

"So what did you think of Carla?" I asked.

"I believed her."

Was he saying that because she thought Tony was innocent? Or was she more believable because Hyperion felt guilty?

"She seemed real," he continued. "Honest."

I sighed. "Yeah. She did to me too. But I still want to check her alibi."

I glanced up. The sky had darkened behind the clouds. "On the positive side, you survived the haunted house."

"It means nothing," Hyperion said. "The curse is sneaky that way. Tearoom?"

I nodded.

We returned to Beanblossom's, and I helped clean up. The staff and

I had a routine by now, and we were done by seven thirty. I watched the other ladies shuffle, laughing, out the door. Then I returned to the kitchen and pulled my keys from my purse.

"Hey," Hyperion said from behind me, and I started.

I pressed the hand holding the keys to my chest. "You're still here?"

He'd changed out of his costume and into a black sweater and slacks. "Yeah. I figured it might be smart to stick around after someone tried to shove you into traffic."

"Thanks. Walk me to my car?"

"I'll follow you to your car and to your house."

"I appreciate the gesture, but—"

"Don't be too flattered. I heard there's a party at Brik's tonight."

Of course there was. I walked into the hall and pushed open the heavy, metal door to the parking lot. At least my neighbor had backed off on the nightly parties, but Brik still threw too many, in my humble opinion. And they were *loud.*

"Besides," Hyperion continued, "there's something I want to show you, and I can't do it here."

I locked the door behind us. "Should I be worried?"

"No, it's not like it's a rash."

At this point, a rash might be preferable.

We strolled to my Mazda hatchback.

I opened my door and rested my hand on it. "So what is it?"

"I told you, I have to show you."

I slid inside the car. "You're sure it's not a rash? Because I really wouldn't mind a rash."

"It's not a rash." He shut my door then jogged to his Jeep.

I waited for his headlights to flash on, then I backed from my spot and drove home.

My neck tightened as I rounded the thickly wooded corner to my bungalow. If any of Brik's guests were blocking my driveway again...

I slowed, passing Brik's modish two-story. He'd recently repainted the exterior a deep blue-gray. The light over his door was on, and Brik's pickup sat in the driveway.

But the front door was closed, and the street wasn't packed with cars. The party mustn't have started yet. Or maybe there wasn't going to be one after all.

Nah. I never got that lucky.

I pulled into my own tiny driveway, stopped short of the coffin mobile, and stepped out. My rear bumper stuck into the sidewalk. I really needed to move that coffin.

Hyperion pulled up at the sidewalk. Frowning, he climbed from the Jeep and checked his watch. "We must be early."

"So what did you want to show me?"

"Oh, right." He reached into his Jeep and pulled out the t-shirt cannon.

"I've seen that already, remember?"

"Not since Razzzor modified it."

My blood turned arctic. "Razzzor? Modified?" I squawked. But I'd *told* Razzzor... to stay away from the coffin mobile, not the cannon. It's the little details that always trip you up.

"Are you ready for a full bucket of awesome?" He brandished the plastic cannon.

I raised my hands in front of my chest, palms out. "No. Hyperion, Razzzor's great with tech, but the robotic stuff he's been working on is military grade."

"That's probably why he converted it into a pumpkin cannon."

"A pumpkin what?"

"For mini pumpkins, of course."

"Mini..." I sputtered. Were they crazy? "*Tell* me that thing isn't loaded."

"Duh. What good would an unloaded pumpkin cannon be?"

"Mini pumpkins are hard as rocks. Why would you shoot them at anyone?"

"I wouldn't. That would be dangerous." He swiveled, aiming. "We can shoot them into the ocean. It will be a Halloween treat for the fish."

I folded my arms. "Fish aren't meant to eat mini pumpkins, and it's got to be illegal."

"What about sharks? I have it on good authority they'll eat anything."

I barely managed not to stomp my foot. "Hyperion—"

"Fine. Be a killjoy. It may be October, but I own the world's first and only mini pumpkin cannon. How cool is that?" He pivoted toward me, the barrel of the cannon aimed roughly at my midsection.

I sucked in my stomach. "Put the pumpkin cannon down."

"Please." He rolled his eyes. "I have trigger discipline."

Sure he did. "May I see it, please?"

"You're going to try to confiscate my cannon, aren't you?"

"No," I lied, edging closer. "You're an adult. You're entitled to whatever possibly illegal weaponry you want. I just want to see what Razzzor did to modify it."

Hyperion aimed at Brik's pickup. "It's something to do with the spring and the trigger mechanism."

Oh, that doesn't sound dangerous. Not at all. "Have you tested it yet?"

"No, I thought we could go into your backyard and try it out. You've got all those high fences."

Despite the cool night air, sweat beaded my brow. "Hyperion. Listen to me very carefully."

"I'm listening."

"I wasn't kidding when I said Razzzor made weapon's grade robotics. There's a good chance that is not a toy." I made an ineffectual grab for the cannon.

Hyperion lurched away.

Thwunk-thwunk-thwunk. Orange blurs shot from the cannon. Mini pumpkins rocketed loudly off the door of Brik's pickup, leaving deep dents in the sides.

We stood in stunned silence.

Hyperion's jaw snapped shut. "Razzzor might have said something about making it an automatic." He thrust the cannon into my arms. "Gotta run. Ta!" He jogged to his Jeep and roared down the tree-lined road.

The door to Brik's house sprang open. Barefoot and bare chested, my neighbor hurried into the street. Brik turned to me. "What was that sound?"

"Nothing."

"What are you holding?"

"Nothing."

He glanced at his pickup and did a double take. "Are those...? Something dented my truck."

"Did it?"

"Are those pumpkins?" He stepped toward me. "Abigail—"

I flinched backward. "I can explain—"

Thwunk. The cannon jerked in my hands.

Brik grunted and doubled over. A mini pumpkin dropped between his feet.

CHAPTER 12

I hate it when I do terrible things. "Oh, no." Face hot, I hurried to my neighbor. "Brik? Are you okay?"

His knees folded inward, and he dropped to the pavement.

"I'm so sorry," I babbled. "It was an accident. I'll get you an ice pack."

Racing to unlock my door, I hurried inside. I dropped the pumpkin cannon on the sofa and jogged into my kitchen.

I threw open the freezer door. Icepacks? No. But I did have a bag of frozen Asian-style vegetables. I grabbed the bag and rushed back outside.

Brik lay on his side in a fetal position.

I knelt and handed Brik the frozen vegetables. "Brik, I—"

"Why?" he gasped.

"Razzzor converted a t-shirt cannon into a pumpkin cannon for Hyperion, and I guess it's now a hair-trigger *and* an automatic, and—"

Pressing the frozen foods to his crotch, he sat up and glared. "Really, Abigail?"

"I didn't—"

"And my truck?"

I snapped my jaw shut. Because as much as Hyperion deserved it, I was no snitch. "That was an accident too. Like I said, it seems to be an automatic—"

"This grudge has gone too far."

"Grudge?" I coughed and wished I were anywhere but here. "I don't have a grudge. It was an accident."

He staggered to his feet, tossed me the frozen vegetables, and hobbled into his house. The front door slammed, and I winced.

It *had* been an accident.

But I could see how it might not look that way from Brik's perspective.

"I'm not holding a grudge," I muttered. There was no *reason* to have a grudge. It wasn't like he'd dumped me. We'd never even dated.

And we never were *going* to date because according to Brik, I was too high-risk. I snatched up a mini pumpkin and returned inside my bungalow.

Okay, maybe I was still a little upset with Brik. Because while I could see his point about the high-risk business, it had been a jerk thing to say.

I set the pumpkin beside my laptop on the dining table, and stared absently at the tableau.

Had shooting him been an accident? After seeing what Hyperion had done, why had my finger been on the trigger at all?

No. I was overthinking this. Of course it had been an accident.

But I kept turning over the sight of Brik crumpling, of the pumpkin dropping between his feet. I needed to clear my head. And if we were going to start making our own scones, I also needed to come up with a scone recipe or two for Halloween.

I wandered into my pantry. Drying herbs hung from the rafters. Scanning the shelves for ingredients, I found a package of mixed chocolate and peanut butter baking chips.

They were orange and yellow and brown, perfect for Halloween. And it's hard to go wrong with chocolate and peanut butter. Unless you were one of those weirdos who hate chocolate and peanut butter, which I definitely was not.

Returning to my living room, I grabbed my laptop and brought it into the kitchen. I pulled up my basic scone recipe, made a few test changes and saved it as Chocolate Peanut Butter Cup scones.

By this time, mixing the basic recipe was old hat. But I loved how versatile it was. Small tweaks created totally different flavors and textures.

I put the scones in the oven and left them to bake.

While the scent of baking chocolate and peanut butter wafted through the kitchen, I nuked a frozen burrito. I braced my elbows on the butcherblock island and nibbled and investigated, searching for articles about the murder.

The only thing new I learned was that Cassius had been driving a Fiat Spider when he'd been killed. If he'd hit Tony's Jeep, the Jeep had to have come out the winner.

There was also a disheartening article about police brutality. It included a long quote from the DA about abusive cops not being tolerated. I was down with that. No one likes a bully with a gun, especially one with the legal authority to use it. But Tony Chase wasn't that guy.

I searched for our other suspects. All I found on Lafayette Grief was the website for his tent company. *Not helpful.*

Several articles featured Dr. Tarrach and his wife, and the charities they were involved with. He even sponsored a kid's baseball team, though it didn't look like he had any kids of his own.

The oven timer dinged, and I removed the scones. I let them cool for five minutes then drizzled chocolate over the top. It just seemed like the right thing to do.

Gingerly, I bit into a scone and closed my eyes, blissing out. It was definitely a dessert scone, and I hadn't been wrong about the chocolate and peanut butter. Or the drizzled chocolate. I'd have to cut them smaller though, or customers would be collapsing in sugar comas.

Feeling slightly better, I packed away the scones, did more fruitless interneting, and went to bed.

*****

"Whoa." Hyperion stepped away from the tearoom's white counter and raised his hands in a warding gesture. "What are you wearing?"

I plucked at my serving-wench skirt. "You should know. You ordered it." And since I couldn't hide in the kitchen on a busy Friday, I'd been stuck wearing the stupid thing. I braced my hands on the counter.

It was our last seating of the day, and the tables were full. Customers sipped tea and nibbled scones. Costumed Tarot readers roamed between the tables.

"I didn't order that," Hyperion said. "We were supposed to match." He adjusted his tricorn hat. "We're supposed to be American revolutionaries." He rubbed his chin. "Though your costume's time period seems right."

"I'm starting to think you're doing this on purpose."

His brown eyes widened. "Are you kidding me? I don't want to be partnered with someone dressed like a... What *are* you supposed to be?"

"Serving wench."

He gripped the lapels of his long coat. "Oddly appropriate for a tearoom."

"No, George Washington. No, it isn't. From now on, I'm getting my own costumes."

"From where? This is the only decent costume shop in town."

"There's that Halloween store—"

He gripped his hat. "You can't. It's blasphemy. Their costumes are made of plastic. You can't possibly slum it in Beanblossom's in that trash."

A headache started behind my eyeballs. But darn it, he was right. "Well, we're wasting money on belly dancer and other revealing costumes I can't wear."

"Oh, I've been getting refunds."

Then why hadn't the store learned? They had to be losing money on costumes that weren't getting rented out.

"Forget about the costume," Hyperion said briskly. "We have bigger fish to fry."

"It's a little hard to forget." I adjusted my busty and itchy vest.

"True." He eyed me askance. "But I have news."

"Me too," I said. "I've been thinking about that little witch who was hanging around just before Tony lost time—"

"Lost time's a UFO thing. Before he was drugged."

I turned and straightened a tea cannister on the shelf. "Maybe we should check out that Halloween store? I know it's a longshot, but that's probably where the costume came from."

"We don't have time for longshots. They won't know whom they sold it to. Listen. I was talking to Tony. He doesn't remember it, but according to the accident investigators, *his* car rammed Cassius's."

So the newspaper had been wrong. *Surprise, surprise.* I rested my elbows on the counter. "That fits our theory. If someone drugged Tony to frame him for the murder, then the killer drove Tony's car and crashed it. But… it should also make Tony look more innocent to the police."

"How do you figure that?"

"Because if Tony had hit Cassius instead of the reverse, then he had even less reason to go road ragey. Have you visited the crash scene yet?"

"No," he said. "And I think we should."

"It does seem like the sort of thing a detective would do." I checked my watch. It would be getting dark soon.

"Er," Hyperion said, "I don't suppose you could…"

I looked around the tearoom. The food had already been delivered to tables for our last seating. All that remained were tea refills and collecting the bills.

"Let me talk to Maricel." *Again.* She was definitely going to get a bonus this year, whether I could afford it or not.

Maricel agreed she could handle closing. I promised to return for the cleanup. And Hyperion and I were off in his Jeep.

Pine Ridge Road is, as you might expect, full of evergreens and on a high ridge. But since cypresses (not pines) block the ocean views, it's not particularly popular unless you're a motorcyclist.

It's gloomy. There's too much shade, too many shadows. The road is narrow and twisty. The bark on the cypress trees is near black, and the low branches are bare and grasping. There are rumors it's haunted, and I half believed them.

Hyperion slowed the Jeep.

"Do you have any idea where the accident happened?" I asked.

"Tony said it was just past the summit."

Where a speeding car might not see an object in its path, like another car.

"Did he say anything else?" I asked.

"He said he woke up on the road, by the driver's side of his car, when a passing driver shook him awake."

I grunted. "Brave motorist."

"Cassius was lying beside his car, off to the side."

"Any idea how long they were lying there?" I asked.

"None. But it could have been minutes or an hour. I mean, have *you* seen any cars since we've been up here?"

We crested the road's summit, and Hyperion pulled to the shoulder beneath the hillside. Trees clung desperately to the steep bank, their roots exposed in the rocky soil.

I stepped out and scanned the pavement. "Did he say what side of the road they crashed on?"

He dropped from the Jeep and shut his door. "No."

"Okay, I'll take the opposite side." I crossed the street and walked slowly, looking for signs of a crash. After a few minutes, I spotted tire tracks in the soft dirt. I followed them onto the road, where they became skid marks.

"I think I found it," I called.

Hyperion hurried to my side, and I pointed.

He snapped a photo of the skid marks and the tire tracks. "A detective would do that too," he said.

"Oh, totally." I studied the road. I didn't see any other skid marks. Crouching, I stared at the tracks in the earth. They went a little sideways, the tracks smearing, like the car had been pushed. "Do you see this?"

"Yeah."

"Could these tracks be from the Spider Cassius was driving?"

"Judging by the axle track, I'd say yes."

"I don't see skid marks from another car. Do you?"

"No, which means—"

"Tony's Jeep didn't brake. This is more support for our theory that the accident was intentional." But I shook my head. I wasn't a professional accident investigator. "I'm going to look around some more."

Hyperion grunted and took another picture with his phone.

I walked further down the shaded road. Across the street was a short dirt driveway. It led to a barbed wire fence with a county sign:

NO PARKING/NO TRESPASSING.

Since I don't like being told what to do, I crossed to the yellow sign.

Another set of deep tracks marked the earth. It looked like someone had driven in and turned around there.

"Find anything?" Hyperion called.

I studied the tracks some more. "I'm not sure," I said slowly.

He strode to join me.

"Those look recent," he said.

"Yeah. I was just thinking—"

"Look how deep those wheel tracks are." He pointed to the spot where the car had turned around. It did look like there were four slightly deeper imprints. "It looks like a car was waiting there." He snapped a photo.

"Tony's Jeep?"

"I don't have his tire tracks memorized."

"Okay, what are we thinking here? That someone was lying in wait for Cassius here? That when they saw Cassius pass, this car—Tony's Jeep—came out of hiding and rammed it?"

"Yes," Hyperion said. "That is an excellent summation of our theory."

"We need to find out if we were right about Tony being drugged."

"He doesn't have the toxicology results back yet."

I shook my head. "If that test comes back positive, it all fits. But… the killer's plan was crazy elaborate. If we're right, someone put a lot of thought into this."

"Someone really hated Cassius."

Someone really hated Tony.

CHAPTER 13

Hyperion and I took more photos of the crash site, largely because we weren't sure what else to do. And then we returned to Hyperion's Jeep and drove down the hill.

The sun had set, a thin, pale line glimmering on the horizon. Slivers of darkening ocean slashed through the trees.

"How's Brik?" Hyperion asked.

I pressed deeper into my seat. "Have you talked to him?"

"No... Don't worry. I'll fess up to the dents in his truck, even if my insurance rates go through the roof again."

"Don't bother," I grumped.

He shot me a glance. "You two still, er...?"

"No. Yes. I might have accidentally shot him with the pumpkin cannon."

Hyperion winced. "Was he hurt?"

"I didn't hit anything important."

Hyperion was silent for all of a minute. "Brik's wrong, you know," he said quietly.

"I can't blame him for being mad about getting hit with a pumpkin."

"Not about the pumpkin, about you."

I sank lower in my seat. I never should have told Hyperion about the Brik situation. But tequila has a powerful effect on me. Hyperion had taken advantage of that a month or so back.

"Some things are worth the risk," Hyperion continued. "People are worth the risk." He turned onto a street paralleling the freeway.

"People like Tony are," I said. And so was Hyperion.

His hands tightened on the wheel. He took the onramp onto the freeway, merging into traffic. "Tony's in real trouble, Abigail. This isn't a good time to be a cop, and it really isn't a good time to be a cop accused of murder."

I thought about the articles I'd read, about how infuriating they'd be if I didn't know Tony, and how infuriating they were because I did. I thought about how easy it was to make decisions based on emotion rather than facts. About the strength of narratives over truth. "He's innocent," I said in a low voice. "We'll figure this out."

"The truth will set him free?" Hyperion's laugh was hollow. "I'm not so sure about that."

"We'll figure this out," I repeated.

His jaw tightened, and he nodded.

A red, Lebaron convertible sped past, and I did a double take. The driver had fluffy orange hair. "Was that the clown from the haunted house?"

The convertible took an exit.

"What?" Hyperion asked.

I pointed. "Follow that clown."

Hyperion swerved across two lanes of traffic. Horns blared behind us.

I gripped the armrest. Now I was *really* glad I'd be driving the coffin racer.

"Why are we following the clown?" Hyperion asked.

"He's friends with the victim's wife. He may have been working at the haunted house the day Cassius was killed. That means he may be able to verify if Carla was there. That clown's a possible witness."

We got jammed up on El Camino (typical), but managed to keep the red car in sight. The Lebaron turned onto a side road and then into the parking lot of a hospital.

"His wife," I said. "Didn't that other clown tell us she'd gone into labor?"

"I hope she's all right." Hyperion frowned. "They usually eject new mothers from the hospital right away, don't they?"

The convertible turned into a parking garage and whizzed up a curving ramp. Hyperion turned to follow.

A VW Bug reversed suddenly from a spot in front of us. Hyperion slammed on the brakes and honked.

The other driver made a rude gesture.

"Of all the—" Hyperion glared. "He should have watched where he was going."

The VW slowly reversed, stopped. Taking its time, it inched forward.

Hyperion swerved around it, tires screeching, and we flew up the ramp.

The Lebaron sat parked beside an elevator, the lucky stiff. We had to go up another ramp to find a parking spot of our own. Hyperion and I raced down the stairs to the hospital.

"He can't be that hard to find." My partner peered through the bustle in the hospital's high-ceilinged entry. "Besides, how fast can he move in those floppy shoes?"

Panting, I jogged to a signboard. "Maternity's on the third floor." I pressed an elevator button.

"No time." Hyperion grabbed my elbow and steered me into a stairwell. We jogged up the steps and into a blue-carpeted waiting area.

A flash of polka dot caught my eye.

"That way." I hurried down a corridor.

The clown stood staring at a window, a bouquet of flowers in his hands.

"Hey, Clown," Hyperion said.

Frank tensed, his red-gloved hands throttling the bouquet. "What?"

"It's us," Hyperion said. "From the haunted house. Carla's friends."

He gasped. "Oh, babies!"

Hyperion pressed his hands to the window and goggled at the infants in their cribs. Most were sleeping. One was yelling. His two infant neighbors stared at the yeller, perplexed expressions on their baby faces.

The clown's shoulders dropped, and he exhaled. "Oh. You. I thought you were—"

"Trained killers?" Hyperion asked. "Oh my God, they're adorable. Which is yours?"

"That one." He pointed at the yeller.

"Good lungs," Hyperion said.

"Yeah." The clown beamed. "It's a girl. I mean, she's a girl. You're sure you're not here to cause trouble?"

"Not in front of the children." Hyperion waved at them through the window.

"Why would we cause trouble?" I asked.

"You wouldn't believe how many people have a thing about clowns," Frank said. "And not a good thing."

"Could be why your haunted house has a circus theme," I said.

"Well, yeah, but those are evil clowns. Not all clowns are evil. Most just want to spread joy. But people are prejudiced. It's unfair. And I'm not even that scary."

"All clowns are scary," Hyperion said, not taking his eyes off the babies.

The clown's blue-painted brows drew downward. "Are you two going to a costume party or something? It's a little early for Halloween."

"Not that early." I tugged my wench's bodice upward. "Our whole tearoom's wearing them. And you're dressed like a *clown*."

"You work in that little tearoom near the beach?"

"Yeah," I said. "Beanblossom's. How's your wife?"

"Recovering. She had a cesarian. There were some complications, but she's doing fine." The clown's smile broadened.

"That's great news," Hyperion said. "Give her our best."

"Were you working at the haunted house last Saturday?" I asked.

"Last Saturday?" Frank scratched his orange wig. "Um, yeah. Why?"

A nurse pushed a tiered food cart, wheels squeaking, down the hall.

"Were you and Carla working together?"

"No. I mean, she was working, in and out, but I was building things, and she was, you know, administering."

"What do you mean *in and out?*" Hyperion asked.

"I mean she was coming and going so much I barely saw her."

"You mean, she left the haunted house?" I asked.

"Yeah. And came back and left again."

"Do you remember what time?" I asked.

"Are you kidding? I wasn't keeping track. Do you have any idea what goes into building a house of mirrors? You wouldn't believe the safety issues." He checked his oversized watch. "Look, I've got to see my wife and get back to the haunted house. Are we good?"

"We're good." Hyperion tapped on the window with one finger. "Buh-bye, babies."

We parted and returned to the parking garage and Hyperion's Jeep.

"I thought you didn't like kids," I said.

"Children are voluminous, enveloping, screaming distortions. But babies are perfect."

"Okay." I strapped on my seatbelt. "So Carla doesn't have an alibi."

"Doesn't look like it." He started the car and reversed from the spot.

"Does Tony know Carla? Does he know any of these people?"

"No," he said. "I gave him our list of suspects – the partner, Johnson, the wife, Carla, and the two disgruntled clients, Dr. Tarrach and Lafayette Grief."

"What did he say?"

Hyperion turned the Jeep down the curved ramp. "He said, *stay out of the case.* I don't think he's appreciating my puckish, whimsical nature. Also, he didn't recognize any of the names. And that's the problem."

"It's *a* problem, but—"

"No, it's *the* problem," he said. "Look, we think he was framed, right? Tony thinks he was framed. The cops have looked at his past cases here in San Borromeo and elsewhere. There are no tie-ins to Tony. No one he arrested or testified against is in the mix so far."

"Then it's got to be something personal," I said.

"But then he'd recognize his enemy, wouldn't he? So either the person who framed him isn't on our suspect list, or..."

"Or?" I prompted.

"Or there's something else going on."

I tasted something sour. What else could possibly be going on? Wasn't this case convoluted enough? "Okay, well, we've just started. What about that guy Gino?"

Hyperion angled his head to the side, chin down, and looked over at me. "Really? You're going there?"

I sputtered. "I'm just saying—"

"Just because Brik is being a deafening dunderhead, doesn't mean you have to throw yourself at every single, good looking, straight, successful guy you find."

Maybe it did. "You do realize how rare that combo is in California?"

He pulled onto the street. "Point taken. Do your worst. Because trust me, that's going to be a lot more fun than your best."

*****

Doing my worst was easier said than done. When you're a business owner with a newish business, there isn't a whole lot of time for a social life. This is especially true on Saturdays. We were packed.

Customers *oohed* and *ahhed* at the paper bats, at the tea trays loaded with orange and black goodies, at the costumes.

Okay, they shuddered and looked away at my costume—barbarian queen. Tomorrow I was really and truly going to bring my own costume.

Pirate costumes are easy.

But even on Saturdays I got a lunch break. And according to their website, Johnson's financial consulting firm was open.

After our 11:30 seating, I packed a pastry box full of scones and tea cakes, and I slipped from the tearoom.

I found a spot on the street and went inside the building. I pushed the button for the elevator, thought better of it, and hurried up the concrete stairs.

The door to the consulting firm stood ajar. Inside, a woman loosed a single sob.

I leaned forward and peeked through the door. Verena sat at the reception desk and dabbed her eyes with a tissue. She looked miserable, and I backed away, suddenly less enthusiastic.

Helping Tony was well and good and definitely a noble cause. But grilling Cassius's weeping secretary wasn't going to fill me with the pride of good works.

Biting my lip, I turned and knocked on Gino's door instead. He probably wasn't there. Why would an estate attorney work on—?

The door opened, and I started.

Gino raised a brow.

"You're open on Saturdays?" I asked.

"No." His gaze traveled from my furry boots to my horned helmet and then returned to my too-tight faux-fur vest. "Is this one of those singing telegrams?"

"Ha, ha. We met the other day. I'm Abigail Beanblossom."

"Beanblossom?" He canted his head. "Are you related to Frank Beanblossom, the CPA?"

"He's my grandfather."

"He's a good man. I was sorry when he retired, though I can't blame him. He's put in his time. I didn't take him for a member of a barbarian tribe though."

"How do you know him?" I asked.

"We had some mutual clients."

"Oh. Right. You're an estate attorney."

He glanced at the pastry box. "Are those for me?"

Not after that singing telegram crack. I hugged the pink box closer. "I just happened to be in the area—"

"Dressed like Xena."

"Xena had a much cooler outfit."

"And a sword."

"That too." Actually, my costume *had* come with a sword, but it got in the way when I was pouring tea. "I wanted to ask you about Cassius."

Gino arched a brow and leaned against the doorframe. "You know, I've read some mysteries about amateur detectives. I have to say, they all seem a little nuts. I mean, why would an amateur get involved when we have police to solve crimes?"

My heart thumped harder. *He reads fiction too!* "I'm not nuts. I'm desperate. The man accused of killing Cassius is a friend of mine."

Gino blew out his breath. "Figures. Come in." He stepped from the doorway, and I followed him into a neat, professional reception area.

Simple but comfortable chairs lined the walls. A low table displayed financial magazines and the latest *Wall Street Journal.* I felt like I was back in my grandfather's office, where I'd worked summers as a kid.

The tension in my back and shoulders leaked out. "So you're not usually open Saturdays?" I asked.

"I came here today to catch up on work. The office isn't open to clients."

I shut the door behind me and followed Gino into his office. Photos of old San Borromeo hung on the walls. He sat in an executive chair behind a plain, wooden desk. I took one of the leather client chairs opposite.

"What do you want to know?" he asked. "I can't tell you anything about our mutual clients. If it has to do with my clients, it's confidential."

"Mutual clients? So you worked with Cassius and Johnson?"

"Yes." He relaxed back in his deluxe chair. "But we weren't friends, and I have no idea who'd want Cassius dead."

"When you say you weren't friends, is that because the relationship was strictly professional? Or is it because Cassius was unpleasant?"

"How do you know I wasn't the one who was unpleasant?"

"You let me in here wearing a barbarian costume." That spoke to a certain easygoing nature.

"You look good in cheap fur."

"Thanks?"

He grinned.

"Look," I said. "Someone killed Cassius, and it wasn't road rage. It was planned. Whoever did it framed a cop, and... The murder was complicated. Careful. Someone took their time figuring out how to pull this off." And I wondered if they'd enjoyed it. Goosebumps shivered my bare arms.

"How do you know the cop wasn't the real target?" he asked.

"I don't." I leaned closer, then realized that wasn't something I wanted to do in my barbarian outfit. I sat back. "But it would take someone who was a whole other level of psychotic to murder one person just to frame someone else."

"And you don't think those types of people exist?"

"I think they're rare. At least, I hope they are. There's got to be a connection between the cop and Cassius."

"You and this cop, you're close?" he asked.

"He's dating my business partner."

"In that case," he said, "want to go out?"

I blinked. "What?"

"On a date. You know, dinner, drinks. That sort of thing. Or if you're the more adventurous sort, we could go skydiving or something."

"Skydiving? Are *you* psychotic?"

"Nah. Like you said, the real psychos are rare. I do have a thing for women who are a little nuts though." He shoved his business card across the desk. "Think about it. Give me a call if you want to meet up."

I took the card and stood. "So... *no* idea who might have had it in for Cassius?"

"Nope."

"Okay. Thanks." I slipped the card into my faux-leather pouch and walked out.

The door to the financial consulting firm was still ajar.

I knocked on it, pushing it wider, and stepped inside.

CHAPTER 14

Verena looked up from the modular, blond-wood reception desk. "Yes? Can I help you?" Blinking rapidly, she grabbed a tissue from the box and blew her nose. Verena glanced toward Johnson's closed office door.

"I, um, brought you scones." I walked to her desk and set the box beside her leather-bound planner. "Are you okay? Sorry, dumb question. You're crying. You're obviously not okay."

"I'm not crying," she snapped. "You're crying."

I wasn't sure whether to laugh or leave. "I'm not... Sorry. Never mind." I began to turn.

"Wait. I shouldn't have…" She sniffed. "Thanks for the scones."

"I've got something close to an endless supply." I sidled around one corner of the desk to get closer to that open planner. "Is Johnson here?"

"No, and I don't know when he'll be back. He called this morning to say he'd be in meetings all day. We have a perfectly good office for meetings." She motioned toward the glass-walled room. "I don't know why he doesn't hold them here."

"Does he meet important clients at their homes?" I frowned. The planner was open to this week instead of the week of the murder. That wasn't helpful at all.

"No, and *all* his clients are important." She released a shuddering breath. "He... Oh, I need to get out of here. Cassius… gone, and sitting here alone… Do you want to grab lunch?"

"I—" *Oh, damn.* I had to get back to the tearoom. But this was the perfect opportunity to pry secrets out of Verena. It was also the worst time, since she was obviously vulnerable.

But so was Tony, sitting in jail.

"Why not?" I said. "Just a quick one though, I've got to get back to work."

"I don't." She opened a drawer and pulled out a purse that matched the color of the couch cushions. Grabbing her matching jacket, she stood, revealing a pencil skirt. Verena slung the purse over one shoulder. "Let's go."

Since there weren't any full-service restaurants nearby, we ended up at the pier. The San Borromeo Pier is so big it has an upper *and* a lower deck. It's also as wide as a two-lane road so supply trucks can drive down it.

You couldn't do that today though. The farmer's market was on, and the pier was packed with stalls decorated for Halloween. The scent of baked pumpkin mingled with Pacific brine.

We wound through the throng, Verena mincing on her high heels, water sloshing beneath us. A half a dozen people leaned over the rail, pointing, and we walked around the stairs leading to the lower deck and stopped beside a red fire hydrant to look too.

A mother sea otter floated on her back on an island of purplish seaweed and groomed her baby on her stomach.

"Okay," Verena said. "That's adorable."

Sealions had taken over a nearby floating dock. One rolled over, pushing a smaller sealion into the dark blue water. The fallen animal popped from the waves and barked indignantly.

The back of my neck prickled, as if I was being watched.

Edging around the stairs, I scanned the cheerful crowd. Gramps and Tomas sat behind tables at their horseradish and salsa stands. Tomas waved, and I relaxed. It must have been his gaze I'd sensed.

I touched Verena's arm. "That's my uncle, selling salsa, and my grandfather, at the horseradish stand. "Do you mind?"

She shook her head and followed me to their stalls.

Gramps sat in a folding chair, his hands laced across his beige knit vest, his eyes closed.

His mallard, Peking, sat on his gently rising and falling stomach. The duck wiggled his tail feathers and quacked.

Gramps started, his blue eyes flashing open. "What?"

"Hi, Gramps." Edging around the table lined with colorfully labeled jars, I kissed his grizzled cheek.

"Abigail, what are you doing here?"

"I'm taking a break with a friend of mine, Verena."

My grandfather tugged on his cabbie's hat. "It's a pleasure to meet you, Verena. Unusual name."

"Nice to meet you, too, sir," she said.

The white curtain between his stand and the one next door was yanked back. Tomas stuck his head through. "Abigail!"

"Hi, Tomas." I walked to him and hugged him briefly, crinkling his Giants windbreaker. "This is Verena. How are sales?"

"My garlic salsa is about to sell out." He gave my grandfather's half-full table a superior look. "A Texan came by and told me it was the best he'd ever tasted. He bought a case."

Gramps snorted. "One lucky sale."

"It's not luck when you make the best garlic salsa in California."

I choked back a laugh and shot Verena an apologetic glance. Tomas's salsa *was* good. It also tended to linger. But it was an argument I'd heard many times before.

"You're just jealous I have the best Halloween decorations in town." My grandfather sneered.

"You hired a ringer," Tomas said.

"Brik did do a good job," Gramps said. "But I wouldn't call him a ringer." He looked up at me.

"Oh, well," Tomas said, "maybe you need a ringer. You're not exactly known for your Halloween skills. Remember that time you tried to make your wife a wreath out of poison oak?"

My grandfather's voice rose. "How was I to know? It's the only plant in these hills that gets any autumn color."

Tomas guffawed.

"How's your neighbor doing?" Gramps asked me.

I winced. Had Gramps heard about the pumpkin-cannon incident? "Good. He's doing good. Excuse us, we were just on our way to the fish restaurant."

We said our goodbyes. I hustled Verena away. We passed beneath a life-sized Dracula, strung between two cables over the pier. His cape flapped loudly.

We walked into the restaurant at the pier's end. It had a name, but everyone just called it the fish restaurant on the pier.

"Your grandfather seems nice," Verena said.

We made our way to the bar, nets hanging above the barstools.

I glanced out the window. Clouds met the ocean on the horizon. "He is." I sat on a barstool beside her. "He raised me."

"Oh." She knotted her fingers on the bar. "You were lucky."

I *had* been lucky. I'd escaped a storm of parental insanity to anchor with the one person in my family who was stable and loving.

"I had parents," she blurted. "Two of them. Of course, everyone has two parents, but I meant they raised me. But I was on my own most of the time."

"Ah. That's rough." Sometimes I forgot I wasn't the only one with abandonment issues.

"They were busy," she said quickly, "successful." She ran her palms along the smooth, wooden bar and laughed uneasily. "Where is that bartender?"

As if she'd heard Verena, a woman in a white shirt, vest, and black bow tie appeared behind the bar. She took our orders and strode away.

"It must be strange, working in that office now," I said. "One partner murdered, and you sitting all alone there while Johnson's out."

"What's worse is wondering... Everything points to that cop. He wouldn't have been arrested if the police didn't think he was guilty. But what if it was someone else? Detective Chase *says* he didn't kill Cassius."

"Says?"

"It was in the news today," she said.

I rubbed my arm. "And you're starting to have doubts about the murder? Why?"

"It just seems—"

The bartender set our drinks in front of us — hard apple cider for me and a martini for Verena. "Can I get you anything else?" the bartender asked.

"A menu," Verena said. "And have you got those beer-battered artichoke hearts?"

The bartender nodded. "Coming right up." She walked away.

"I love those." She swigged her drink.

"Me too." Verena and I had all sorts of things in common. I cleared my throat. "You were saying you had doubts. About the murder, I mean."

"It just seems like Carla is a much more likely suspect. I mean, now that Cassius is dead, she doesn't have to go through a messy divorce."

"Whose idea was the divorce?"

"Cassius's, of course." She rolled her eyes. "He was such a..." Her mouth compressed.

"Some people seem made to cause problems."

"Exactly. Cassius kept Johnson down. He didn't want to do anything new. He didn't want to—" She drummed her fingers on the bar.

"What?"

"Nothing. But that office could have been a lot more than it was with a different partner. Maybe now it will be."

"Different how?"

"Just... different." She motioned to the bartender for a refill. Verena sniffed again. "Have you ever loved someone who didn't love you back?"

A crust of ice formed over my heart. But I *didn't* love Brik. I was over him. And my finger most definitely had not made a Freudian slip on the trigger of that pumpkin cannon. If Brik thought I was too risky, that was his problem.

I forced a smile. "Yes, I have, and it stinks."

"How did you get over it?"

"Denial. Alcohol. Throwing myself at other unavailable men." *Huh.* That might not be so healthy either. "So there was tension between Cassius and Johnson?"

"Why would you say that?" she asked quickly.

"It's just something I heard."

"From Carla, right?" She scowled. "Johnson did tell Cassius to step up a time or two, but I wouldn't say there was tension."

"Why did Cassius need to step up?"

"He just… Johnson wanted to expand their offerings. Cassius didn't. He was happy just going along the way they were."

It didn't sound like a motive for murder.

Unfortunately, I couldn't get much more out of Verena than that. We ate, paid our bills, and ambled from the restaurant. Verena seemed more relaxed, her muscles looser.

A seagull swooped low, and we both ducked, then laughed, embarrassed.

"This was just what I needed," Verena said. A breeze tossed her red hair. "Thanks for getting me out of the office."

A wave of guilt crashed down on me. I smiled weakly. "Yeah. I guess I needed the break from the tearoom too."

"I really do want to stop in at Beanblossom's. Why don't we—?" She stiffened and gasped.

"What?"

"It's Johnson."

"Where?" I craned my neck.

"He can't see me." She darted into the crowd.

"Ver— Wait!"

So much for Verena not having to work. She obviously didn't want to get caught out of the office. But what was Johnson doing at the pier?

I moved through the crowd. A pointed black hat bobbed away on my left, and I oriented on it, my eyes narrowing. That hat had looked a lot like the witch's from the tearoom.

It was Halloween season though, and it was an off-the-shelf costume.

Lots of people probably had hats like that. But I wove through the crowd in pursuit.

Another ripple of black caught my eye, and I glanced up. High in the air, the vampire bobbled and swayed on its cables. A gust of wind caught its cloak and wrapped it around the vampire's wooden head.

"Abigail!" Hyperion shouted from behind me. My partner wound through the shoppers. "What are you doing here?"

"What are *you* doing here?"

"Following Dr. Tarrach," he said. "Have you seen him?"

"No, but Johnson's here too. Do you think they're meeting?"

"If we find them, we can ask," he said. "Come on. Let's search together."

We wandered past a stand specializing in all things pumpkin — pumpkin butter, pumpkin muffins, and actual pumpkins. I told Hyperion what I'd learned from Verena.

Hyperion swiveled his head, scanning the pier and not watching where he was going. He moved toward the stairs leading to the lower level.

"Careful." I grabbed his elbow.

He teetered at the edge of the steps. "Whoa. Thanks."

A breeze whisked off the ocean. It ruffled the back of my hair and raised gooseflesh.

I glanced over my shoulder and got a quick impression of something black and membranous billowing toward us.

I launched myself sideways at Hyperion. Something slammed into my shoulder and knocked me off balance.

Hyperion and I tumbled down the stairs in a tangle of arms and legs.

CHAPTER 15

Toppling down the stairs wasn't as bad as it sounded. Not for me, at least. Hyperion cushioned my fall. Our tumble ended abruptly at the base of the pier's grimy wooden stairs, and for a couple seconds, I lost track of what was going on.

Then Hyperion groaned, so I (a) knew he was still alive, and (b) could take a moment to figure out if *I* was alive.

Something splashed near my head. Involuntarily, I turned to look, setting off sparks of pain along my neck and back.

A dolphin stuck its head from the lapping waves and chittered. I'm pretty sure it was laughing.

Hyperion groaned and sat up. "Cursed. Have I mentioned how much I hate Halloween? Anything broken?"

The dolphin whisked around and slapped its tail, soaking me. It dove, vanishing into the murky Pacific.

I wiped saltwater from my stinging eyes and sat up. I wiggled my fingers and toes. Everything hurt. Everything also seemed to be in working order. "I'm okay."

Two murky human silhouettes, backlit by the sun streaming through the gap in the pier, peered down at us.

"Abigail?" Tomas asked, and I squinted, the figures resolving themselves.

"Are you all right?" Gramps adjusted the mallard beneath one arm.

Peking quacked.

I staggered to standing. "I'm fine."

"Lawsuit!" Tomas turned, his back to us, hands on his hips. "Who was responsible for that vampire?" He strode away.

Back aching, I followed Hyperion up the stairs. I could tell these were going to be those fun types of bruises that felt worse on Day Two than Day One.

"You two were lucky." My grandfather stroked Peking's back. The vampire decoration that had once hung above the pier swayed, head on the pier, feet in the air, on its remaining cable.

Hyperion rubbed the back of his head, ruffling his near-black hair. "Yeah. Lucky. But I don't think we need to sue anyone."

"We won't," Gramps said. "It's just Tomas's scare tactic to get answers."

Tomas emerged from the crowd with a worried-looking middle-aged woman.

"I don't know how it could have come loose." She scooped up the vampire and unhooked it from the other cable. "Are you two all right?"

I opened my mouth.

"Don't say anything," Tomas barked. He picked up the end of a cable she'd dropped. "Where did this hook in?"

"Behind the photo stand." The woman pointed toward wooden photo cutouts decorated with pumpkins and mummies and werewolves.

Tomas handed the end of the cable to my grandfather, who frowned at it.

"The carabiner looks undamaged," Gramps said.

I made my way through the crowd to the photo cutouts. A wooden haunted-forest backdrop stood behind them. Each cutout cleverly blended with the forest, giving it a 3-D effect. A high wooden pole rose behind the cartoon forest.

I stepped behind it and looked up. A metal hook jutted from the pole, just above the top of the backdrop. From the front, looking up, the hook was invisible. And whoever had unhooked the carabiner would have been hidden as well.

Experimentally, I climbed onto the first rail and stretched upward. The hook was out of my reach. I climbed onto the second rail.

"Careful," Hyperion said sharply, and I started.

My foot slipped on the rail. I gasped, lurched forward, and grabbed the rough pole. Heart thudding, I hugged it close. Waves splashed twenty feet below me.

"I said *careful*," Hyperion said.

"Well, you didn't have to sneak up on me." I touched the hook. If I could reach it, pretty much any adult could.

"So," Hyperion said. "Not an accident."

"No," I said, grim.

I climbed down, and we returned to Gramps and Tomas. The latter was still grilling the hapless pier manager, who now had a cable looped around one shoulder.

"Who could have unhooked it?" Tomas asked.

"I have no idea." She looked around wildly, as if the saboteur might emerge from one of the stalls. "No one has any right to unhook that vampire."

"Who's manning this photo booth?" Tomas asked.

"No one," she said. "That's the whole point of the cutouts. People don't need help or to pay money to take a photo."

I pointed to a stand selling pumpkins and other harvest vegetables beneath a canopy tent. "She may have seen something."

Hyperion strode to the vegetable seller, and I limped along behind him.

The redheaded seller looked up and smiled. "Can I help you?"

"Someone detached the vampire's cable from that pillar." Hyperion pointed. "Did you see anyone on the pole back there?"

She shook her head. "Sorry. No."

I bent to pick up a Cinderella pumpkin, and pain blazed in my mid-back. More carefully, I straightened. I left the pumpkin.

"You didn't notice anyone going behind the creepy forest backdrop?" Hyperion persisted.

"I'm sorry," she said, "I haven't been paying attention to the photo stand."

Ooh, zucchinis. I grabbed two and handed it to the woman. "I'll take these."

Hyperion scowled. "You're shopping? Now?"

"It's called multitasking." Above us, the canopy flapped, the sound like running footsteps. A green patch on it caught my eye, and I stepped closer, sucked in my breath.

"Hyperion—"

"And what are you going to do with zucchinis?" he asked.

"I'll make a quiche. *Look.*" I stabbed a finger at the green patch. It read, *LAFAYETTE, INC.*

Hyperion rubbed his chin. "A suspicious coincidence, but there can't be that many local tent rental companies. I'll bet Lafayette has rented tents all over the pier for the farmers market."

"Oh," the vegetable seller said, "he has. His prices are very reasonable. And that will be one-twenty-five."

"You know Lafayette?" I asked her.

"I wouldn't say I know him," she said. "I just rent a tent from him once a week."

"I don't suppose you've seen him around the pier today?" I handed her some cash.

"Yeah, he's been around." The woman made change from a rusted metal cash box. "He was here about fifteen minutes ago."

Hairs stood up on my scalp. "Is that... normal?"

"No." She handed me my change. "It's the first time I've seen him at the pier. He said he wanted some vegetables, but he didn't buy anything. I think it was more a customer service thing, just checking in. Why?"

"No reason." I put the coins into my wallet and dropped it in my purse. "Thanks."

We wandered from the booth.

"So Lafayette Grief, Johnson, and Dr. Tarrach were here," Hyperion said. "Any of them could have unhooked that vampire."

"Don't forget Verena. She ran off when she spotted Johnson." Unless she hadn't really spotted Johnson. I only had her word for it that he'd been here. "And in this crowd, who knows? Carla could have been here too."

"I'm going to talk to the vendor on the other side of the photo booth." Hyperion strode through the milling crowd.

I joined Gramps and Tomas.

The duck wriggled in Gramps arms. "I'm not putting you down around all these people," he told the duck. "You'll get stepped on."

"Learn anything?" Tomas asked.

"Not really," I said. "I hope you weren't too rough on the farmers market manager." To me, Tomas was a kindly pseudo-father figure. But he had a reputation as a fierce lawyer.

"Threatening a lawsuit was the quickest way to get answers." Tomas elbowed my grandfather's side. "Plus, she gave us twenty percent off for the next three months of space rental."

Gramps shook his head, his gaze flicking to the gray sky.

"And did she help?" I asked.

"She said she doesn't know anything." His shoulders slumped inside his Giants windbreaker. "I think she figured out I was retired. I've lost my legal mojo."

"At least you can still kill someone with a bottle cap," Gramps said.

Tomas nodded. "That is true."

I rolled my eyes. Tomas claimed to have killed someone with a bottle cap in the war. I could never tell if he was teasing about it, but he had some mean bottle cap skills.

Hyperion reappeared at my side. "No luck. No one saw anything."

"I've got to get back to the tearoom," I said. "I've been gone too long as it is."

"I'll walk with you," Hyperion said.

I hugged Gramps and Tomas. "Thanks for everything. I hope this time away from your stalls hasn't cut into your sales too much."

"The jam and honey seller on the right is watching our stands," Gramps said. "We're fine. You get back to work."

Hyperion and I walked down the pier.

"Whoever did it had a good understanding of geometry," Hyperion said. "Not everyone could have figured out how to aim that vampire."

"I'll add that to my list of suspect qualities. How do you think we can casually work that into an interrogation?" I snapped my fingers. "I know, we can take all our suspects out for a game of pool."

"Sarcasm does not become a woman who interrupted an investigation to buy zucchinis."

"Nag, nag, nag." I snorted, and pain rippled along my spine. I winced. "Ow."

"The bad news is the curse will only intensify the closer we get to Halloween."

"I need more details on this curse," I said. "How did it start?"

"It started when I was thirteen."

"An unlucky age."

We reached the end of the pier and stepped onto the sloping cement leading to the sidewalk.

"Not for me," he said. "At least, not until Halloween. Some friends and I got the bright idea of trick-or-treating in the rich section of town. We thought we'd get more candy."

"Let me guess. You didn't." We walked through the parking lot, packed with cars, and new aches made themselves known.

"There's a reason rich people are rich. They keep their money close. But that wasn't the problem."

"Go on."

"The neighborhood was full of old houses and big, twisty oaks. There weren't many streetlights, so it was dark— Isn't that the tent guy?"

I looked in the direction he was pointing. Lafayette Grief closed the back doors of his van and walked toward the driver's side. He pulled a tissue from his pocket and wiped the top of his balding head.

"Hey, Lafayette," Hyperion shouted.

Lafayette jumped and flattened himself against the white van. He sagged against its side. "Oh. It's you," he said, straightening off the van.

"Who did you think it was?" Ignoring my screaming muscles, I strode through the cars.

"No one." Lafayette bounced up on his toes and dropped back down. It didn't make much difference in the little man's height.

I arched a brow. He was awfully jumpy. "What's going on, Lafayette?"

"Nothing." Lafayette looked exhausted, his shoulders slumped, his face pale.

"What were you doing near those photo cutouts on the pier?" Hyperion asked.

"What?"

"You were seen," I said darkly.

Lafayette's right eyelid twitched. "I was avoiding someone, if you must know."

Ah, ha. So he *had* been there.

"Who were you avoiding?" Hyperion asked.

"Johnson."

"You were avoiding Johnson on the pier?" Then Verena hadn't been lying. I sent her a silent apology.

"So what if I was? There's no law against it."

But the zucchini lady had said Lafayette's presence on the pier was unusual. I stabbed a finger in Lafayette's direction. "Avoiding him or following him?" Okay, it was a jump, and maybe I was projecting. But I had a feeling I was right.

"Following?" Lafayette blotted his face with the handkerchief.

Hyperion raised a brow. "Oh, you were totally following Johnson."

"Okay, okay. You got me. Sheesh." Lafayette jerked his hand toward the pier and let it drop to his side. "Are you happy?"

"Why follow Johnson?" Hyperion asked.

He exhaled a heavy breath. "Because I think there's something funny about that company."

"Funny how?" Hyperion asked.

"Well, you know, they deal with money," Lafayette said vaguely.

"Yes," I said. "That is what financial consulting companies do."

"Listen, a month or so ago I overheard someone on the phone outside my office. He'd left Cassius and Johnson's, and he was angry, talking about money being moved without his permission."

"Who was it?" I asked. Doctor Tarrach, or another dissatisfied client?

"I didn't see him, I only heard him."

"And that's when you decided to start asking about your money," Hyperion said.

He blinked rapidly. "Look, I don't have a lot, okay? But I don't want to lose what I have."

"So you decided to follow Johnson," I said. It sounded like paranoiac behavior, but… glass houses, stones, etc., etc. "Did you see anything interesting?"

"No. I lost him. But yesterday he went into that big, six-story building downtown. The one that looks like it was designed by J. Edgar Hoover."

There was only one six-story building in San Benedetto, the one where Beatrice Carlson worked. I stiffened, and my back protested. Right now, what I needed was a hot water bottle, aspirin, and a beer—*not* to mix it up again with Beatrice. "Did you see what floor he got off on?"

"No. Why?"

Hyperion's gaze met mine. Beatrice Carlson's office was on the third floor. Beatrice worked with Gino, across the hall from the financial consulting firm. Beatrice might have been working with Johnson and Cassius too.

A seagull whirled overhead. The scent of baking ice cream cones and pumpkin pie wafted on the breeze.

"We can't possibly accuse Beatrice of murder again," I said, flatly.

Hyperion lifted his shoulders and winced. "Third time's a charm?"

CHAPTER 16

Running a tearoom can complicate amateur detecting. After all the afternoons I'd left Maricel to manage, I couldn't play hooky the whole weekend. Saturdays and Sundays were our busiest times. So when I wasn't lying on a heating pad, I spent the rest of the weekend in Beanblossom's.

Tony Chase spent the weekend in jail.

I have no idea where Hyperion spent his time. He was conspicuously absent from the tearoom for the rest of Saturday and Sunday. That worried me.

Monday, heating pad between my chair and my aching back, I breakfasted on an apricot and coconut scone and contemplated the fog swirling beyond my French doors. I'd been right; the bruises from the pier had felt worse on day two. But day three was improving.

A knock sounded at my front door.

I walked to it and peered through its peephole. Hyperion's eyeball goggled back at me. He always did that, pressing his eye close. It was like staring into the enormous orb of some Eldritch fiend.

That Lovecraft calendar was starting to get to me.

I levered out the front door's security brace. A killer had found their way into my house a couple months back. That disaster had inspired me to buy steel security braces.

I opened the door. "Good morning."

He brushed past me. "We have to talk to Beatrice." Hyperion wore what I'd come to recognize as his casual wear — charcoal slacks and a collarless white shirt.

"Do we?" I asked warily. "There are lots of offices in that building. Odds are Johnson didn't go to see Beatrice."

"But what if he did?" Hyperion asked. "Beatrice is a player. She knows all the businessowners in San Borromeo worth knowing. Why wouldn't she try to get Gino's office neighbors as clients too?"

"She's going to sue us for harassment."

"That's what Tomas is for."

"He's retired."

Hyperion folded his arms. "Are you going to help me help Tony or not?"

I blew out my breath. "Yes." Of course I was. I owed Tony, and he was innocent. He deserved friends in his corner.

"Now?" he asked pointedly.

I looked down at my soft gray sweats. There are some super-confident women who don't care how they look. I was not one of them. No way I'd face the PR consultant looking like this. "Give me a few minutes to change."

I slapped one of those adhesive heating pads on my lower back, then dressed in wide-legged, brown slacks, a white blouse, and a cognac-colored sweater duster. Looping a matching plaid scarf around my neck, I studied the effect in the mirror.

Then I dropped onto the bed, tugged off my boots, and slipped into sneakers. They'd be more practical if we had to run. I'd once seen Beatrice throw a javelin into a wall. She kept one in her office. Because *that* was normal.

Hyperion paced my living room while I made sure there was a notepad and pen in my purse. "Are you ready yet?" he asked.

"Better late than unprepared."

Hyperion and I drove to the office building where Beatrice worked. Well, Hyperion drove. I passengered in style.

"Why do you smell like eucalyptus?" he asked.

"It's my stick-on heating pad. How are you doing after the fall?"

Hyperion shrugged. "I tucked and rolled. And spent Sunday with an ice pack."

He ushered me into the building and into a waiting elevator. The elevator doors closed on us, and Hyperion pushed the button for the third floor. "At the very least," he said, "we can talk smack about the coffin race."

"That *would* be worth the trip."

"Have you practiced with the coffin racer yet?"

"Practiced?"

"I told you, I can't possibly drive. Cursed. Remember?"

"You never told me how the—"

The doors slid open. I closed my mouth. We stepped into a mid-century modern reception area, decorated in orange and blue.

The receptionist, a youngish brunette wearing a headset, looked up.

Her smile froze, the color draining from her face. "You."

"Hi," I said. "We're here to see—"

She scrambled up from behind her glass desk. The headset caught on something, yanking her head, sideways. She wrenched it free and jogged down a carpeted hallway.

A door slammed. Footsteps echoed on metal stairs.

"—Beatrice," I finished. "That's—"

"Irregular? Lunatic? Awry?" Hyperion asked.

I closed my eyes. Less than three months until his word-of-the-day calendar was finished. I could handle three more months.

Right?

"Yeah." I strode to the wooden double doors to Beatrice's private office and knocked.

"Yes?" she called. "Come in."

I opened the door and stepped inside. "Hi, Beatrice."

She looked up from her smoked-glass desk. "You two." Her hemlock eyes narrowed. "Where's Giselle?" She tugged down the hem of her emerald vintage blouse. It had black piping and looked like something Katherine Hepburn might wear.

Hyperion edged in behind me. "Um, we didn't see her at her desk."

Beatrice swore. "This had better be about the coffin race."

"We're going to beat you like a drum." Hyperion made a moue. "So sad."

She arched an elegant brow. "Is that the best you've got?"

"We'll beat you like the Colts at the Super Bowl?" he said.

"Is Johnson Warszowski a client of yours?" I tried not to stare at the javelin mounted behind her desk.

She brushed back her streak of gray hair. "Good God, you really are investigating the murder."

Hyperion's expression hardened. "Tony Chase didn't kill anyone."

She arched a brow. "Are you so sure about that?"

"Of course I'm—" A thoughtful expression crossed Hyperion's face. "He didn't kill Cassius Santori."

"Then I hope your friend has a good lawyer. And a good PR firm." She smiled. "Is he looking for one?"

"No," Hyperion said shortly. "He doesn't need good press. He needs to clear his name."

She shook her head. "I suppose he thinks proving his innocence will be enough."

"It should be," I said. But my chest tightened, fear, anger, and embarrassment mingling. I knew better. It had been a stupid thing to say, even if it was right.

"You can't be that naïve." Her lip curled. "Ask the police chief how much the truth has to do with anything. They're pressuring him to step down, saying he's been too hands off, the department's out of control."

"Really?" I asked, aghast. My grandfather knew the old chief slightly, and I thought he'd liked him. If this case had gotten that political, what chance did Tony have?

Hyperion shook his head, his brow creasing, his jaw tight.

"I wasn't kidding about Chase needing a good PR team," she said. "Though he's probably done in any case. And being a police officer, I doubt he could afford my rates."

I shook my head, bewildered. It was so easy to say he was done. But this was Tony's life—his livelihood, his freedom… "Look," I said, "we just want to know if you work with Johnson, and we'll get out of your hair."

"I don't." She leaned back in her executive chair. "Financial planners and consultants have a whole raft of rules and regulations they have to operate under when it comes to marketing. I'd rather not deal with them."

"So Johnson asked you to work with him?" I said.

"No. I barely know the man." She brushed an invisible speck of lint off her wide sleeve.

"Barely?" Hyperion asked.

"We've met at various networking and social events. That's all. It's inevitable in a small town like this."

"What's your impression of him?" I asked.

"What does my impression have to do with anything?"

Maybe nothing, but despite our spat, I respected Beatrice. She hadn't gotten where she was for nothing. The consultant understood human nature.

"If you want to learn about Johnson," she said, "I suggest you talk to Johnson. And I hope you've found some serious donors. You're going to have a lot of funds to match when you lose that coffin race."

"LOL. In your dreams." Hyperion sauntered from the office.

I glared at Beatrice. "What you did, telling everyone we'd match your donations, was—"

"For a good cause."

Dammit. It really was. But that didn't make it right. "Beatrice, you've put me in a real spot. Beanblossom's is still a start-up. Good cause or not, I don't have that kind of money to throw around."

"That's what sponsors are for."

"I don't know any— It doesn't matter, because I'm going to win that race. But can't you just let it go?"

"You treat me like a suspect every time there's a murder. What do *you* think?"

"I don't think you're a suspect," I said.

"Oh?"

"We came to you today as a possible witness."

The PR consultant cocked her head, her expression disbelieving.

"Seriously," I said. "You're not a suspect."

Beatrice sighed. "Please go."

"Abigail," Hyperion shouted. "We've got to bounce."

I hustled through the lobby and into the elevator.

"That went well. *Not.*" Hyperion pushed the button for the ground floor. "What were you two talking about?"

"I told her she's not a suspect, she's a possible witness."

"In her mind, it's a distinction without a difference."

We stepped into the lobby, and I stopped to study a signboard by the elevator bank. None of the names triggered any associations. Johnson could have visited any of them.

"She's right, you know," Hyperion said. "We should talk to Johnson again. If Cassius was killed because of funny business at that office, then Johnson's in it up to his neck."

"Why not?" Besides, I had nothing better to do with the tearoom closed on Mondays. And that was kind of depressing.

We drove to Johnson's office building. Thick fog surrounded it, the mist seeming to collect in the depression.

A Tesla backed from a spot in the small lot, and Hyperion whipped into it.

"You weren't kidding about a direct line to the parking gods," I said. "How can I get them on *my* side?"

Hyperion stared out the windshield. "Beatrice was right." He dropped his hands from the wheel and exhaled slowly, his shoulders hunched. "Even if we do prove Tony innocent, no one will care."

"The law will care," I said. "He won't be in jail."

"Yes. That. And I have to believe we'll succeed. But I don't think it's going to be the end of it. Not for Tony."

I tasted acid. Hyperion was right. It was a lot easier to destroy a reputation than repair one.

We got out of the Jeep. Footsteps dragging, I followed my partner up the steps to the financial firm's office. Its door stood ajar.

I rapped on it with my knuckles and gently pushed it open. No one sat behind the reception desk. No one sat on the turquoise couch.

"Hello?" Hyperion called.

No one answered.

"Verena's probably gone to get coffee," I said.

Hyperion strode across the reception area to Johnson's office and knocked.

No one answered there either.

The skin twitched on the back of my neck. "We should come back."

"And pass up an opportunity for snooping? No way." He opened the door and froze. Hyperion yanked it shut and stared at his hand.

"What did you see?" I moved toward the door.

"No, Abigail. Don't open it." He pulled his phone from the rear pocket of his charcoal slacks.

I pushed past him and opened the door.

Johnson lay on the sisal carpet, blood pooling about his head.

CHAPTER 17

A tremor shuddered through my body. "No. No-no-no." I hurried to Johnson and pressed my fingers to his neck, looking for a pulse. I didn't find one. His skin was cool. His eyes were half-open. I swallowed and stepped away.

Hyperion's voice murmured into his phone as if from a distance. I swayed.

Get it together. I looked away and drew a long, shaky breath, my throat aching.

It wasn't the first dead body I'd found. The others were scored into my mind. I knew Johnson's would be too. I knew one night I'd turn a corner in a dream and find his body, just like I found the others before my dreams morphed into nightmares.

And right now it felt like I was in one. We were in over our heads, and I was scared. I was scared that a killer was out there and out maneuvering us. I was angry another life had been taken. And I was sorrowful. Johnson had seemed like an okay guy, and now he was lying there, frail and broken. He hadn't deserved to have his life cut short.

And none of these feelings would help Tony. Swallowing, I pulled my own phone out and took photos. It was easier observing the scene through my camera. It put a fraction of distance between the horror and me, and I'd take that fraction.

The leather chair I'd sat in nearly a week ago had been pushed back, as if to make room for Johnson's corpse. The pyramid I'd held, now stained with blood, lay on the sisal carpet beside him.

The pyramid I'd held. The pyramid would have my prints on it.

I felt myself starting to hyperventilate. I backed from the room before I did something stupid.

Hyperion met my gaze. "The police are on the way."

"It looks like someone hit him over the head with his paperweight." My voice quavered. I scanned the empty office. A puffy blue jacket hung over the back of the receptionist's chair. "And where's Verena?"

"I suppose we should look for her. In case she's hurt."

Or dead. Limbs heavy, I opened the door to Cassius's office. "Verena?" I whispered and stepped inside.

The walls were a cool gray. Three modernist watercolors, geometric shapes in gray tones, had been mounted behind a blond-wood desk. The desk's legs pegged outward. The floors were grayish wood. The office was sleek, soothing, and Verena wasn't in it.

I edged around the desk. A photo beside a blotter showed a man at the beach with two smiling younger people—Cassius and his children, I guessed. It was the first photo I'd seen of the dead man. His hair was flecked with silver. He looked happy.

It just goes to show how unexpectedly things can end.

I returned to the reception area.

Hyperion shook his head. "She's not hiding in any of the closets." He angled his head toward the glass-walled meeting room. "That's empty too. Think she clonked him on the head and ran?"

"What are you two doing here?" Verena said from the open doorway. She held two paper coffee cups sporting green mermaids in her hands.

"Waiting for the police," Hyperion said quietly.

Her face turned a shade lighter. "The police? Why? What's happened?" A gray purse was slung over one shoulder. She wore a smart, turquoise jacket over a white blouse and gray slacks. Her high heels were turquoise as well.

"Verena..." I shook my head. "We just got here and found... I'm sorry. Johnson's dead."

The cups slipped from her hands. Brown liquid splashed across the thin carpet, splattered her high heels. "No," she said, hoarse. "That's impossible."

"I'm sorry," I repeated. What do you say? How do you comfort someone you don't know all that well? I stood there, drained and useless.

Verena rocked back on her high heels. "No." She shook her head. "This is a bad joke. He's not dead." She started for his office door.

Hyperion stepped in front of her, his hands outstretched. "It's better if you don't go in there. The police will want to see it undisturbed."

"It's... no." She stared, wide-eyed.

"When did you last see Johnson?" I asked.

"You're not joking," Verena whispered. She groped her way to the turquoise couch and dropped onto it, knocking a lime green cushion to the floor. "Johnson." Her voice broke.

"Can you tell me when you last saw him?" I repeated.

Verena buried her head in her hands. "Saturday," she said, voice muffled. "He didn't show up for work today."

"But you have two coffee cups," I pointed out.

She sat up. Tears trickled down her cheeks. "I thought he was late. I was angry when he didn't show up, but he didn't have any appointments scheduled. Mondays are his paperwork days. So I left to get coffee. And then I felt guilty and got him one too, for when he did arrive."

I nodded. It made sense. But it also made a plausible lie.

"What are you doing here?" Verena asked.

"Someone attacked us with a vampire at the pier," Hyperion said.

"The pier?" She looked to me. "Not... not the day *we* were there?"

"Yes," I said.

"It's a long story," Hyperion said. "We saw Johnson at the pier—"

"Wait, did you say *vampire*?" she asked.

"Remember? The vampire decoration hanging above the pier," I said. "Someone unhooked its cable."

"Johnson wouldn't have done that," she said.

"We thought he might have seen something," Hyperion said smoothly.

That was... not entirely a lie. I met Hyperion's gaze, and he nodded.

We did need a reason to be here, one that did not involve investigating a murder. Police got sensitive about that sort of thing, throwing around words like *interfering* and *handcuffs*. Asking about a pier vampire made a better story.

"How do you know he wasn't here before you left for coffee?" I asked.

"Because he wasn't," she said.

"You checked his office?" Hyperion asked.

"No, I knocked on the door and he didn't answer, so I knew he wasn't here..." She blanched, realization dawning. "Oh." Her face turned greenish. "Oh."

Because he could have been inside, dead, when she'd knocked. We had no idea when he'd really gotten to the office.

The police arrived, separated us, and took our statements. Paramedics came and went, empty handed. We watched, and we waited.

A tall man in a rumpled business suit strode into the room, and the activity stilled. He stood there for a long moment, his gaze roaming over the office. It landed on me, and I felt myself shrinking backward in my chair. His gray-blue eyes snapped with repressed anger.

And I recognized him. He'd arrested Tony in the tearoom.

His face was ruddy, his brown hair in a comb over. His jaw worked rapidly on a wad of chewing gum.

And then his gaze fell upon a hapless man in blue. "You," he barked. "Who's in charge?"

The policeman's Adam's apple bobbed. "Um, I am, Sir."

"Wrong answer. I'm in charge. Where's the body?"

"This way, Detective Baranko." He hurried into the office where Johnson lay, and the newcomer followed.

Hyperion leaned across a potted fern. "You recognize him?" he whispered to me.

"Wasn't he the guy who arrested Tony?"

"And he's in plain clothes, so he's a detective. He must be the one they brought in from Santa Cruz."

After a few minutes, Baranko and the policeman walked from the office. The cop thrust a thick finger at Hyperion and me.

Baranko came to loom over us. "Which one of you found the body?"

"I did," Hyperion said.

"And you called the cops?"

"Yeah," Hyperion said.

The detective's bullet-like head swiveled in my direction. "And what did you do?"

I clutched my purse closer. "I checked to see if Johnson was still alive. He wasn't. And then we went to look for Verena, the receptionist. She wasn't in the office."

"She's here now," the detective said.

"Um, yeah." I glanced at the office door. "She returned from getting coffee about five minutes before the police arrived."

"And the office door was open?"

"The front door was open," I said, gesturing.

"What were you two doing here?"

We'd gone over all of this with the cops earlier. I had a feeling we'd be going over it a lot more.

"Someone unhooked a cable on the vampire above the San Borromeo pier on Saturday." Hyperion sat up straighter. "It nearly killed us. We'd seen Johnson at the pier earlier, so we came to ask him if he'd noticed anything."

"You were nearly killed." The detective lifted a single eyebrow. "By a Halloween decoration."

Hyperion tugged on his collarless white shirt. "It's not as strange as it sounds when you understand that for me, October is a curse—"

I stepped on Hyperion's foot. "The vampire was weighted," I said.

"The pier can get windy."

"And your appearance here has nothing to do with your relationship with Detective Chase?" He made the question sound like a statement—one he didn't believe.

"Relationship?" I asked.

"You were in the tearoom where we arrested him," Baranko said. He pointed a thick finger at Hyperion. "And you're dating him."

"Ye-es," Hyperion said.

"It's pure coincidence that Detective Chase is accused of murdering Mr. Warszowski's business partner, Cassius Santori?" The detective's eyes narrowed. "And you found Warszowski's body."

My insides burned. "Well," I said, "we did get to know Mr. Warszowski after his partner's death."

"Why?" he barked.

"We wanted to give him our condolences," I said. It sounded weak, even to me.

"I used to work in this building," Hyperion said quickly. "I knew them both, though I hadn't seen either since I moved out. I dragged Abigail along on my condolence visit."

"Why?" the detective repeated.

"Why?" Hyperion asked.

"I have a crush on the guy across the hall," I blurted.

Hyperion nodded enthusiastically. "And then when we saw Johnson—I mean, Mr. Warszowski at the pier—"

The detective made a slashing motion with one beefy hand, silencing us. "Enough." He pointed at two uniformed cops. "You and you. Take them down to the station. Separate cars."

"The station?" I squeaked.

"No talking," he said.

I subsided against the wall.

We were escorted to separate police cars and driven to Santa Cruz.

Santa Cruz is a lovely town. Even the police station is charming—adobe-looking with arches and a red-tile roof. The interior isn't as beguiling, at least, not the interrogation rooms.

I sat in one for two hours before Detective Baranko returned. They were long hours.

I straightened in my chair, my abused back muscles protesting against the heavy plastic. After that fall on the pier, it was amazing I wasn't in traction. "Can I go now?"

"No."

The detective dropped a manilla file on the metal table in front of me. "This isn't your first run-in with the law."

"I wouldn't say run-in—"

"You were a suspect in a murder investigation earlier this year."

"Not for very long. The killer was caught."

"And then you stuck your nose into another murder. Later, you were brought into the station for interfering in a different investigation."

"The prosecutor dropped those charges. We didn't even see a courtroom," I babbled. "It was all a misunderstanding."

He smiled insincerely. "I do hope you're not interfering in Mr. Santori's murder investigation."

"Gosh, no." I widened my eyes and considered throwing in a *golly* for good measure. Nah, that would be overkill.

"Because I'm not as patient as your *friend* at the San Borromeo PD. Not that he'll be there for much longer," he muttered.

"Tony Chase didn't kill anyone."

"The evidence says otherwise."

I opened my mouth to argue, thought better of it, and shut my trap.

"Now," he said, "tell me about your visit to Mr. Warszowski's office."

I told him. And I told him again. And again, and again, and again, my back aching against that uncomfortable chair. I knew what he was doing, trying to trip me up. And there were a few moments, when a triumphant gleam appeared in his eyes, where I worried he might have.

The detective closed his file folder and stared hard at me. My skin felt like it was being peeled back to reveal something unpleasant. "You can go," he said.

"I can?"

"Mr. Redmond confirmed that you have a crush on him."

Heat blistered my face. "He... What?" He'd talked to Gino?

"You can go." He glanced toward the door.

I grabbed my purse and moved so quickly, I banged my hip on the table. At the door, I turned. "Tony Chase is a good cop."

His face darkened. "Good cops don't kill people. And killers don't belong on the police force."

I nodded and fled.

In the courtyard, I stopped short beside its modern-art fountain. I didn't have a ride home. It was late afternoon. The fog had thickened and the temperature dropped. I shivered, cool droplets splattering my face.

"Abigail!" Hyperion jogged across the street. "I was waiting for you."

"Thanks." I didn't want to admit how vulnerable I'd felt standing there.

He glanced toward the adobe station. "How'd it go?"

"Baranko knows we weren't there to find out about a vampire."

"You told him?" he asked, his expression appalled.

"Of course not. But I could tell he wasn't buying it."

His shoulders slumped. "Yeah. Me too. Did you get the manila folder treatment?"

"Yeah."

We stood in silence for a long moment.

Finally, I said, "I'll call a ride share." I dug my phone from my purse.

"There's something else," Hyperion said in a low voice. "The detective implied—"

"Look what the cat dragged in," a familiar voice drawled from behind us.

We turned, and Hyperion froze.

Tony strode across the courtyard and stopped beside the fountain. He shoved back his cowboy hat with one thumb. "It's almost like you don't listen when I tell you to stay out of police investigations."

CHAPTER 18

Tony rested his hand on Hyperion's shoulder. The two men said nothing to each other for a long moment, as if in silent communication. Then Tony sighed and released my partner.

Tony didn't look bad for someone who'd spent the week in jail. His navy blazer was unwrinkled, his jeans and denim shirt fresh.

I shivered again, glad I'd worn my sweater duster, and glanced at Hyperion, jacketless in his white, collarless shirt. The guy was impervious to cold.

"You're out," Hyperion said briskly. "Good. What happened?"

"I finally scared up the bail money." He rested his hands on his belt, which, I noticed, was weapon-free, aside from the massive buckle. You could put an eye out with that thing.

"I've got an aunt in Amarillo with a soft spot for me," he continued.

"Nice aunt," I said. Even if she'd only had to put up ten percent for the bail, it had still been pretty steep.

"She's in oil."

A thuggish looking man with greasy hair and bare, muscular arms trotted down the steps. He gave Tony a hard stare.

Tony began to draw aside his jacket, where his badge and gun would be. Then, he seemed to realize they weren't there anymore. He gave the man a granite stare back.

The man looked away and hurried on.

"You two didn't kill anyone to suggest my innocence, did you?" the detective drawled.

"I don't like you *that* much," I said. "You obviously heard what happened. It's awful, but at least they've got to drop the charges now."

"Why?" the detective asked.

"Because someone killed Johnson," Hyperion said. "The two murders are linked."

Tony shoved back his cowboy hat. "Are they?"

"It does seem likely," I said slowly. "We don't have so many murders in this town. When two business partners die, there's got to be a connection."

"When did they kick you loose?" Hyperion asked.

"This afternoon."

Hyperion's face cleared. "Then they can't blame you for this. You couldn't have done it. We found his body in the morning."

"Someone who cared about me could have killed Mr. Warszowski to make me look innocent."

Hyperion's face tightened.

"Baranko tried to get you to confess," Tony continued. "Didn't he?"

"It doesn't matter," Hyperion said.

The detective nodded. "All right. In spite of everything I told you, you two are in it up to your necks. We may as well have a sit down somewhere private."

"Abigail's house," Hyperion said, and I looked at him in surprise.

We piled into Tony's Jeep Commander and drove to my bungalow. Tony parked on the street in front of Brik's house.

My neighbor's windows were dark. His pickup wasn't in the driveway. Not that I cared or anything.

Tony stopped in front of the coffin racer and studied its black-painted sides. "I'm not sure what to think about this."

"It's Beanblossom's entry in the coffin race," Hyperion said.

Tony's eyes widened. "You're going to coffin race? What about the curse?"

"Abigail's driving."

"Is she now?" He shot me a doubtful look. "You're going to let her drive that great big coffin all by herself?"

"I'm right here," I said, annoyed. Is it because I'm short I get talked over? It's gotta be because I'm short.

"Of course she won't be alone," Hyperion said. "I'm the ballast."

Tony folded his arms over his blazer and turned to me. "You know how to drive this thing?"

"I don't think there's much actual *driving* involved. It's gravity powered."

"Huh."

I hurried up the steps and let the two men into my house. They sat around the dining table. I went into the kitchen and made peppermint tea. But I did it more to give the men some privacy than because anyone actually wanted a drink.

After what I hoped was a suitable amount of time, I returned to the narrow dining room with three steaming mugs.

Tony leaned back in his wooden chair. "What can you tell me?"

"The body was cold when we found it." I set the mugs on the table.

"And what time was that?" Tony asked.

Hyperion checked his phone. "I called the police at eleven-fifteen this morning."

My stomach wheezed like an espresso machine. I realized I was starving.

The men stared at me.

Oh, come on. It hadn't been that loud. "Anyone for pizza?"

"I wouldn't say no," the detective said.

"Vegetarian for me," Hyperion said.

Tony rolled his eyes.

I slid my laptop closer on the dining table and pulled up a local pizza parlor's website. "Since the body was cold, do you think Johnson was killed the night before?"

"Most likely," Tony said. "But what was he doing in his office on a Sunday night?"

"That does seem abnormal," Hyperion said.

"Was it a personal meeting?" Tony asked. "Or business?"

"Why have a personal meeting in the office?" I entered the order and dug my credit card out of my pink wallet. Don't laugh. Its bright color once saved me from a pickpocket in San Francisco.

"Who else have you been talking to?" Tony asked.

"The wife, Carla," Hyperion said. "The receptionist, Verena, who we all think had a serious thing for Johnson. A—"

"Why?" he asked.

"Why what?" Hyperion asked.

I sipped my tea and scalded my tongue. Grimacing, I returned the mug to the table.

"Why do you think she had a thing for Johnson?" the detective said.

"Because everyone who knows her hinted at it," I said. "And she basically admitted it to me."

"All right." The detective leaned back in the wooden chair, and it creaked. "Go on."

Hyperion went on. "And two clients who'd argued with them recently—Dr. Tarrach and Lafayette Grief. And we spotted all of them minus Carla at the pier."

"What happened at the pier?"

"Someone dropped a heavy Halloween decoration on us," I said. My ribs still ached. "Oh, and I have crime scene photos." I unlocked my phone and held it out to the detective.

"When's the last time you cleaned that?" Tony asked.

I drew a deep breath and held it in, released it. *Save me from germaphobes.* "I'll be right back." I tromped to the kitchen, got a cannister of bleach wipes, returned to the dining table, and wiped the phone down in front of him.

"Thank you." He scrolled through the photos. "Looks like he was bludgeoned with that pyramid. Egyptian alabaster is my guess." He squinted. "What's that?" He made the photo bigger, and we leaned in eagerly.

A lipstick lay on the carpet beside a potted parlor palm.

"Verena's?" Hyperion asked.

"That's strange," I said.

"Why is it strange?" Tony said.

"Well, women don't generally wander around with loose lipsticks in their hands, especially at the office. It usually stays in your purse until you bring it out to use it."

"What are you saying?" Hyperion asked.

"I'm saying I can't picture Verena strolling into Johnson's office carrying lipstick, and then banging him over the head with an alabaster pyramid."

"And yet," Hyperion said, "the lipstick is there."

"And she was the only woman working at the office?" Tony asked.

"Yes." Hyperion frowned. "I suppose Carla could have dropped it when she was in there last week, but you'd think someone would have noticed."

"Look," I said, "the murder of Cassius was carefully planned. Maniacally planned, even, to frame Tony. But Johnson's murder looked like a spur of the moment thing. What if it wasn't? What if that was planned too?"

"And you think the lipstick was planted there?" Tony raised a brow. "Seems a stretch."

I sputtered. "Someone drugged you and set you up in a fake road rage accident." I sat at the end of the table. "Tony, what happened to you the night Cassius died? We never got a chance to really talk."

He set my cellphone on the dining table between us. "I don't know. That's the problem. I remember walking into your tearoom, and then nothing."

"What happened after… when you discovered Cassius?" I asked.

"A motorist woke me up. It was dark. I was lying beside my car feeling like I'd eaten bad chili. My gun was in my hand. I was groggy. The victim was in the road too, shot dead."

And the police had arrested Tony the next day. I pushed my palms down the legs of my wide-legged slacks. "Did you recognize the victim at all? Did you have any connection to Cassius Santori?"

"Not that I can figure."

"All right," I said, staring blankly at the French windows. "Let's assume you didn't shoot Cassius."

"Assumed," Tony said.

"That you were drugged or something at the tearoom or maybe in our parking lot," I continued rapidly. "Then someone drove you and your car up to the murder site, lay in wait, and somehow caused an accident. They shot Cassius, then dragged you out of your car. Is that plausible?" It *had* to be plausible.

"It's a lot of work," Tony said. "How big is Cassius's wife?"

"Not very," Hyperion said.

"Then she would have had trouble moving me around."

He was right. Tony was over six-feet of lean muscle. I sure wouldn't want to try to move his dead weight. Carla was taller than me, but not by much.

"And how did the killer get away?" Hyperion asked. "After he or she shot Cassius, did they just walk away? That road is far up on the hill, and there's not much activity. A hitchhiker might have been noticed."

"There are a lot of trails up there," I said. "They could have put a backpack on and hiked down one of the trails. No one would have given them a second glance. Even at night."

Tony nodded. "It's a thought."

One which I guessed he'd probably already had. That was the problem with amateur detecting. We were *amateurs.*

The pizza arrived. We ate and talked well into the night, going round and round and understanding nothing.

*****

I fluffed the frilly collar of my pirate costume and scanned my reservation book. Our four-o-clock seating was nearly fully booked, which was pretty amazing for a Tuesday. Our Halloween-themed menu seemed to be paying off.

I scanned the tables. A few walk-ins loitered, drinking tea and eating cinnamon-pumpkin scones. The clear tables had been prepped. Their white tablecloths were pristine. Cauldron centerpieces overflowed with flowers and plastic skeletons.

Self-conscious, I adjusted my bandana. My pirate costume was, admittedly, a little lame. A single hoop earring, baggy white blouse, big belt, and jeans. But it beat the alternative from Hyperion's costume shop.

The bell over the door jangled, and I looked up, smiling.

Gino strolled into the tearoom, and my heart gave a funny jump. His dark-eyed gaze raked me up and down. "Pirate queen?"

"Argh."

"I have to say, I was expecting something a little more..."

"Ridiculous?" *That barbarian costume...*

"Unusual."

"There *is* a naughty nurse costume in the kitchen." Hyperion had promised to deliver it to the costume shop, along with a piece of his mind.

He raised a brow. "Intriguing."

"What can I do for you?"

Gino braced his elbow on the hostess podium and leaned close enough for me to smell his spicy cologne. "Since you've admitted you've got a crush on me—"

"I didn't—"

"You perjured yourself?"

"I was under duress," I sputtered.

"How do you feel about Chinese food?"

"I like it," I said, wary.

"There's a great place on the corner of Oceanside and Seal Avenue. You know it?"

"Yes."

"What time do you get off?"

I shut the reservation book, mainly to have something to do with my hands. "I don't think going out is a good idea."

"Why not? I'm a suspect, aren't I? What better way to pump me for information?" He waggled his brows.

Despite myself, I laughed. "That's a better reason *not* to go out with you."

He pressed a broad palm to the front of his white, button-down shirt. "I'm a gentleman. Sometimes. I won't even drive you home. You can save me gas money and bring your own car. It'll be dinner and nothing else. Unless you want to bring the naughty nurse costume."

I hesitated. This was a bad idea. I didn't know Gino. And though the odds were low he really was a murder suspect, I wasn't exactly feeling lucky.

A movement at the window caught my eye.

Brik walked past. He stared straight ahead, careful not to glance in Beanblossom's windows. If he could feel my gaze on him, he didn't react.

He just walked past, like he didn't care at all. And he'd *remodeled* Beanblossom's. But that wasn't why I suddenly felt hollow.

"Abigail?" Gino said.

"What?" I refocused on the lawyer. "Oh. Sorry. I was just thinking. Um... I get off at seven."

"Meet you at the restaurant at seven-thirty?"

"Yes," I said. "Sure. Why not?" A girl's gotta eat, right? "I love a good interrogation over Kung Pao Chicken."

"Great. I'll see you then." He grinned. "And I wasn't kidding about that nurse costume."

And I wasn't kidding about the interrogation.

CHAPTER 19

A bead of sweat trickled down my spine. Sitting back on my heels in front of the lower refrigerator, I adjusted my wide black belt. I checked my blurred reflection in the door. Did I have time to go home and change before my meeting with Gino?

And it *was* only a meeting. Maybe an interrogation.

Definitely not a date.

Even though I sort of wanted it to be a date.

But I wasn't sure I had any business going on a date. Not when as much as I tried to tell myself otherwise, I still had feelings for Brik.

And that was dumb. We didn't have a relationship beyond being neighbors, and we weren't going to have one.

I understood why Brik was gun shy. He had good reason. But I *wasn't* high-risk, like he'd claimed.

"Evening, Abigail," my grandfather said behind me.

I started, squeezing the towel and dripping cleaner in the fridge. "Gramps. What are you doing here?" Hastily, I wiped up the cleaner.

Tomas emerged in the doorway behind my grandfather. He struggled with the zipper on his Giants windbreaker.

"Hi, Tomas," I said and stood.

"We're taking you to dinner," Gramps said.

"Oh. Thanks guys. But I, um, can't tonight."

"Why?" Gramps asked. "What's going on?"

"You're not ashamed of going out in that pirate costume," Tomas said. "Are you?"

"Um, no. I just have plans."

"Detecting plans?" Gramps asked, his bushy brows lowering.

"No. Just. Plans." I rested one hand on the long table, removed it, brushed a crumb off the metal.

"A date?" Tomas looked around the kitchen like he expected a likely candidate to emerge.

Heat crept across my face. "It's just, I mean, not really—"

"You and Brik?" Gramps asked.

A stab of guilt came and went. "No," I said. "I think you know him though—Gino Redmond. We're just grabbing a bite at that Chinese place on Oceanside."

"They have good garlic eggplant," Tomas said.

"I know Gino," Gramps said. "We shared a client. Good man."

My shoulders relaxed.

"Have you got high heels?" Tomas asked.

"They wouldn't go with her pirate costume," Gramps said. "That *is* a pirate costume, right?" he asked me, and I nodded.

Tomas rubbed his chin. "I guess you're right."

"Just don't tell him you want to get married," Gramps said.

I sputtered. "Why would I do that?"

"Or that you want children," Tomas said. "It's way too soon."

"I'm not a total romantic incompetent. Why do you think I'd...?" *Oh.* They thought I'd screwed up things with Brik. "That's not why Brik and I aren't together."

Tomas and Gramps looked at each other. Gramps shuffled his feet.

"He's just not looking for a relationship right now," I hedged, because Brik's reasons were his to tell, not mine.

I looked down at my black tennis shoes. *Huh.* The shoes weren't doing anything for my pirate look either, but they were more comfortable than my boots.

"You mean because of his girlfriend getting killed back in Eureka?" Gramps said.

My head jerked up. I goggled at him. "How did you—?"

"Hyperion told us," Tomas said. "Nasty business. And then being suspected in her death?" He shook his head. "That would do something to a man, that's for sure."

"But Brik needs to get over it," Gramps said.

The refrigerator made a mechanical rattle, and I glanced at it.

"It's not exactly easy to just *get over* being accused of killing the person you loved," I said. And it had only been a few years ago.

"No," my grandfather said, dragging out the word. "But life is short. It may not seem that way to you young folks now, but trust me, it will. And a life without joy isn't worth living, if you ask me."

"Abigail already knows that." Tomas patted my cheek. "And I'm glad you're moving on. But if that Gino gives you any problems, I've got a bottlecap with his name on it."

"It's only Chinese food. And I'm taking my own car."

"Smart girl," Tomas said.

The men waited for me to gather my things, and they walked with me into the dark parking lot.

"I don't know if you heard," I said, locking the tearoom's back door. "Detective Chase is out on bail."

"That's good news," Gramps said.

But Tomas looked thoughtful.

I told them about Johnson's murder, and our time in the police station. We walked toward my hatchback.

"Why didn't you call me?" Tomas asked.

"Because you're retired, and they let us go."

"Unless you're reporting something," Tomas said, "never talk to the police without a lawyer."

"He's right," Gramps said.

If only I had a lawyer who *wasn't* retired on speed dial. "They'll have to drop the charges against Detective Chase now, right?" I rubbed my arms. "He was in jail when the second murder was committed."

The men shared a look.

Tomas cleared his throat. "I've still got some contacts in the prosecutor's office. I'll have a word with them."

I released a long breath and nodded. "Thanks." I got into my Mazda.

"Don't stay out too late," Gramps said and shut my door.

As I pulled from my spot, I watched the two men laughing, and warmth replaced some of my cold anxiety. Those two knew joy. They knew how to eke it out of every day. I couldn't imagine better examples of how to live.

Smiling, I drove the few blocks to the restaurant and parked on the street. I could have walked, but having a quick exit on a first date always seems like a smart play.

I walked into the restaurant's red and gold foyer and looked around.

Gino stood up from behind a round table in the center of the room and waved. I smiled and made my way to him.

"So you stuck with the pirate costume." He rose and pulled out an ornately carved wooden chair. "Interesting choice."

"It came with a cutlass." I adjusted the curving, plastic blade in my belt, sat and scooted the chair forward. "Also, I came straight here from Beanblossom's and didn't have time to change."

He sat across from me and motioned to a waitress. "Can I get you a drink?"

I scanned the paper menu and ordered a beer.

"So." He braced his chin on his hands. "Tell me all about being an amateur detective."

"It's not as glamorous as most people think. In fact, it's generally frowned upon."

"Is that why you do it?"

"Partly," I admitted. I also had authority issues, but that probably wasn't first-date discussion material either.

"And why take up Detective Chase's case?"

"I owe him. He saved my life." And it mattered to Hyperion.

"And you pay your debts, no matter how uncomfortable?"

The waitress returned with my beer, and I took a sip.

"What makes you think it's uncomfortable?" I cocked my head and slowly adjusted the napkin in my lap.

"I looked you up online—don't worry, only some light cyber-stalking. Some of the situations you've gotten yourself into sounded... rough."

"I take it you're not interested in hearing about the in's-and-out's of tearoom management?" I asked.

He relaxed in his high-backed wooden chair. "I'm assuming there's a lot of hard work involved. There generally is in the restaurant industry."

"A tearoom's hours are more reasonable than most other restaurants."

"Really?" He arched a brow. "You don't put in twelve-hour days?"

"Only on weekends. And they're more like eleven and a half. You?"

"I try to keep normal hours. I love what I do. Estate planning is important—more important for the people who are left behind. But life is short, and I don't want to spend it all behind a desk."

He stared at me. "What?"

I shook my head. "Nothing. Someone said nearly the same thing to me not twenty minutes ago."

"Cliché or not, it's true." He smiled. "What else did this mysterious someone tell you?"

"That joy was worth the risk. Not in those words, but—"

"And do you feel joy?"

I shifted on my chair. This seemed a little deep for a first date, but I hadn't been on a first date in ages.

Was I happy? I wasn't whistling while I worked, but I loved Beanblossom's. I loved the Tarot readers and Hyperion's antics and yes, even the costume mix-ups. I drew breath to speak.

Gino frowned. "Isn't that your grandfather?"

I looked over my shoulder. Gramps and Tomas stood in the red-arched entry, chatting with the hostess.

I sank in my chair. They wouldn't.

Gino waved to them. My grandfather saw us and grinned.

The two older men ambled to our table, and Gino rose to shake their hands.

"Gino," my grandfather said. "Long time no see. Do you know Tomas Salazar?"

"I know *of* you," Gino said. "You're famous among San Borromeo lawyers."

"And I see you know my granddaughter, Abigail." Gramps pressed his hand to my shoulder.

I smiled weakly. "What a surprise to see you here."

"Someone mentioned Chinese food," Tomas said, "and we thought, why not?"

"Would you like to join us?" Gino asked.

"Don't mind if we do." Tomas sat beside me. He reached into the pocket of his Giants windbreaker and pulled out a bottlecap. Tomas set it meaningfully within reach on the tablecloth.

I stifled a groan. *Seriously?*

Gramps sat on my other side. "What's good here?"

"They do amazing things with eggplant," Gino said, sitting down.

"Told ya," Tomas said.

"So," Gramps said. "What did we interrupt?"

"We were talking about the murder investigation," I said quickly. "Detective Chase has no memory of anything after he left the tearoom the day of the murder. We think someone drugged him—"

"We?" Gino asked.

"Hyperion and me. And Detective Chase, I think."

"What sort of drug could do that?" Tomas asked.

"Let me ask my sister," Gino said.

I looked around wildly. "Is she here too?"

"She's in Idaho." Gino drew a phone from the pocket of his blazer. "She's a pharmacologist."

"That's a good career," Tomas said.

Gino dialed and pressed the phone to his ear. "Hey, sis, it's Gino." He smiled. "Yeah... Yeah... Hey, I've got a drug question for you. Can I put you on speaker?" He set the phone on the red tablecloth and pressed a button.

"I can't give out medical advice over the phone," a woman's voice said.

"We don't want advice, just information," Gino said. "What sort of drug are people using these days to knock people out? We're looking for something that would mess with their memory."

"You're talking about something someone would slip into a drink?" she asked. "That sort of thing?"

He glanced at me, and I shrugged.

"Sure," I said.

"Well," she said, "there's— Why are you asking?"

"A local cop may have been dosed." Gino glanced up at me.

"Rohypnol is popular," she said, "and it can cause amnesia."

"How fast does it work?" I asked.

"Fifteen to thirty minutes. They're adding blue dye to it so people see it in their drinks. Though of course, the blue dye is invisible in darker drinks, like coffee."

Or chai? I shifted in my chair.

"There's also ketamine," she continued. "That takes affect more quickly, but you get more of an out-of-body experience."

"I don't think he went out of body," I said. "He thinks he lost consciousness."

"He can't remember anything?" she asked. In the background, a child gave a gleeful shout.

"No," I said. "He did mention waking up with an upset stomach. But where would someone get ketamine?"

"Vets use it," she said. "But that and rohypnol seem to have made their way to the street too. Are you sure something was put in his drink?" she asked.

I glanced at my grandfather. "I'm not sure of anything."

"Well, if he lost consciousness and woke up nauseated, that sounds more like a benzodiazepine or a hypnotic. Has he had a blood test?"

I shook my head and realized she couldn't see the movement. "I don't know."

"When did this happen?" she asked.

"About a week ago," I said.

"If he hasn't had a toxicology test," she said, "it's not too late. They can still test his hair follicles for the drug."

My pulse quickened. "Really? That's great news. I'll tell him. Thanks."

"No problem. Um, can I speak to my brother for a minute?"

Gino picked up the phone and turned off the speaker. He turned slightly away from us and spoke in low tones to his sister.

"This is good news." Tomas turned the bottlecap between his gnarled fingers. "If he was drugged, there'll be evidence."

"But you'd think the police would have tested for that already." Of course, they weren't sharing their test results with me. I drew back in my chair and pushed one finger into the red tablecloth, making a small bubble in the fabric.

Tomas looked ill at ease. "I don't think the police are trying to prove his innocence."

"What?" My hand fisted on the red cloth napkin. "But he's a cop. Tony's one of them."

"But he's still new to the department," Tomas said, "and—"

Gino hung up. "Is that what you needed?"

"Yeah," I said. "Thank you. Your sister was really helpful."

A waitress hustled past carrying a tray laden with food. It smelled heavenly.

Gino took a slug of beer from his bottle and set it down. "For what it's worth. I don't think they were doing anything wrong in that consulting firm."

"Both Johnson and Cassius were murdered," I said. "There's got to be some connection, and their business is the most likely point." *Unless...*

Could Tony be connected to them *both* somehow? He'd denied it, and I didn't know why he'd lie. But maybe there was something he wasn't aware of.

"I hear what you're saying," Gino said. "But we shared a lot of clients, and I reviewed all their investment recommendations. Cassius and Johnson always matched the client's risk tolerance and timing with the investments. I never heard any complaints."

I closed the menu. "Maybe it doesn't matter. Detective Chase was in jail when Johnson was killed. That's got to make the police look twice."

Tomas cleared his throat.

"What?" I said. "What's wrong?"

"Before we came here, I called my friend in the DA's office. They're treating the murders as two unconnected cases."

"But... That's stupid," I said. "They're obviously connected."

"They're not dropping the charges," Tomas said. "I hope Detective Chase has a good lawyer. He's going to need one."

CHAPTER 20

"What?" I throttled the napkin in my lap. But Tony must have had an inkling this would happen. I wondered if Hyperion knew.

Tomas nodded. "I'm sorry."

"This isn't right," I said, my voice low and intense. I'm pretty used to things not going my way. You learn to roll with it. But I couldn't stand watching bad things happen to my friends.

A trial would destroy Tony. Even if he was found innocent, his name would always be under a cloud. And to a man like Tony, name mattered.

Around us, diners spoke in low voices. Waitresses wound between tables. Life went on.

"No," Gramps said. "It doesn't seem right at all."

"Does the prosecutor have some evidence you don't know about?" Gino asked. "Or do you think this is politics?"

"The latter," Tomas said. "The prosecutor can't look weak on dirty cops."

My jaw hardened. "But Detective Chase isn't—"

Tomas laid his wrinkled hand over mine and squeezed. "I know."

"The murders have to have something to do with that investment company," I insisted.

"How much do you know about how consulting firms like that work?" Gino asked me.

I folded my arms. "I know I can't afford to hire one."

"Okay," Gino said, "there are layers on layers of regulation of these firms. Individual investors have direct access to their investing accounts. They can see exactly what's going on with their money, and they can buy and sell on their own. The money isn't even held by the consulting firm. It's held by a separate brokerage."

"What about the other side of their business?" I asked. "Dr. Tarrach said they were managing the finances for his office."

Gino shook his head. "Same. That consulting firm doesn't hold any money for clients. They can recommend investments and make trades on the client's behalf. But that only happens with the client's permission."

"What if they don't get permission for a trade?" I asked.

"Then there'd be a paper trail of forged signatures," Gramps said. "You wouldn't believe the paperwork involved these days."

After talking to Lafayette Grief, I thought I might.

The waitress returned. The four of us ordered, but my appetite had fled.

"I saw the coffin in your driveway," Tomas said to me. He unfurled his cloth napkin and arranged it on his lap. "Are you entered in the coffin race?"

"Beanblossom's is." I nodded. "But I don't know how to drive the thing yet."

"You'd better figure it out," Gramps said. "That hill you'll be racing on doesn't look steep, but it has a good grade."

For the rest of the dinner, our conversation was relaxed and easy and murder-free. Or at least it was on the surface. Thoughts of the murder kept spinning through my mind.

The way I thought the world should work would never match reality. But politics had no business in a criminal case. It wasn't fair, wasn't right.

Gino insisted on paying the bill, and the three men walked me to my Mazda on the well-lit street.

"What happens to all their clients now that both Johnson and Cassius are dead?" I asked.

"Their company is an affiliate of another, larger firm," Gino said. "I suspect someone from that firm will step in."

And then maybe they'd figure out if something odd was going on at the company. But how long would that take?

Beneath the suspicious gazes of Gramps and Tomas, Gino gave me a chaste peck on my cheek and helped me into my car. "See you around?"

"I hope so." I shut my Mazda's door and drove home.

*****

The next day, Hyperion was still AWOL and not answering his phone. I'd left three messages. He hadn't answered any of them. Gnawing my bottom lip, I watched the Tarot readers mingle among the tables.

Sierra rose from her chair and slipped her cards into their colorful cloth bag. Her black t-shirt read: *This Is My Costume.*

I walked around the counter and touched her slender arm. "Got a minute?" I angled my head toward the counter, and she followed me there.

"What's up?" Sierra asked.

"Have you heard from Hyperion?"

She shook her head. "I haven't talked to him since Saturday, when he sent out the reading schedule. But there's that whole October curse thing. He's probably lying low."

"I'm sure that's what it is," I fibbed, mouth dry. "Thanks."

An elderly woman at a table for six raised a hand and motioned her over. Sierra nodded and bustled to their table.

I swallowed and checked my phone. Nothing from Hyperion. My partner wasn't the type to go into hiding. He was up to something. Or in trouble. I really hoped he was up to something.

So I didn't race from the tearoom to track him down. Instead, I forced myself to stay put and do the job I got paid for.

That resolution lasted until we stopped serving food at four o'clock. I *still* hadn't heard from my partner.

"Enough," I muttered. I strode into the kitchen and pulled off my pirate vest, unhooked my single hoop earring.

Janet looked up from the opposite side of the giant metal table.

I undid the oversized belt from around my waist and dropped it and my plastic cutlass on the counter. "I'm sorry, I've got to take off for an hour." I tucked my white blouse into my jeans.

"The food's all out," she said. "We can manage."

Feet aching, I pulled my black jeans out from the tops of my boots. I should have stuck to sneakers. "Thanks."

Grabbing my purse, I hurried out the back door. *Please let him be investigating.*

I drove to Hyperion's modest condo and rang the bell at the gate. And I waited. Staring at the boxy, metal intercom, I shifted my weight from one foot to the other. I jingled my keys in my hand.

No answer.

Investigating. He's investigating and not lying hurt in his condo.

After five minutes, I gave up and drove to his old office building. Hyperion's car was not in the lot.

But since I was here, I hurried to the fourth floor and to Lafayette's office. I knocked on the door. No one answered there either.

I hesitated outside Gino's office. Then I turned to the door opposite and went inside the consulting firm.

Dr. Tarrach and Verena faced off. Her face was splotchy. She'd taken a defensive position behind a fortification of cardboard boxes surrounding her desk. Verena pressed her fingers into the modular wood.

The dentist glowered, his chiseled face a study in annoyance. He folded his arms over his neat, button-down shirt.

"Someone from our parent company will be in touch," she was saying. "But if you want to close your account and move your money elsewhere, I can assist you with that."

His face reddened. "And once the account's closed, all the records will be gone. There'll be no trace of what Johnson and Cassius did, will there?"

"No," she said, "closing the account won't delete the records. The brokerage firm has to send you all the records for tax—"

"But they won't be detailed."

She glanced at me. "If you'd like to keep the account, you can work with someone from our parent company."

"Huh. Maybe *they'll* figure out what's really going on," he snarled. Turning quickly, he stepped toward the door, his shoulder banging into mine.

"Sorry," he muttered and moved to brush past.

"It's okay," I said to him. "I see your poison oak free." I motioned toward his bandage free arm.

He blinked and looked down at his wrist. "It's better."

"Say," I said, "did Hyperion come by your office today?"

"Hyperion?" He glanced at the clock above the door.

"My business partner. You met him in your office the other day. He mentioned he might stop by again." That wasn't true, but if Hyperion was investigating, he may have stopped by the dentist's.

Dr. Tarrach shook his head. "No. I haven't seen him."

I clawed my hands through my hair, knocking off the bandana. "Okay." I bent and grabbed the square of red fabric off the carpet. "Thanks."

Dr. Tarrach strode from the office.

Verena dropped into her chair. "This is awful. Working without Cassius and… All their clients…" She blinked rapidly and looked toward Johnson's door.

"I can only imagine." I studied the stacked boxes. "How are you coping?"

"The parent company's going to send someone tomorrow to help," she said dully.

"I don't suppose Hyperion's been by here?"

"No. Why? Is everything okay?"

"Probably. Sorry for interrupting your work." I hurried out the door.

I jammed the red bandana into the pocket of my jeans. Asking people if they'd seen Hyperion was a fool's errand. If they'd done something to him, they wouldn't admit it. But running into Dr. Tarrach was a surveillance opportunity too good to pass up.

I hustled down the stairs. Stopping on the second-floor landing, I knelt and peered through the metal railing into the foyer. The elevator doors creaked opened on the ground floor. Dr. Tarrach walked out and toward the glass exit doors.

Heart banging, I descended to the foyer. The dentist didn't turn around as he walked into the parking lot.

I got into my Mazda and watched him get into a BMW SUV. He pulled out and turned right onto the street.

I started my car and followed, keeping well back. It was one of those unnaturally warm October afternoons, and I rolled down my window.

He headed toward a freeway onramp and into the lowering sun. I twisted my hands back and forth on the wheel. How far was he going?

But instead of taking the ramp, he drove past it. I relaxed. He was staying in the area.

I followed him to Beach Street, a chic road along the beach. It had recently undergone a lot of new construction. The old, California bungalows were gone, replaced with anodyne condos built above shops and bars. I missed the old mission-style homes.

Beach was one of those odd roads that started out with one name, and then at a bend, changed to another, in this case, Sunset. The locals called the street BS, because it was so impossible parking on it.

A familiar dark-haired figure strode down the sidewalk. I sucked in a breath, took my foot off the accelerator, and craned my neck toward the window. *Hyperion?*

I braked and looked again. Yes, it *was* him. My head dropped against the rest, my grip relaxing on the wheel. He was okay. A jerk who wasn't returning my calls, but he was okay.

My jaw tightened. I'd deal with him later. I focused forward and stepped on the accelerator.

The BMW was gone.

"What the...?" Slowing, I scanned the street and blew out my cheeks. The dentist had been two cars ahead, and now the street was clear.

Behind me, a Prius honked.

I made an apology wave and pulled into an empty spot. At least I knew Hyperion was still alive. But what was he up to?

I stepped from my car and looked around.

Hyperion was gone too.

"Are you kidding me?" My nostrils flared, my lips flattening. I jammed my hands on my hips and imagined them around Hyperion's neck.

I crossed the street to the sidewalk where he'd been walking. A nearby wine bar looked promising. I hurried inside.

No Hyperion.

"Can I help you?" the hostess asked from behind her podium.

"Sorry. No." I walked out.

A concrete walkway led alongside the gray-painted building and down to the beach. Maybe he'd gone for an oceanside stroll?

Striding down the walkway, I raised one hand above my eyes and squinted at the beach. A few hardy souls lay on towels and blankets. People walked their dogs. But no one was foolish enough to swim. The ocean here was beautiful and cold. A lone surfer in a wetsuit bobbed in the Pacific.

My boots crunched on the sand, and I plodded closer to the water. A breeze whipped my hair into my eyes, stinging. I knotted it into a loose bun and continued on.

Beneath a massive white awning stood rows of white folding chairs. A woman hooked small floral arrangements to the chair at the end of each row. A beach wedding?

I walked toward her and passed a kid with a slingshot. He shot a rock toward the water, his mouth moving silently.

"Kevin!" A woman, presumably his mother, ran to him and grabbed the slingshot from his hand.

He stared at her emptily, and I shivered.

"Where did you get that?" his mother scolded. "You could hurt someone." She marched the silent Kevin toward a garbage can and dropped the slingshot inside.

I trudged onward toward the awning.

The woman working inside frowned at an arrangement of three pink roses and hooked it to a chair.

"Hi," I said. "What's going on?"

"Wedding." She checked her slim watch and gave me an I'm-busy look. "It starts in thirty minutes."

"Sorry to interrupt, but can I ask where you got that tent?"

"Lafayette, Inc. They've got the best prices, and they're right here in town."

That guy was everywhere. "But he didn't help you set it up?" I asked.

"He did. In fact, he just left. If you're quick, you might catch him." She nodded toward another walkway further down the beach that led back to the street.

"Thanks." Slogging hurriedly in that direction, I scanned the beach for Lafayette and Hyperion.

October curse. Hyperion was going to wish he'd encountered the curse when I got through with him. I passed a determined couple with a beach umbrella setup. Another garbage bin stood close by.

"Grab him! Grab him!" a woman shouted behind me.

I turned. A golden retriever loped past me, his leash snaking in the sand. A white-haired woman in a pink velour sweatsuit jogged after him, one arm outstretched. The dog looked behind himself playfully.

I lunged and turfed it, spitting sand, but I managed to grab the leash. The dog sat, now obedient and grinning. Brushing sand off my jeans, I clambered to my feet.

"Oh." The elderly woman stopped beside me. Panting, she braced her hands on her knees, and suddenly we were both laughing.

I handed her the leash. "I think this belongs to you?"

"He's too much dog for a woman my age. But isn't that the point?" Still chuckling, she turned and the two went back the way they came.

I stared up the beach. It had taken on that misty quality you sometimes get on the Pacific. The edges of objects seemed to blur. My footsteps slowed, my annoyance at Hyperion evaporating. I wanted to wear pink velour when I got old.

But as soon as I'd let thoughts of Hyperion go, Brik popped into my head. There was no *reason* for a wedding tent by the ocean to make me think about Brik. We'd never even dated.

But I thought about him anyway. About the loss he must have felt when his girlfriend had died, and how hard it was to move forward. As much as I hated to admit it, kicking me to the curb had been the rational choice for Brik. In his mind, he'd done it for a good reason, a logical one even.

But my grandfather was right. Brik *should* move on, for his own sake. But *should* and *can* are often oceans apart. I sighed. The Pacific rolled on.

A whistling sound. Hot pain slashed my ear. I gasped, staggered, and fell to one knee. I clapped my hand to my head. Heat, wetness, stickiness met my touch.

I pulled my hand away, stunned. My palm was painted with blood.

CHAPTER 21

Head wounds bleed like crazy. The same seemed to be true of ear wounds.

Heat dripped down my wrist. Stumbling to standing, clutching my ear, I looked around the beach, dazed. My ear stung like crazy.

Hyperion jogged easily toward me in the sand, the hems of his gray hip-length coat flapping. "Abigail! What happened?"

"Oh, hey," I said with as much sangfroid as I could muster. I studied his outfit. A charcoal tee over black denim and suede boots. "I was looking for you."

"Why are you bleeding?" He whipped a clean, white handkerchief from the rear pocket of his jeans and handed it to me.

"How retro. And thanks."

"Your grandfather gave it to me for my birthday. It's monogrammed."

I clapped it to my ear. "I'll get you a new one."

"What happened?" he repeated.

"I don't know. I was walking, and then there was this sort of whizzing sound, and something hit me."

"Here? That makes zero sense. Was it a seagull? I hate seagulls. Ever since I saw that movie in junior high school science class—"

"What hit me wasn't a seagull," I gritted out. I wanted to throw myself into his arms for comfort and simultaneously wring his neck. "It was hard. Like a rock."

Whatever had struck me had been moving fast. Muscles in my face hardened. I knew anger never led me anywhere good, and I should let that shitake go. But if it had hit my head and not my ear... I'd be unconscious or worse.

And it was more than that. I was furious I hadn't sensed it coming. That I'd just been walking along, lost in thought like a big fat sitting duck.

"Help me look for it," I said, pointing. "It was moving in that direction."

We searched the sand, but all we found were shells and stones and bits of plastic.

"This is useless," Hyperion said. "We don't even know what we're looking for."

"Something covered in my blood."

"And then what?" He lifted a dark brow. "Take it to the police?"

I drew in a breath to shout my frustration, but he had a point. I couldn't imagine the police taking me seriously.

"We need Tony," he said. "Let's go."

"Go where?"

"To his condo. It's on Beach Street." He nodded toward the buildings lining the beach.

We trudged back the way we came. I stopped beside a public garbage can.

"Don't throw that handkerchief away," Hyperion said. "I can get bloodstains out of *anything*."

Good to know. I pointed at a yellow plastic and rubber toy lying on top of the trash. "That kid's slingshot." I looked up. The couple with the beach umbrella watched me curiously.

I'd swear that boy's mother had tossed the slingshot into the bin closer to the wedding awning. "This isn't the right garbage bin."

"There's a *right* garbage bin?"

"There was a kid playing with this slingshot earlier. His mother threw it in a garbage bin between that walkway and the wedding thing." I jerked my chin in that direction. "Now it's here."

"Someone moved the slingshot." He rubbed his chin. "Suspicious."

"It *is*," I snapped, then I realized he wasn't being a smart ass. He was frowning at the toy, his brows drawn downward in thought. In a quieter tone, I asked, "Have you got another handkerchief?"

Hyperion drew himself up. "A gentleman never carries more than one."

"I don't think that's a rule," I said dryly. Pulling the frills of my white sleeve over my hand, I lifted out the slingshot, careful not to touch it with my skin.

Hyperion strode to the couple beneath the umbrella, and I trailed after him. "Did you see anyone using a slingshot within the last five minutes and dumping it in that garbage can?" he asked.

They shook their heads.

"Did you see *anyone*?" Hyperion asked.

The man looped his arm around the woman's shoulders. "We weren't really paying attention."

Hyperion made a disgusted sound. "Romance. The bane of investigation."

"Huh?" the man said.

"Never mind," I said and staggered past Hyperion.

Together we made our way to the sidewalk, and Hyperion led me to a doorway beside the wine bar. Two miniature topiaries shaped like seals stood on each side of the entry.

Hyperion typed a code into the pad beside the door, and we walked into a simple carpeted foyer. He pressed the button for the elevator.

"Tony's got an ocean view?" I asked. Cops made more than I thought in pokey San Borromeo.

Hyperion shook his head. "Street view. Don't bring it up. It's a sore spot."

The elevator binged, the doors sliding open. We stepped inside, and Hyperion pressed a button for the second floor.

"Where have you been?" I asked, as the doors slid shut. "I've been calling and calling. I thought something might have happened to you."

Hyperion carefully didn't look at me. "Tony thought it was best if I stayed incommunicado," he said.

"Why? Are you in danger?"

He folded his arms, rolled his eyes, and dropped his head in my direction, all at the same time. "Seriously? You've been pushed in front of a car, attacked by a vampire, and now assaulted with a slingshot. The killer's focused on *you*."

I thought about that. It didn't feel good.

At home, even with the metal braces in my doors, I never slept well. I'd start at every creak, at the soft thuds of animals scampering across my roof.

I swallowed. "In the interests of accuracy, you were attacked by the vampire too."

He stared at the elevator buttons like he might find the meaning of life there. "The point is, he doesn't want you on the case."

"What?" I asked, outraged. "He may have been drugged in *our* tearoom."

A bead of sweat trickled down his temple. "Yes, but—"

"You're trying to chisel me out of our case. *Our* case?"

"We don't want to get you killed. Is that so awful?"

"Yes." I fumed. "Tony's my friend too."

He wrinkled his face, his head waggling. "Well..."

"I don't appreciate you ghosting me, and I'm not dropping this." And especially not now. I'd never get to sleep again. Not with a killer out there, knowing who I was while I stumbled around blind and vulnerable.

Hyperion shifted his weight and sighed. "I guess I can't stop you. Did you see any of our suspects nearby before this happened?" He motioned toward the handkerchief clasped to my ear.

I huffed a breath. "I was following Dr. Tarrach. He could have seen me and turned around. But I'd just left Verena at the office. She could have followed me too. And that wedding awning thing was set up by Lafayette not that long ago. He could still be in the area."

"This is ludicrous. Those are *all* our suspects. We can't wait for more people to die to write them off as persons of interest. That's not a solid investigation technique."

"No," I agreed. "And it's hard on the suspects."

The elevator doors slid open, and we stepped into a carpeted hallway. Black and white photos of beach landscapes graced the walls.

"Oh, I have an idea." One-handed, I dug my phone from my purse, looked up the number online, and called Verena's office.

"You have reached the offices of Santori and Warszowski," Verena said. "Our offices are currently closed. If you—"

I hung up and checked the clock on my phone. It was just after five, so Verena had a totally reasonable reason not to be at work. I swore. *Work.* "I've got to get back to the tearoom." The staff would revolt if I wasn't there to cleanup.

Okay, they wouldn't revolt. But I was sure they'd *feel* like revolting.

"You can't go looking like that," Hyperion said. "You'll horrify the staff. They'll think an unspeakable, shuffling convolution walked in."

"It's not that bad." I pulled the bloody handkerchief away. There was a lot of blood. I swayed. Maybe it *was* that bad.

Hyperion knocked on a door. After a moment, Tony opened it.

The detective's gray eyes widened slightly, then narrowed. "Why, oh, why, does no one take my advice?"

"I don't remember you giving me any," I said.

"She's delirious." Hyperion hauled me inside the condo.

The walls were that sandy-beigy color that's so popular these days. A longhorn skull with a lariat wrapped around it hung from one wall. A few neutral abstract paintings decorated the opposite wall, covered in shiplap. The chairs were brown leather. A black coffee table between them was piled with manila folders. A cowhide rug lay on the wood floor. A small balcony looked over the street. The condo smelled of bleach wipes and lemon.

"Nice place," I said.

"You're dripping," the detective drawled. "Hyperion, show her to the medicine cabinet in the bathroom."

"Here." I held out the slingshot.

Tony recoiled, his nose wrinkling. "What is that?"

"Evidence," I said. "Someone shot me with it."

"Put it on the table."

My partner led me into a gleaming white bathroom that smelled of bleach. He opened the mirror over the sink, exposing a deconstructed first-aid kit. The items on each row appeared to have been organized by size. "You okay here?"

"Yeah. I can manage."

Hyperion vanished into the other room, and I got busy. Tony had an astonishing array of disinfectants, even for a germaphobe. I chose the one that seemed the least likely to sting, and dabbed at my ear with a soaked cotton ball.

It hurt like crazy.

I cleaned myself up and returned to the men on twin leather chairs in the living room. They huddled over the coffee table and frowned at open manila folders. The slingshot had vanished.

"What are those?" I pointed to three, foot-high stacks of more folders on the table.

"People I've arrested," Tony said.

I blinked. "You mean, total? In Texas too?"

"Nope, just here."

I gaped. "You've lived here a year. There can't be more than twenty-thousand people in San Borromeo. How can you have arrested so many people?" Was San Borromeo more crime ridden than I'd thought?

"I've arrested people outside town too."

"But still..." I looked aghast at the files. That was a *lot* of arrestees.

"Pull up a chair," Tony said. "We're trying to figure out who I've arrested who's also got a beef against Cassius Santori or his firm."

"But... I have to get back to the tearoom." I flushed. After that scene I'd made about being part of the investigation, that just sounded silly.

"No you don't," Tony said. "If you're going to do reckless things, you may as well do them where I can keep an eye on you."

"I can be reckless wherever I want," I muttered.

"What?" Tony asked.

"Were you tested for drugs when you were arrested?" I asked.

"Yes."

"And?" I asked.

"They lost the results."

"Lost...?" Red heat flushed through my skull. Was the San Borromeo PD totally incompetent or *trying* to send him to jail? I remembered what Gino's sister had said. "It's not too late—"

"I know. My lawyer's on it."

My stomach rumbled.

The men looked at me.

"I can't help it," I said.

"There are some chips on top of the refrigerator," Tony said.

I walked into the kitchen. Now, I keep a clean kitchen. You have to in food service, and the cleanliness habit has crossed over into my home kitchen as well. But I really think you could have eaten off the floor in Tony's. The countertops and appliances gleamed.

I grabbed a bag of chips from the top of the fridge. "Ooh. Barbecue." My favorite. Next to ranch. And those lime tortilla chips. And pretty much anything with cheese dust on it. I opened the bag and returned to the living room.

Hyperion handed me a file. "Read."

"I've got to call the tearoom." I popped a chip into my mouth.

I called and told them I'd been delayed, but I'd be there by seven at the latest to finish cleaning up. Then I started reading.

An hour later, I flopped backward on the brown leather couch. "This is going nowhere. There's nothing obvious. I mean, if we had the client files for the financial consulting firm..." I glanced into the bag of chips. It was half empty. "Oh, my God."

"What's wrong?" Tony looked up.

"Half these chips are gone, and I don't remember eating them. I've lost time. My head wound must be worse than I thought. I must have blacked out."

"While eating?" Hyperion asked.

"I'm about ready to lose consciousness too." Tony tossed his file onto the coffee table. "I pride myself on being able to make connections, but there's a lot of info here to process."

"What we need," Hyperion said, "is one of those super computers."

I jolted on the couch. "Razzzor."

"You're nutty tech friend?" Tony asked.

I roughly flipped back my hair. It was slightly sticky. "He's not nutty. He's an eccentric genius. He could probably put together some program that will... I'm going to call him, if that's okay." It was Tony's case, after all.

Tony sighed and relaxed back on the leather couch. "Why not?"

Hyperion shot me a worried look.

I walked onto the balcony and called Razzzor.

"Where've you been?" my friend asked. "I haven't seen you since the Centauri system. And you didn't tell me how you liked the pumpkin cannon."

"It's really cool, but, um, a little too aggressive for the parade." I stared at the condos across the street. Several, higher-up balconies had telescopes. I was willing to bet they had ocean views and much higher property taxes.

"Have you tried out the coffin car yet?"

"I haven't had time." But I really did need to start practicing if I was going to beat Beatrice. And I *was* going to beat Beatrice. *Heh.*

Razzzor blew out his breath. "Well, hurry up, will you? I want you to tell me how it drives."

"Why?" I asked, my skin prickling.

"So I can make any adjustments. If I'm sponsoring you, you'd better win."

I braced an elbow on the wrought-iron railing. "Well, as long as the adjustments are within legal limits."

"Duh."

"How are you with databases?" I asked.

"I could build one with my right and left brain tied behind my back. Why?"

I explained.

"So you're thinking something that could cross-reference public records and the internet? Something that would include the dark web?"

"Um. Yes?"

"And I'd be a part of the investigation?"

I pinched the bridge of my nose and looked down at the patio tiles. "Ah..." Tony wasn't going to like this. "Since you'd have to show us how to use the database..." I winced. "Yes?"

"In the interests of justice, I'm in."

"How long do you think it'll take?"

Razzzor didn't answer. I checked the phone. He'd already hung up.

When I returned to the men in the living room, they were again reviewing case files.

"Razzzor's going to build us a database," I said. "It will cross-reference public records and the dark web and stuff."

Tony quirked a brow. "And stuff?"

"You know," I said. "Internet stuff. And now I've really got to get back to the tearoom."

"Abigail." The detective set his folder on the coffee table. "It strikes me that whoever is doing this is seriously disturbed. You do not want a disturbed person angry at you. Do you hear what I'm saying?"

I shivered. I heard.

"Better walk her to her car," Tony said to Hyperion.

My partner shot me a resigned look and escorted me to my hatchback. "That went better than I expected," he said. "Think Razzzor's program will make a difference?"

"I don't know." I slid into my car. "It's a lot of data to sift through. Anything that can give us a leg up is worth a try."

I sped to the tearoom and guiltily helped clean up. Then I drove home, with that irritating, vague, nagging feeling that I'd missed something.

Since the coffin racer was in my driveway, I parked on the street and walked to the short flight of steps to my front door.

At their base, I stopped, turned, and studied the coffin. I set my purse on the wooden steps and walked to the racer.

There was no time like the present. The alternative to winning that race was losing to Beatrice and more debt. The thought nauseated me.

I studied the coffin's interior. The seats were red plastic. Two sticks were on each side of the front seat for steering. A wooden brake pad was where the brake would be in a real car.

I pushed the coffin into the quiet street. This would actually be a pretty good place to practice. There was a gentle slope and not a lot of traffic.

I climbed inside. The car rolled forward an inch, and I grimaced. I'd forgotten it needed a push start.

Stepping from the coffin, I squinted up the darkened street. What this thing needed was...

I walked to the front of the racer.

Headlights. It actually had two safety headlights. Maybe this race wasn't as hairbrained as I'd initially thought. Someone had put some thought into building this coffin.

I fumbled inside the racer and found a switch. The headlights snapped on.

"Let's try you out," I muttered. Bracing my hands on each side of the coffin, I gave it a gentle push, and we were rolling. My chest made a sharp, panicked squeeze. Hastily, I hopped inside and tested the brake.

The coffin slowed, and I blew out a relieved breath. I should have checked the brake before launching it down the hill.

The coffin picked up speed, and a cool breeze tossed my hair. I pulled gently on the right stick. The coffin rattled to the right.

I sped down the road, laughter bubbling up inside me. My heart pounded. I felt out of control and in control at the same time. The wind tossed my hair. "Whoo hoo!"

The heck with Brik and Hyperion and Tony. They might be well intentioned, but I was flying. I was *free*. "I can be reckless wherever I want," I shouted to the street. "Woot!"

I flashed past a parked car, and my insides clenched. There was reckless, and then there was driving too fast in a residential area.

I stepped on the brake, and the coffin slowed. *Snap!* The brake went slack beneath my shoe and slammed against the coffin's wood floor.

Frantically, I stepped on the useless brake again.

The coffin picked up speed. My stomach dropped.

"Oh. Hell."

CHAPTER 22

There had actually been several good reasons for testing the coffin on my own street. First, I knew its turns. Second, there was a massive blackberry bush at the bottom of the first curve. If that botanical beast couldn't stop me, nothing would.

Another good thing about the blackberry bush was that instead of sidewalk, a patch of dirt led up to it. The dirt itself might slow me a bit before I even hit the tangle of thorns.

I tried not to think of the fact that no one harvested berries from that bush. The thorns just weren't worth it. Even the racoons avoided that bush. Its berries just hung there, limp and rotting.

Lit windows whipped past on the dark street. I bit back a moan. Maybe this sense of high speed was only the rollercoaster effect? Rollercoasters are never as fast as they feel. Still, I wouldn't want to go flying off one.

Also, I hate rollercoasters.

The coffin rattled and bumped across a manhole cover. My hands gripped the steering sticks hard enough to give me splinters.

The blackberry thicket rose up before me, a monstrous tangle in the darkness. My heartbeat hammered in my ears. Vocabulary from Hyperion's word-of-the-day calendar floated through my head. *Colossal. Ominous. Appalling.*

I braced and realized my foot was still pressing the useless brake.

Low headlights flared in front of me.

I shouted, yanking on the left steering stick. The coffin swerved out of the way of the oncoming car and hit the curb. The racer's back-end reared upward.

I couldn't scream. I was too terrified. The rear of the coffin rose in slow motion, until the coffin stood on its non-existent bumper. I stared straight down at unforgiving pavement.

The coffin turned once, the pavement spiraling around me. There was a grinding sound— its headlights being pulverized. The racer managed another half-rotation.

And then the back of the coffin dropped to the ground with a teeth-rattling thud. The rear wheels shot from the racer and spun into the darkness.

I sat, panting, mouth open, heart pounding, hands fisted on the steering sticks. I was alive. There was a slim chance I might not even have whiplash.

Razzzor jogged easily toward me. He might not get a lot of sun, but he was in shape, sinewy muscles pumping. "Whoa. Whoa! Did you... Did you *see* that?"

I patted my head, neck, and chest, checking for damage.

"I never would have believed a coffin could *do* that," he went on. "Two rotations!"

It took me two or three tries to clamber from the coffin.

"You okay?" he asked.

"No brake." I bent, breathing deeply, and pressed my hands to my thighs. "I'm fine."

Razzzor prowled around the coffin, then flipped it on its back. He clicked the flashlight on his keychain and studied its underside. "Huh. Looks like your basic go-kart design." He reached inside and pulled out a rope. "Here's your problem. No wonder the brakes went out."

"Yeah." I gasped. "No wonder." I studied the rope uneasily. It looked like it had been cut most of the way through. Only one edge of the rope was frayed.

"Good thing I stopped by," he said. "I can fix this."

I wasn't sure I wanted him to. "Why *are* you here?"

"Oh." He reached into the pocket of his khakis and handed me a thumb drive. "That program you wanted."

"You finished it already?"

He sneered. "A glorified database? Please. It was easy. All I had to do was..." He rattled off a bunch of programming terms I'd long ago and happily ever after forgotten.

I nodded and went to look for the missing wheels. One had landed deep in the blackberry bush. Arms limp, I stared at it, a dark circle beneath a tangle of branches. "Of course, that's where you landed," I muttered.

"What?" Razzzor called.

"Nothing."

Resigned, I reached into the bush. Thorns clawed my puffy, white pirate sleeve. There was a ripping sound, and I winced. So much for that part of my pirate costume. And I'd *liked* that shirt.

I grasped the wheel, carefully pulling it free. There was another sound of fabric tearing.

I located the second wheel at the base of a eucalyptus tree and set it on the coffin's red seat.

"You know," Razzzor said thoughtfully. "There are other things I could do to improve this coffin."

"There are strict rules on what the coffins can and can't do," I said more shrilly than I liked.

"I wouldn't electrify it or anything. But we can definitely improve the aerodynamics and handling. You want to win, don't you?"

I groaned. "I *have* to win."

"Why do you have to?"

"Nothing. Never mind. It's only my pride." He didn't need to know about the bet. If he did, he'd just offer to cover it, and I couldn't let him. Not if he was doing it out of guilt. Also, he'd asked me out a couple times. I was pretty sure he'd moved on, but I didn't want that obligation between us.

I drove Razzzor's Tesla up to my house, while he maneuvered the coffin up the street, handling it like a wheelbarrow. He pushed it into Brik's driveway, and a porch light flashed on.

"Um," I said, "that's not my house."

"I know, but Brik's got the tools to repair this bad boy. You don't." He set down his end of the coffin and adjusted his glasses.

"How do *you* know I don't?"

Razzzor arched his brows. "I've seen your toolbox. No offense, but it's pathetic."

"How am I not supposed to take offense at that? Just because it's pink—"

Brik opened the door and stepped, barefoot, onto the wide cement step. "What's going on?"

"That toolbox was on sale," I told Razzzor hotly. Really, it wasn't a bad tool box for the price.

"Hey, Brik," Razzzor said. "What do you know about go-kart design?"

"I used to know a thing or two. I had one when I was a kid." He walked down the steps. "What happened to the wheels?"

"Training accident," Razzzor said smartly.

Brik looked me over. His deep-water eyes widened with concern. "Did you just do that?" He pointed to my head.

"What?" I touched the bandage on my ear. "No, this was..." I shook my head. "I'm fine."

"Anyway," Razzzor said, "*she* can't fix the racer."

Brik laughed. "Tell me about it."

"I can fix things." I'd fixed my toilet the other day, thanks to the internet, and I was proud of that fix. There are answers to *everything* online.

"Move it into my garage." Brik ambled to his garage door and pushed some buttons on the keypad. The door glided upward.

Razzzor and I gasped.

Now, I'm not exactly handy. But even I can appreciate a well-organized garage.

Brik's had been turned into a workshop/gym. Tools hung in neat rows on wire racks on one wall. On the opposite, a free-weight set fit into a rack beside a weight machine. A work table with a circular saw stood beside shelves lined with labeled drawers of various sizes.

"Nice." Razzzor wheeled the coffin inside.

The garage door glided down, leaving me standing alone on the sidewalk.

"Is this about the pumpkin cannon?" I shouted to the door. "Because Razzzor made that hair trigger."

No one answered.

I grabbed my purse off my steps and marched inside my yellow bungalow.

Grabbing the steel security brace by the door, I jammed it beneath the doorknob. I dropped onto the arm of my couch by the door, my legs suddenly trembling.

Someone had cut the brake rope. It wouldn't have been hard. The coffin had been sitting in my driveway for days. There'd been ample opportunities for sabotage.

I stood and nudged the brace's rubber stopper closer to the door with my foot.

Whoever was gunning for me knew where I lived.

*****

At nine a.m. that morning I snuck out of the tearoom and drove to the temporary Halloween store. As Hyperion had predicted, they'd sold so many witch costumes no one remembered who'd bought them. None of the photos of my suspects raised any eyebrows. I bought an eyepatch and a pirate hat and returned to the tearoom.

My puffy pirate blouse was a total loss. I had other white blouses, but they didn't have that certain something. Hence the eyepatch and pirate hat.

Later, when Hyperion arrived, I gave him the news about the coffin car sabotage.

"It turned on its *bumper?*" Hyperion looked up skeptically from his laptop.

A familiar-looking stack of manila folders lay by his elbow. On the altar against the wall, Bastet lashed his tail.

"The coffin doesn't have a bumper," Hyperion continued.

"You know what I mean. On the front. It rotated on its front." I touched my fingers against the palm of one hand and swiveled my hand back and forth.

He bent his head to his computer on the table. "And you're certain the rope was cut?"

"I'm not certain. Nothing's a hundred percent."

The tabby growled.

"But I'm pretty sure," I amended. "The break was clean except at the very edge of the rope. Like someone had cut most of the way through. One minute the brakes were working, the next, they weren't."

"Tony's not going to like this." He cocked his head. "You could have been badly hurt. Tell me you at least got some blackberries."

I adjusted my eyepatch. It was a little tight. "Trust me, they're not worth the trouble."

"They're organic."

"They're a menace. No way I'm going near those blackberries again."

Hyperion's office door opened, and Brik strode inside the crimson room. "Hey."

"Hi, Brik." Hyperion waved vaguely and returned his attention to the laptop.

Brik nodded toward Hyperion then turned to me. "They told me you were in here. I took a look at that brake rope." His voice vibrated with anger. "Someone cut it."

"Good Lord." Hyperion widened his eyes. "Abigail could have been killed."

I compressed my lips. Hyperion smirked.

Brik folded his arms over his white tee. "You can see it's a clean cut except for the last eighth of an inch. Why would someone target you? What's going on?"

I folded my arms. "Detective Chase—"

He raised his hands. "No. Forget it. I've changed my mind. I don't want to know. We'll keep your coffin racer in my garage until the race. I don't want some neighbor kid to sneak inside and learn the hard way it's not working."

"You and Razzzor weren't able to fix it?" Hyperion asked anxiously.

Brik snorted. "We fixed it. Now we're working on some improvements. But I don't want whoever sabotaged the racer to come back and do it again."

My flesh pebbled. "Improvements?"

"There's no way you'll lose now," Brik said. "If you don't get yourself killed first." He stalked from the office.

At the end of the hallway, the rear door slammed.

"Cool," Hyperion said.

"Not cool." *What improvements?* I tore my gaze from the door and angled my head toward the laptop on the round table. "What are you doing?"

"Data entry. Razzzor's program may well be the next big thing in law enforcement. But for it to work I need to enter the basic data for all our suspects and everyone Tony's arrested. It's a lot of info." He slapped shut a manila folder. "And that's the last one."

With a flourish, Hyperion pressed the ENTER key on his computer. A chime pinged.

"Well?" I edged around the table, close enough to rustle its wine-colored cloth.

Hyperion's dark brows slashed downward. "It's not working."

"What do you mean it's not working?" I looked over his shoulder at the screen.

NO MATCHES.

Hyperion opened a tab and frowned. "All the data is there. There *has* to be a connection."

"Hold on." I phoned Razzzor.

"Hey, Abs. You're going to love what we did to your coffin car."

"What did—?" *Never mind.* "We're having some trouble with your program. I'm putting you on speaker." I set the phone on the table.

"What's the problem?" Razzzor asked.

"It says there are no matches," Hyperion said.

"Did you put the info for the detective and the other victims in the alpha category?"

"Yes," Hyperion said.

"And the suspects in the beta category?" Razzzor asked.

"Duh," Hyperion said. "That was obvious."

"Then there aren't any connections."

"But..." Hyperion sputtered. "That's not possible."

"Look," Razzzor said, "the program doesn't search for connections between suspects. And it doesn't search for connections between suspects and one or two of your victims—assuming Chase is a victim."

"Then what does it search for?" I sat across from Hyperion.

"It looks for connections between any of your suspects and *all three* of your victims. If it says nothing's there, then nothing's there."

I sucked in a breath. "Wait. What if Johnson's death was because he saw or knew something? He might not have a direct connection with the killer. The connection may be more tangential."

"So take him out," Razzzor said. "He's throwing the results."

"I'm on it," Hyperion said, typing furiously. He pushed the delete key. "Done. Johnson's out of the mix."

"Okay," Razzzor said. "Now re-sort the data."

Hyperion pushed more keys.

NO MATCHES.

My stomach hollowed. It wasn't working. We'd failed. "It's still saying no matches."

"Then there aren't any matches," Razzzor said. "Or it's a garbage-in, garbage-out situation."

"I double-checked everything," Hyperion said.

But it *had* been a good idea. And there had to be a match. It was only logical. "Could we send everything over to you, just in case we did something wrong?"

Hyperion straightened in his high-backed chair and shot me an irritated look. "I didn't make any mistakes."

I covered the phone with my hand. "I know," I whispered, "but Razzzor might have." Actually, either man could have. But I wasn't dumb enough to say that out loud.

"Oh," Hyperion said, mollified. He waved his hand negligently at the screen. "Send away then."

"What was that?" Razzzor asked.

"Nothing," I said. "Can we email everything to you?"

My ex-boss exhaled heavily. "Fine. Send it."

I rose and moved to Hyperion's open laptop.

"I've got his email," Hyperion said, and tapped away. "Okay. I've just sent it."

"Message received." After a minute, Razzzor grunted. "Huh."

"Did you find a problem?" I asked.

"No. It's working perfectly."

My mouth went dry. "Are you sure?"

"Abigail, do you think I didn't test this before I sent it to you? It's based off some of my existing software. All I had to do was make a few tweaks. I tested it. My beta team tested it. I'm telling you, there are no connections between your suspects, your detective, and Cassius Santori."

Hyperion and I met each other's gaze.

"But... That makes no sense," I said. "There *has* to be a connection."

"Why?" Razzzor asked.

"Because..." Because if this was all random, there was no way we were going to be able to find the killer.

CHAPTER 23

It's not easy arguing with a tech genius about his own software. But I did it anyway.

Razzzor double-checked the code and retested it over the weekend. I poured tea and baked scones and refreshed the tearoom's Halloween decorations. We each play to our strengths.

But Razzzor didn't find anything wrong with the program.

Monday morning, I drove to Hyperion's old office building. Razzzor might be a tech genius, but the answer had to be here, where Cassius and Johnson had worked. I stared up at the building's cement-colored sides.

Jaw set, I walked inside and up the stairs. At this point, I was a little surprised no one had filed a harassment suit against me.

I knocked on the Santori and Warszowski office door.

"Come in," Verena called.

I stepped inside. More boxes were piled around her desk, stacked with files.

"Oh, hi." Expression vacant, she brushed a coil of red hair off her forehead. Beneath her porcelain-blue eyes, her skin was the color of a bruise. "Did you find Hyperion?"

"I did. It turns out I was panicking over nothing." I lifted my shoulders, dropped them. "Go figure."

"And I should have panicked more," she said in a near whisper. "I still can't believe Johnson was..." Her gaze traveled to his closed office door.

"You couldn't have done anything."

"If I'd just opened the door..." Her mouth flattened into a line. She shook her head.

"You're packing up?"

She nodded. "We're transferring the paper files to our parent company."

"What will happen to you?"

"I guess I'll find a new job. Got any openings at the tearoom?"

I smiled faintly. "I suspect you're over qualified. What did Dr. Tarrach decide to do? Is his account transferring over to your parent company?"

"Yes." She braced her fingertips on a clear space on the desk and leaned toward me. "He's their problem now."

"Was he that big of a problem?"

She gulped and looked away, blinking rapidly. "Johnson was getting sick of him. He was a difficult man to work with."

"And Lafayette Grief?"

She bobbed her head. "He's going to a new advisor elsewhere."

"Did he say why?"

"He said he wanted to find his own advisor rather than just be shuffled over. I guess I can't blame him." She picked up a file and studied the label. "I went through Lafayette's files," she said, not meeting my gaze.

"Oh?"

"After you were asking about who might have wanted them both..." She swallowed. "There was nothing wrong. Every transaction was accounted for. I checked Dr. Tarrach's records too. There were no red flags."

"Why did Dr. Tarrach think something was wrong? Were his investments not panning out?"

A spark of anger lit her eyes. "He was crazy. There was no *reason* for him to be unhappy. After everything Johnson and Cassius did for him..." Roughly, she shoved the file into an open, cardboard box.

"What did they do for him?"

"I'm not supposed to—" Her mouth compressed. "Oh, I don't even care anymore. My last day is tomorrow. Dr. Tarrach may be a great dentist, but he's no businessman. He ran his practice into the ground. He has a lot of Medi-Cal patients, which is very noble, but he couldn't collect on the insurance."

"And so Johnson and Cassius helped him?"

She raised her chin. "They managed his practice and his investments. At least they *thought* they were. Then last year we found out he'd gone and bought a beach condo for his mistress—"

"Whoa." *Mistress?* That was still a thing?

"I know." She motioned violently toward Johnson's office door. "How is any financial advisor supposed to be able to stick to a plan if their client goes spending his money on beach condos? Even if it *was* a good investment," she said, grudging.

I'd actually been thinking more about the cheating on his wife part of the story being a problem, but okay. I guess buying random properties *would* make managing someone's finances difficult. But Tarrach had already admitted to that.

The door behind me opened, and I turned.

Detective Baranko hulked in the open doorway. "What are you doing here?" He glowered impressively, his jaw jutted forward, his eyes narrowed.

"Leaving," I said.

"Uh, uh." He folded his bulky arms, straining the fabric of his blue suit jacket. "What. Were. You. Doing here?"

Oh, boy. "Gossiping with Verena."

"About what?"

"The murders," I said, exasperated.

"So you admit you're interfering in an investigation," he said.

"No. I'm not interfering. I'm gossiping. Anyone can gossip. It's not illegal. And what are you doing back here?"

"I'm asking the questions."

I rolled my eyes. "Detective Chase could not have killed Johnson. He was in jail. And the idea that he could have killed Cassius Santori is ridiculous. It might be easier to pin this on an innocent man, but maybe you should do your job and try to figure out who's really responsible?"

"No one's pinning anything on anyone."

"Really?" I crossed my arms, because he didn't have a monopoly on that move. "Then how did your office lose the results of Detective Chase's drug test?"

Blood suffused his face, but I kept going, muscles quivering, voice rising. "While you were focused on Chase, you let the real murderer run free to kill Johnson."

He stepped closer, but I didn't step back. "Do you know the one thing I hate more than mouthy women?"

"I can't wait to find out."

"Dirty cops. They warp the system. They make the good cops look bad. And the community loses faith."

"And what about DAs trying to make a name for themselves?" My breath came hard and fast. I tilted my head up to meet his eyes. "Or suspiciously incompetent lab techs? How far do those go to build faith in the system?"

Veins bulged in his neck. "Santori was shot with Chase's gun. Chase could have drugged himself anytime afterward."

An impatient noise burst from my throat. "Who carries around knock-out drugs on the off chance they may need an alibi after shooting someone in a random road rage incident?"

"Wait," Verena said slowly. "Knock-out drugs? What's going on?"

"Get out," Baranko said through clenched teeth. "Before I arrest you."

I planted my feet on the thick carpet. He couldn't tell me what to do. I had just as much right to be here as he did. A file folder slipped from Verena's desk, its pages whispering to the floor.

And then I remembered that, yes, he could tell me what to, and I'd have to take it. Furious, I hitched my purse over my shoulder and strode out the door.

The elevator doors slid open. Pulse thudding in my ears, I stepped toward them and stumbled into Gino, exiting.

"Hey," he said. "I was just going to call you."

I blew out my breath and tried to calm down. "Oh, hey." *Casual. I could do casual.*

The elevator door tried to close on me, and I stepped backward, into the gray-carpeted hall.

"Come to my office," he said.

"I can't." I angled my head toward Verena's door. "The detective in there threatened to arrest me if I didn't leave the building. I think he meant it."

"Why would he arrest you?" The elevator door made another attempt to close, this time on his shoulders.

"Oh, you know..."

"That amateur detecting thing?" An odd look crossed his face.

"What?" I said. "Why are you looking at me like that?

"I'm just trying to figure out if you like taking risks, or if you're codependent."

Every muscle from my heart to my head tightened. What was with the box-top psychoanalysis? "What's that supposed to mean?"

"It means taking the need to be needed to unhealthy levels."

"I know what codependency means. Why would you think...? No. There's a difference between codependency and helping a friend. This isn't about being needed."

"Then what is it about?" The doors bounced off his broad shoulders. I pushed past him into the elevator. "It's about friendship," I said.

Gino nodded. "Fair enough."

"Thanks for your permission," I said acidly and stabbed the button for the first floor.

He grimaced. "I didn't mean to offend you. I'm just trying to figure out what makes you tick."

I grunted. Was I supposed to be flattered by that? Maybe I was. Maybe I was still so angry and yes, rattled, by Baranko that my reactions were off. Maybe I *was* acting like a crazy person. "It's fine."

He braced one hand on the closing doors. "Want to try dinner again? This time without your grandfather and Tomas?"

"I've got your number. I'll call if I'm free."

He released the door and it closed. The elevator rattled and bumped downward.

I should have taken the stairs.

I tugged my bottom lip. *Was* it codependency? People raised by narcissists did tend to have dependency issues. I'd spent college in a self-pitying, self-analysis phase researching those issues. My twenties had not been good years.

But my narcissistic parents had abandoned me at too young age for that to influence me. Too bad the abandonment had created its own bucketful of neuroses. A distrust of authority figures, independence, and a tendency to sabotage relationships.

Which I'd sort of just done. No, *Gino* had done that.

Heat flushed through me. Why was I so angry?

Answer: because Gino had struck a nerve. Maybe I wasn't being nobly loyal to Hyperion and Tony? Maybe I was being driven by fear, fear of letting people down the way my parents had let me down?

Nah.

I stepped from the elevator and walked into Detective Chase.

"Gagh," I stepped backward. Twice? I'd walked into someone twice? I needed to get my head in the game.

"What are you doing here?" Tony drawled.

"Not plunging to an untimely death."

He cocked his head.

"The elevator's iffy," I explained. "And I was looking for clues. What are you doing here?"

"Same."

"I wouldn't go up there. Detective Baranko just threw me out."

"Ah." He smoothed his navy tie. "Thanks for the heads up. Any luck with Razzzor's software?"

I shook my head. "Razzzor swears it's working. Didn't you have a meeting with your lawyer today?"

He nodded. "Just finished."

"Any word on the drug test results?"

"We'll get them back tomorrow."

I shifted my weight beside a Ficus tree. "Baranko said the test wouldn't matter. You could have dosed yourself after the murder."

"That will be a hard argument to make since I've got no other connection to the victims. Aside from Hyperion once sharing an office building with them."

I glanced up the concrete stairs. *Codependency. Ha.* "And the whole dating thing," I said absently.

Chase's face went carefully blank. "Dating thing?"

I focused on the detective. "You know. Hyperion and Cassius."

"Hyperion and Cassius," he said flatly.

I swallowed. *Oh. Oh, damn.* He hadn't known. "It was only one or two dates," I said quickly. "It was no big thing." It *was* no big thing. Wasn't it?

"Did you mention this to Detective Baranko?"

"No. What do you take me for? I'm not going to help him take you down..." But I'd just dropped the dime on Hyperion.

So much for loyalty.

CHAPTER 24

I studied the bill for the new oven and rubbed the back of my neck. If I wore a lot of sweaters and didn't use the heater this winter, maybe I'd save a few hundred bucks on my electric bill. That would help.

Hyperion burst into the tearoom's kitchen, his cowboy hat askew. He wore a plaid shirt, jeans, and a six-shooter holstered low around his hips. His eyes were blazing.

"How could you?" he hissed. "You told Tony about Cassius."

Setting the bill down, I straightened from the metal table and turned to face him. "I'm sorry," I said quietly. "I didn't know it was a secret."

"Would you talk about your exes with your current boyfriend?"

"Well, no, but—"

"Then why would you bring up mine?"

"We were talking about Razzzor's software and the lack of connections, and..." I closed my eyes. There was no excuse. I'd been flustered by Baranko and then Gino, and I hadn't been thinking and shot off my mouth. I'd failed him. Thoughtlessness was no excuse. "You're right. I should have kept my mouth shut. I'm sorry."

Hyperion sagged against the long, metal work table in the middle of the kitchen. He closed his eyes. "No, it's my fault. I should have told him myself."

"Hyperion—"

He scuffed his cowboy boot on the linoleum. "What is wrong with me? It's been years since I've met someone who—" He shook his head. "It's irony. Or hubris, or whatever."

"What is?"

"I've spent the last five years playing the field, telling myself I just wanted to have fun. And now, all that fun could ruin the single best relationship—real relationship—I've ever had."

"That's not fair. How are you supposed to meet the right person if you don't get out and meet people?" I blinked. I was talking about myself again. Which was doubly narcissistic because this mess was about Hyperion and Tony, not me.

"And are you sure you *have* ruined things?" I asked. "Judging by the number of arrests he's made, Tony has to know nobody's perfect."

"It's because of all those arrests that he prizes honesty in relationships."

"You were embarrassed," I said. "It was only one date."

"A date that could give him a motive in a murder investigation."

"Only assuming Tony's crazy," I said, "which he's not. I've never met a more logical, orderly person."

"Tell that to the DA."

"You and Tony didn't break up, did you?" I asked anxiously.

"I'm not sure what happened between us." Hyperion straightened off the table. "And now I'm going to stop freaking out like a tween girl who couldn't get Jonas Brothers tickets."

He pointed toward the open door, where a feathered costume hung in its plastic bag. "What is that?"

"The latest costume of the day. A Vegas showgirl." I frowned. Usually our costumes had some sort of thematic match, and Hyperion was a cowboy from the old west.

I studied the feathers.

Oh.

It wasn't a showgirl costume.

"I canceled your costumes," he fretted. "Now I have to get a refund for that one too? Why do you hate me, October?" He shook his fist at the ceiling.

"I'll take care of it," I said quickly. "I'll return it to the shop today."

"It doesn't matter. A costume is the least of my problems." He picked the bill off the long table. "What's this?"

My throat thickened. "The, um, bill for the new oven."

His eyes bugged. "It cost that much? It's an oven, not a Maserati."

"I'm sorry. I should have told you sooner—"

He shook his head. "But I've been preoccupied. And it's none of my business how you spend your money."

"Actually, it kind of is." I swallowed. "I didn't just use this month's share of my marketing budget. I used the next six months. That means no ads, nothing but guerrilla tactics on my part to market Beanblossom's. And the Tarot readers rely on—"

"It's okay. I know you'll figure out something." He trudged from the kitchen.

My heart twisted. *No. Yell at me about the oven. Be angry, don't be defeated.* I took a step to follow him and stopped.

I'd been so stupid. All I'd wanted was to help Hyperion, and I'd done just the opposite. If I'd just thought a little faster and kept my trap shut...

I hung my head. Then I spent the next fifteen minutes cleaning the kitchen, kicking myself, and waiting for the next batch of scones to come out of my overpriced oven.

The scones came out perfect. Dammit, the oven was flawless. I managed to refrain from kicking its door shut. How could the Platonic ideal of an oven cause me so much angst?

Maricel bustled into the kitchen. "Perfect timing." She leaned over the tray of scones and inhaled. "Think I can get one of these ovens for my apartment?" she joked. "Because this new oven is savage."

I sighed. "If only."

We filled tiered trays with scones, Halloween treats, and tiny sandwiches. Maricel and the other servers carried them into the tearoom for our first serving of the day.

I checked my watch. We had thirty minutes before things got busy again, and the costume shop was only a five-minute walk.

I told Maricel I'd be back in twenty and hung my apron on the hook behind the kitchen door. Pirates don't wear aprons. I was getting a little tired of my outfit.

Maybe I needed a better hat.

Grabbing the saloon-girl costume, I strode through the tearoom and out the front door. From the doorway of the t-shirt shop opposite, Mr. Jamison waved and ran a hand over his blond hair.

I waved back. Lengthening my strides, I passed shops selling whirligigs and windsocks, blown glass and beachwear.

I ducked down an attractive, cobbled alley to a small, arched pink door and went inside.

Mrs. Henderson looked up from behind the cash register. She was an older woman, with wavy gray hair, a stout figure, and cat-eye glasses.

She adjusted them now and peered at me. "Ah, Abigail. Is there something wrong with the saloon harlot costume?"

Yes. The problem is it's a saloon harlot costume. "Um. I didn't try it on. Hyperion canceled the costumes for me." I glanced around the room. The costumes hanging on the walls were worthy of theaters and opera houses. No plastic witch masks. Wherever that little witch had gotten her costume, it hadn't been here.

"Yes, but your friend reinstated the contract and paid for it in full through the end of the month."

"No," I said politely, fighting back my annoyance. "He didn't.

Hyperion canceled it."

"Not Hyperion, Beatrice."

I stared. "Beatrice? Beatrice Carlson?"

"Isn't she delightful? We're sponsoring her in the coffin race."

My jaw clenched. "Delightful," I ground out. "Please can—" *Hold on.* There's a saying about not stopping your enemy when they're in the middle of doing something dumb. If Beatrice wanted to waste her money on costumes I wasn't going to wear, she could be my guest.

Yes, I *was* being petty. But I could live with that today.

"Sorry about the confusion," I said. "Have a good day."

I stalked from the store and onto the brick sidewalk. *Beatrice.* As pranks went, this one was... less painful than the time she'd sent a flash mob into the tearoom. Maybe there was something subtle going on that I didn't understand. But the costume prank didn't inconvenience me much at all.

I hurried back to the tearoom and stopped short half a block away. A crowd had massed in front of our sky-blue door, and my heart gave an unpleasant jump.

"What now?" I muttered and jogged toward the group.

There was a flare of light, and a woman screamed.

Dreading what I'd find, I pushed through the crowd. "What's going..."

Razzzor and Brik sat in the coffin car. Razzzor wore a leather helmet and goggles. Brik was... Brik, in his usual white t-shirt and jeans.

"What's Halloween without a little fire, amiright?" Razzzor pushed a button on the coffin, and flames leapt from its rear.

"What the...?" I shooed customers away from the flamethrower.

Mr. Jamison grinned. "That's some racer, Abigail. You'll make the street proud."

"Thanks." I turned to Razzzor. "What did you do?"

"The fire was my idea," Brik said modestly.

Razzzor hopped from the coffin.

"How did you get this all the way to the tearoom?" I asked.

"We drove it." Razzzor patted the hood. "This is now the Tesla of coffins."

"The— You put a battery in it?"

"We put the wheels back on too," Brik said.

"Thanks." I struggled to control my temper. "But now the car's illegal."

"Well, it probably violates some code—" Razzzor began.

"I meant for the race." I had to work not to throttle him. "I told you, it has to be gravity-powered only."

"Oh, that's no problem—"

My chest heaved. "It's a problem!"

The crowd eyed me and backed away.

"He means the battery can be removed," Brik said.

"Oh." Prickling heat washed from my throat to my face. "Oh."

Razzzor clapped a hand on my shoulder. "No worries, Abs. We got you. Push the button again, Brik."

Grinning, Brik raised himself up and leaned into the front seat. Double checking there was no one behind him, he pushed the red button. Flames roared from the back of the racer.

"Okay," I said, grudging. "That is pretty awesome." They'd even painted *Beanblossom's Tea & Tarot* on the sides, and in our brand lettering.

"I do not sponsor basic coffins." Razzzor pointed to half a dozen *Zombie Nazis in Space* stickers around the lettering.

"Wow," Gino's voice said in my ear, and I jumped.

Cool as a cucumber, I adjusted my felt pirate hat. "Oh, hi."

The lawyer whistled and raised both hands to his curling, dark hair. "That's some coffin. Is that your entry in the race?"

"Yeah," I said. "What are you doing here?"

Gino leaned closer, lowering his voice. "I came to apologize for that codependency crack. It was out of line."

I'd been out of line quite a bit lately too, and I drew breath to say so.

"I guess I…" Gino hesitated. "The problem's mine. I try to figure out what's wrong with the women I meet before whatever's wrong with them bites me in the butt. I'm sorry."

"Accepted," I said. "I've been a little on edge. I might have reacted more strongly than I should have."

"Nah. No one likes being analyzed without an invitation. But we're good?"

"We're good. Nobody's perfect. Especially me," I added. Because when it comes to dating, I'm all about lowering expectations. "But I'm watching you."

He grinned.

I glanced at the coffin. Brik glowered from the back seat, and a worm of guilt wriggled inside my chest.

A uniformed cop approached. "What's going on here?"

"It's our entry in the coffin race," Razzzor said. "Want to take it for a spin?"

"You can't race a go-cart on a city street," the cop said. "Not in this traffic."

"Oh, this isn't your typical go-cart," Razzzor said. "It's *temporarily* battery powered. We can get this up to thirty-five miles an hour."

The cop's eyes narrowed. "You drove this here?"

Brik shook his head.

I pivoted, looking for escape. But people clustered around me, blocking my exit.

"Yep," Razzzor said. "Pretty amazing, huh?"

"Who does it belong to?" the policeman asked.

Razzzor looped an arm over my shoulder. "Abigail Beanblossom of Beanblossom's Tea and Tarot." He released me, leaned into the car, and pushed the red button.

Flames burst from the back of the coffin.

The cop jumped. "Good God, is that a flame thrower?"

Razzzor shrugged modestly. Brik groaned. I closed my eyes. *Why? Why?*

The cop unlatched what looked like a credit card reader from his belt. "I'm going to have to give you a ticket, Ms. Beanblossom."

Brik covered his eyes.

"Wait," Razzzor said. "What?"

"Fine," I said. "Let's get this over with." Like I said, there's a point where you just expect disaster. There's no sense fighting it.

"Hold on," Razzzor said. "That's not fair. It's like a motor scooter or a motorized bicycle. You wouldn't give them a ticket."

"Motor scooters and motorized bicycles are built to strict code," the cop said. "They don't shoot flames out the back, and yours can reach speeds over twenty-five miles an hour. This is a threat to public safety."

The crowd muttered and backed further away. Nodding and pointing, the ladies in the tearoom window leaned closer to the glass.

"But it's a *coffin*," Razzzor said.

The cop raised a brow. "You want to keep going? I don't see any headlights."

"We haven't gotten around to fixing them," Razzzor argued.

"And no seatbelts."

"Well," Razzzor sputtered, "that's just—"

"Right," the cop said, punching buttons on the small machine. It spat out a ticket over a foot long. He handed it to me. "Payable in thirty days. Have a good morning."

I stared at the ticket. I know the police are only being polite. But telling you to have a good morning after handing you a ticket is just salt in the wound.

"Razzzor?" I said.

"Yes, Abigail?"

"What have we learned today?"

"To keep my mouth shut when getting a ticket?" he said meekly.

"Yes," I said. "That's right."

CHAPTER 25

Let's summarize.

I'd possibly caused the breakup between my business partner and the man of his dreams. The DA still hadn't dropped the charges against Tony. And I'd been fined in front of the tearoom for possessing a reckless coffin.

At least Razzzor paid the ticket. And I'd let him because it had totally been his fault.

But I felt a little guilty about that. That's the thing with guilt. It piles on.

And since work is often the best medicine, I got back to mine.

Around lunchtime, Gramps and Tomas shuffled into the tearoom. They settled themselves at the quartz bar. Gramps removed his cabbie hat and set it on the counter.

"What have you got in the way of sandwiches?" My grandfather braced his patched elbows on the counter. He'd missed a button in his cardigan, and its hem hung at an endearing, off-kilter angle.

"Chicken salad, salmon dill with avocado, and roast turkey and bacon with pesto." I didn't bother telling them the vegetarian options. They'd never order anything meat-free. I also didn't bother explaining that the chicken had been smoked with earl-gray tea. They wouldn't care.

"Turkey for me," Gramps said.

"I'll try the salmon." Tomas laid down his Giants cap, exposing his wispy, graying hair. "Extra avocado."

Gramps made a face. He hated avocado.

"Coming right up." Returning to the kitchen, I put together their sandwiches and favorite teas. I carried their orders to the counter.

Gramps motioned to the full tables. "Looks like business is booming."

"The Halloween season has been good for us." Though I was starting to wonder if Hyperion's curse was contagious.

"So why do you look so low?" Gramps bit into the sandwich.

I grimaced and leaned closer over the quartz counter. "It's Tony," I said quietly. "The two of us were talking over the case. I let slip that Hyperion had briefly—very briefly, like once—gone out with Cassius Santori."

"And Hyperion hadn't mentioned that to him?" Tomas set down his salmon sandwich. "Because he told us."

"No." I studied the white counter. When Hyperion and then Tony had come bursting into my life, all they'd been to me were problems. Now I couldn't imagine San Borromeo without them. And it killed me to think that I was the cause of their pain.

"It's caused some issues between them," I said quietly. "I'm not sure how bad."

Tomas sipped his tea. "So, theoretically, that's the connection between Tony and the murder victim. If Tony was the insanely jealous type, he had a motive to kill Cassius."

Gramps opened his sandwich and squinted at it, searching for stray avocado. "He never struck me as the insanely jealous type."

No, the detective seemed more like the insanely-laid-back-until-he-had-to-shoot-you type.

"Has the DA gotten ahold of this news?" Tomas bit into his sandwich.

"I don't know." I poured myself a glass of cucumber water from a carafe and chugged it down.

"Hyperion's not stupid," Gramps said. "He knows he should have told Tony after he was charged. If your partner's angry at anyone, it's likely himself."

"But I still screwed up. I feel like… like I betrayed Hyperion." Because I *had* betrayed him. Sudden anger burned through me. I was sitting in that airport again, waiting for my parents who'd never come, staring at my little shoes.

But this time, *I* was the betrayer. I had abandoned myself, the person I wanted to be, someone you could depend on. I'd become my unreliable parents.

I shook myself. *Never mind.* What I'd done had been an accident. And unlike my parents, I'd apologized and meant it.

Gramps patted my hand. "This will pass. They're two grown men. They can work it out."

The bell over the front door tinkled, and Carla Santori walked into the tearoom. She wore a puffy down jacket over a black, knee-high knit skirt and boots.

"Will you excuse me?" I said to the two men, and they nodded.

I hurried from behind the counter to the hostess stand. "Hi, can I help you?"

"Yes, I have a reservation."

I skimmed our reservation book. She did indeed have a spot reserved for one, and I hadn't noticed. But I hadn't taken the reservation either. I grabbed a menu. "Right this way."

I showed her to a table, and she sat, looping her purse over the back of the chair.

"I love the Halloween décor." She shrugged out of her black jacket and put that over the back of her chair too. "Your tearoom is lovely."

"Thank you." I handed her a menu. But I didn't believe for a minute she'd made that reservation on a whim. "We have a full tea menu. I'll give you some time to look it over and be back."

I headed toward the counter, stopping a waitress on the way. "I'll take table three," I said. "She's a friend of mine. Any tip is yours though."

Sally smiled. "Thanks."

Thoughtful, I returned to the counter.

"Everything okay?" Gramps asked.

"That's Cassius Santori's wife, Carla." I nodded casually toward her.

Tomas took a careful glance over his shoulder. "Good looking woman."

"She's never been in here before," I said.

"You think she wants to talk?" Tomas asked.

"I'm not sure what she wants."

I puttered behind the counter until Carla set down her menu. "Here we go." I beelined for her table. "What can I get for you?"

"I'll try the Royal Halloween Tea with Earl Gray."

Carla had ordered the most expensive thing on the menu. So she couldn't be all bad. "Sure thing."

Speeding to the counter, I brewed her a pot of tea. I deposited it at Carla's table then strode to the kitchen. I built her order, arranging quartered sandwiches, scones, and other goodies on the tiered plates.

I adjusted a tiny jam jar, clipped paper bats to the tray's metal holders, and delivered it to her table.

She set down her teacup. "That looks marvelous."

"Let me know how it tastes." I faked a smile.

"I've been thinking of starting my own business."

"A tearoom?" *Please, not a tearoom.* San Borromeo couldn't handle two.

"No. Interior design. You've done a good job with the flow here."

"I had some help." I hated to say it, but Hyperion had more flare for design than I had. And Brik had had some good ideas too.

"Please." She motioned to the empty seat opposite. "Sit down, if you have time."

Feeling like a guest in my own tearoom, I sat and rested my hands on the table. "I didn't realize you had a background in interior design."

"A degree from a community college." She waved it away with her hand. "But I was working for an interior designer when I met Cassius. I thought I'd keep it up, but when we had kids... They just seemed more important. They *were* more important."

I nodded.

"When our youngest went off to college," she continued, "I thought I'd get back to it. But I seemed to have lost the urgency. Sometimes," she continued grimly, "you need a push."

I nodded, remembering when I'd tried to start the tearoom on my own and everything had fallen apart. If I hadn't been forced to work with Hyperion, Beanblossom's wouldn't have happened. "Necessity is the mother of a lot of small businesses, including this one."

"I think what you've done here is inspirational." She gazed into her tea. "What made you take the leap?"

"I've wanted to open a tearoom since I was a kid," I admitted. "It was always a dream of mine. I even worked in one as a teenager—you can call that product research." And then I'd done well with some stock options, thanks to Razzzor. "The timing seemed right."

"And the Tarot readers?" She glanced at a reader in an orange and black caftan walking past with a deck of cards.

"That was a fluke. Hyperion and I both rented the building from a con artist. He ran off with our upfront rent payments. The only way we could make it work after that was to go in on the tearoom together."

She put her hand over her mouth and choked back a laugh. "Seriously? Oh, I'm sorry. I shouldn't laugh, but... What a story."

"I know, but it worked out perfectly. Tearooms close fairly early, so Hyperion can use the space in the evenings for Tarot classes. But tell me about your plans."

Her toffee-colored eyes lit. "I found a tiny little building at the edge of town. It's a bit neglected, but the rent is cheap and the landlord won't mind if I redecorate." She laughed. "I think he's counting on it."

Carla plucked a paper bat from the tiered tray. She turned the decoration in her fingers. "I'm selling the house. It's too big for me. And there are too many..." Her voice hitched.

Memories, I silently finished for her. "You *will* get through this," I said in a low voice.

She bit her bottom lip. "I know. I just don't... know if I can trust myself again."

"What do you mean?"

"Cassius fooled me for two decades." Her face darkened, her jaw hardening. "And I let myself be fooled."

Ah. So she *had* found out about his cheating. But before or after her husband had been killed?

"That's what hits the hardest," Carla said, "you know? Not that he betrayed me, but that I let him. I think... a part of me always knew? So really, I was betraying myself. I don't want to do that ever again." She shook her head. "Sorry. You don't want to hear all that."

"Trust is tough after you've been burned."

"It's all so... strange. One day, everything's normal. And the next, your world's upside down. First Cassius and then Johnson, and they say their deaths aren't connected. But how is that possible?"

She was fishing. *But why?* "It does seem like a strange coincidence," I said neutrally. "Two men murdered within a week of each other and who worked closely together. Is there anyone who had a grudge against them both?"

"I don't know." Her gaze lost its focus. "Sometimes I wonder if it's all worth it," she muttered and shook herself. "Was this worth it?" She motioned around the room.

I glanced up at the bats rotating slowly above us and smiled. I couldn't imagine a better job.

"Definitely," I said. "I'm doing what I want and working with people I like. Yes, it can be stressful. And there've been unexpected expenses. But you plan and you save and you try not to freak out too much when the plans go sideways."

Her hands twined around her teacup. "And it's yours."

"And it's mine."

"And it won't turn on you," she said, "because it can't."

"There is that," I agreed. "Carla, I get the feeling there's something else you want to ask me about."

"No," she said. "I've taken up enough of your time. Thanks for letting me get clear on some things."

I nodded, scooting back my chair, and stood. Why had she really come? I hesitated, then walked away.

CHAPTER 26

I walked toward the tearoom kitchen. The hall light flickered out. Slowing, I lightly dragged my fingers along the wall until I touched the supply closet door. I fumbled for the knob.

A shadowy figure rose from the gloom, and I froze. It was late afternoon, and the tearoom was bustling. I wasn't alone or vulnerable. But there was something about the stillness of the figure that raised the hair on my arms.

Then the figure turned, stepping from the shadows. It was the Tarot reader, Sierra.

My muscles relaxed. "Oh, it's you."

She pressed a finger to her lips and nodded to the kitchen.

Bemused, I followed her inside and leaned one hip against the long, metal work table. "What's going on?"

Sierra adjusted her pumpkin t-shirt. "Hyperion's not answering my knock." She glanced over her shoulder at the open doorway.

"Hyperion's in his office?" I exhaled unsteadily. "Are you sure?"

"He came in five hours ago, when you were out running your errand."

"Five...?" Worried, I stared into the hall. "But his twinkle lights aren't on."

"I know," she said. "I'm worried. I mean, I know October is cursed for him and everything—"

"It probably isn't."

"—but this is worse than last year."

"What happened last year?"

"Poison oak," she said. "A fender bender. And his biggest client switched to his arch nemesis."

"Isn't his arch nemesis dead?"

"His other arch nemesis. But even after he got poison oak, he never went into hiding. He just wore long sleeves. It's why he doesn't read cards in October."

"I'm not tracking," I said. "I thought it was because his readings were off in October."

"No, because they're too *on*. All he gets are terrible predictions, and they all come true. He'd rather not know what's coming."

I rubbed my temple. "Okay. This is getting out of control. I'm going to talk to him." I strode across the hallway and knocked on his office door. When no one answered, I walked in anyway.

Hyperion lolled in his throne-like red-velvet chair, a yoga pillow over his eyes. Bastet, on the altar beside the wall, lashed his striped tail.

"You'd better not be dead," I said.

Hyperion lifted the blue silk pillow from his face and glared. "Is a little privacy too much to ask?"

"Yes, when you're in hiding."

"If I'm going to be struck by lightning, this is the safest place for it. Kids live in my complex."

"Don't tell me you drew the Tower card." It depicted people falling from a lightning-struck tower.

"I'm not drawing any cards. Not until Halloween is in the rearview mirror."

I jerked down a cuff, and there was another faint tearing sound. *Oh, come on.* "Maybe you *should* draw some cards." I pulled out the chair opposite and dropped into it.

"Trust me, ignorance is bliss."

"Hm." I picked up the deck in the center of the table and shuffled.

"You shouldn't do that." He leaned back and dropped the silk pillow over his eyes. "I'm not responsible for what will happen."

"I like to live dangerously."

"That explains your fetish for carbs."

"Skinny people are easier to kidnap. I'm just taking precautions." I drew a card and laid it on the table. It was the six of swords, a man pushing a boat from rough water into smooth. "Hm..."

"Don't tell me."

"Okay, I won't." I drew another card. Three men consulted a scroll beneath three pentacles. This usually represented people working together. "Interesting."

"You're not interesting me at all." He adjusted his eye pillow.

I rubbed my chin. "*Very* interesting."

"I know what you're doing. It's not going to work."

"Hey, these are my cards, my reading. It's got nothing to do with you."

He lifted one corner of the pillow. "What question did you ask?"

I drew another card and laid it beside the two.

"It's unethical to do readings about other people without their permission," he warned. "You can't ask about me."

"Rules are for suckers."

He straightened in his chair and dropped the pillow onto the table. Hyperion frowned at the cards. "What did you ask?"

"I asked about *our* investigation." I tapped the last card. A crowned woman in red sat on a throne, sword in one hand and scales of justice in the other. "This was the third card I drew. So what do you see?"

I thought the cards said things would get better, soon, but we needed to work together for justice to be done. Not that I necessarily believed in Tarot. But Hyperion did.

He shrugged. "It's a meaningless jumble."

I looked at the cards again.

"You can't help it." he continued in a patronizing tone. "It's the curse. Also, you're untrained."

I imagined playing fifty-two-pickup with the seventy-eight card Tarot deck and shooting it into his smug face. Instead, I decided to be a marginally bigger person, and I reshuffled the cards. "Now I'm going to ask if I've completely screwed up your relationship with Tony."

"Don't." He lunged across the table and grabbed my wrist. "Please."

For a long moment, we gazed into each other's eyes. I could feel the pulse in my wrist beneath his fingers. I looked away.

He released me, and I sat back in my chair. "Okay," I said. Maybe some things were better left a mystery. "I'll stop pushing."

He drummed his fingers on the table and looked away, jaw tight.

Bastet yawned.

"Maybe you shouldn't," he finally said. "Sitting around and feeling sorry for myself isn't helping anyone."

I widened my eyes. "Is that what you were doing?"

"Don't press your luck, partner." He stood and paced the room. "Okay. Okay. What have we missed?"

I checked my watch. The day was almost over anyway. "Whatever's going on, it's centered in your old office building. Why don't we head over there before everyone closes shop, and see what we can shake loose?"

"We'll take my Jeep."

I told the staff where I was going and when I'd be back, and to leave cleaning the kitchen to me in case my timing was off. Then I met Hyperion in the parking lot.

The ocean fog had moved in, darkening the sky. A thin layer of droplets coated the windshield of his Jeep.

He handed me the tabby. "Bastet's still feeling rocky. We can't leave him alone."

"Oh, good."

Hyperion squinted at me.

"Good for us, not for Bastet," I explained, and we drove off.

Near the squat building, Hyperion slowed the Jeep. "What exactly is our goal here?" he asked. "Because we've been going back and forth to that building a lot and getting nowhere."

"I vote for harassing suspects until they call the cops on us."

"Hands down, that's your best idea yet."

Lafayette's white van darted from the parking lot. The van sped off in the other direction.

"Or we could follow that van," I said.

We sped onto the freeway and promptly slowed, the commute traffic doing its thing. Bastet braked by digging his claws into my jeans. We moved and stopped, moved and stopped. The cat sheathed and unsheathed his claws. I watched him warily.

Finally, we edged off the freeway into downtown Santa Cruz. It was just as congested, because, California.

I fiddled with my seatbelt and tried not to check my watch.

We crawled through Santa Cruz, and I bounced my heel on the car's floor. I expected the van to turn. But it continued through town, over the train tracks, and city streets turned to Pacific highway.

"Where is he going?" Hyperion muttered. "There isn't a whole lot out here, aside from pumpkin farms."

We rolled past one, orange gourds dotting grass the color of an Irish hillside.

"Ooh!" I pointed. I *love* pumpkin patches.

"No."

I rolled my eyes. "Well, no, of course not now. We're tailing someone. But later—"

"No. They're cursed."

"But I haven't gotten any pumpkins for my house yet."

"What don't you understand about *cursed?*"

I didn't understand how someone as sharp as Hyperion could buy into a curse. But I kept my mouth shut and pulled my phone from my purse.

"Who are you calling?" he asked.

"I'm calling Verena."

"Why?"

"Multitasking."

"Hello?" she said.

"Hi, Verena, it's Abigail. I just wanted to check in," I lied.

A sign for pumpkins and jam flashed past on the right, and I pointed again.

Hyperion's lips tightened. He shook his head.

"It's my last day," Verena said. "You caught me just before I turned out the lights."

Poor Verena. Leaving one job, didn't have another one lined up, and the man of her dreams was dead. "That's got to have a lot of emotions attached."

She sighed. "You're not kidding."

"How are you doing?"

"Right now," she said, "I just want to get out of here."

"Sorry, I don't mean to keep you."

We bumped over a pothole, and I lurched sideways, banging my shoulder into the door. I frowned at Hyperion, and he shrugged.

"You're not," she said. "How are things going?"

"My coffin car got a ticket, but aside from that, good."

She laughed. "You're joking."

"I'm not. Hey, I've got a question for you. This beach condo Dr. Tarrach bought, do you know where it is?"

"Somewhere on Sunset."

That was the other end of the road where I'd lost Dr. Tarrach the other day. Had he been going to visit his girlfriend?

"Why?" she asked.

"I saw Dr. Tarrach down there the other day. That's probably where he was going. This woman he bought it for, do you know her name?"

"I could hardly forget it."

"Why not?"

"Her name..." She paused. "...is Tara Dactyl."

"You're—you *are* kidding, right?"

We drove past a pumpkin patch with a pony ride. Hyperion shook his head.

"Nope," she said. "That's Tara with one *r.*"

"Wow." That was... Wow. And I'd thought my parents had been cruel. Though mine would never give me a name that might divert attention from them.

"If she's hoping to become Tara Tarrach though, I think she's out of luck," Verena said.

"Why?"

"Just... history. Not the dentist's, just history in general."

"Yeah." The other woman rarely got the ring, and history tended to repeat itself. "Hey, the coffin race is this Saturday night. If you're free, why don't you come by. We're having either a victory party or a drown-your-sorrows party at Beanblossom's afterward."

"Yes, a thousand times yes. I need something to get my mind off... everything."

"Good. I'll be in the Beanblossom's coffin. See you Saturday."

"Bye."

We hung up.

"So?" Hyperion asked.

"Did you see that pony ride? You love ponies."

"No ponies. What did she say?"

"Dr. Tarrach's girlfriend is Ms. Tara Dactyl."

"She's a dinosaur?" he asked.

"She's got parents with a warped sense of humor."

"So she's probably insecure. We can work with that."

Lafayette's van pulled onto a rutted road advertising a corn maze. I shot a wary glance at my partner.

Hyperion's knuckles whitened on the wheel. "It's okay. He's an adult and he's alone. It's not like he's going to go *into* the corn maze."

"Would that be so bad?" I'd never been inside a corn maze, but it sounded fun.

"Are you kidding me? Haven't you seen that Stephen King movie?"

He slowed the Jeep, putting more space between us and the van. The van vanished over a low rise.

Hyperion decelerated some more. "You know what this means, don't you?"

"Yes, corn mazes may be creepy, but they're not criminal. Lafayette's probably here to put up another tent."

"And that means we came here for nothing," he said glumly.

"But we're here. We may as well see what's up."

Hyperion pulled into a dirt parking lot and swung into a spot half-hidden by a pickup and a cypress. We sunk down in our seats and watched the van, parked beside a scarecrow.

After a moment, Lafayette emerged and shrugged into a red windbreaker. He walked to a wooden arch with a ghost painted on it, paid the ticket taker, and walked inside.

"Maybe he's not putting up a tent," I said.

Hyperion gulped. "Maybe he just likes corn mazes."

"Or maybe there *is* something going on." I detached the cat from my jeans and stepped from the Jeep. "Come on." I set Bastet on my empty seat.

Hyperion shot me a pleading look. "Abigail, it's a corn maze."

"Can we focus here? Our suspect is *inside* the corn maze."

"The haunted house was bad, but it wasn't finished. This... This..."

"Is a corn maze."

"Exactly! Do you understand how much bad juju is attached to corn mazes?"

"Don't worry about it. You stay here. I'll let you know what I find." I strode toward the ticket taker.

It was the adult equivalent of a triple-dog-dare. There was no way Hyperion would let me go alone. But if he did, I'd manage.

A car door slammed behind me, and I smiled.

"Wait," Hyperion called.

He strode past me, a leashed Bastet trotting beside him. "*You're* paying for the entrance tickets."

I bought two tickets and joined him at the arched, wooden entrance to the corn maze. A foggy breeze tossed my hair and dampened my skin. The amber corn stalks rustled, rippling like a wave toward low, green mountains.

Hyperion shuddered.

And we walked into the corn maze.

CHAPTER 27

"We're lost." Hyperion folded his arms and stuck out his jaw mutinously.

Bastet meowed. A ceiling of fog pressed against the tops of the corn.

I pressed a finger to my lips and cocked my head, listening. Footsteps moved away from us. "This way," I whispered and darted down one of the maze's narrow aisles.

The footsteps could have been made by a phantom. They crunched, sure and swift, across the dried cornstalk floor. But whoever was walking ahead of us remained out of view. It was more than a little unnerving, because I *had* seen that Stephen King movie.

"So how did the curse start?" I asked in a low voice. "You never finished the story."

"Right. When we left our hero, he was trick-or-treating through a spooky, rich-person neighborhood."

"Right. Spooky rich neighborhood."

"There was a house that obviously had a party going on. Cars filled the curving driveway and music streamed from the house. We went to the door, and a woman dressed like a gypsy answered. She had wild, piercing eyes and smelled awful."

I peered around a corner and walked forward. "And she cursed you?"

"I didn't think it was real. It was Halloween after all, but the curse was oddly specific. And then every October since…" He shuddered.

"Wait. Seriously? That's how you got cursed? By some rich partier?"

"I don't think she was a guest."

We rounded a corner in the maze. Lafayette moved down the aisle, his red windbreaker fluttering. I stepped backward, out of sight, and onto Hyperion's foot.

"Ouch," he hissed.

Bastet growled a warning.

"He's right there," I mouthed.

Hyperion nodded and rotated his ankle.

We crept forward.

The red windbreaker vanished around a bend in the cornstalks.

Lengthening our strides—okay, *I* lengthened *my* strides—we hurried forward. Hyperion and I peered around the next corner.

Lafayette was gone.

Hyperion raised his hands in a baffled gesture. Another gust of Pacific breeze shivered the corn stalks, churned the fog above our heads.

"I'm not saying this is the perfect hunting ground for an ax murderer," Hyperion whispered. "But this is the perfect hunting ground for an ax murderer."

I edged forward and pointed at a break in the corn that had been invisible from where we'd been a step earlier.

He nodded, and we moved toward the opening.

Through the corn stalks drifted a murmur of masculine voices. We tiptoed closer, dried stalks crackling beneath our shoes.

Hyperion ducked his head around the edge of the wall of corn and popped back, his expression hard. "We need to go," he said in a low voice.

"What?" I whispered. "Why?"

He picked up the tabby. "It's a drug deal."

I mentally smacked my forehead. Why hadn't I seen it before? The vampiric eyes, the jittery movements... "Oh, sh—"

A lanky man with blond dreadlocks sauntered out of the cornstalks. "Hey, man." He saluted Bastet with two fingers. "Chill cat." The man nodded and strode away.

"Too late," I said. "Looks like the deal's been done." Angry now, I strode around the corner. I know it's a disease, an addiction, and I should be sympathetic. And I *was* sympathetic toward people trying to quit.

My college roommate had become addicted to some sort of uppers. She'd gone from degree candidate to dropout to dead. My stomach tightened, nausea turning in my throat. If she'd quit... But she hadn't, and I hadn't been able to convince her to. I guess I still felt angry about that. Angry. Depressed. Guilty.

I hadn't found out about the dead part until two years after I'd graduated. We'd lost touch. I'd given up on her after she'd stolen my wallet one too many times, and I shouldn't have. And I guess she'd eventually given up on herself.

Lafayette hastily pocketed a small plastic bag filled with white powder.

"You're a drug addict," I said flatly.

"No. I can quit anytime—" Lafayette's jaw jutted forward. "What are you two doing here? What do you want?" His hands trembled. Beads of sweat dotted his forehead, and his face was a sickly color.

"You don't look so good," I said, my disgust morphing into worry.

Hyperion looped an arm around my shoulder. "Abigail, let's leave the man alone."

"No," I said. If Hyperion had confronted him alone, he'd be pushing for the answers we needed. He wasn't going to lose his shot now out of some desire to protect me. "Is this why you and Cassius argued? Did he know about the drugs?"

Lafayette shifted his weight. His eyes darted about the narrow enclosure, but we blocked the only exit. "It was none of his business." His nostrils flared. "I just wanted him to manage my money, not tell me how to spend it."

"So he did know," I said, "didn't he?"

"Yes, okay, okay. He wouldn't stop hassling me about getting help. Are you happy?"

"You *should* get help, you know," Hyperion said. "Buying in a corn maze? There are kids around here. What if one of them saw?"

"Marijuana's legal. I don't see what the big deal is."

I shook my head. That wasn't marijuana. "You're sneaking around a corn maze. Your financial advisor figured out you had a problem. You don't think that's worth some self-reflection?"

Muscles corded in Lafayette's neck. "Why do you care?"

"Because two men are dead," I said.

"Not because of me." He thumped his chest. "I liked Cassius and Johnson. They were good at their job. They kept me in business."

"Wait," I said, "so they were managing your business too?"

"Only the bills. That's why I stuck with them, even if Cassius was hassling me."

"And they did a good job?" I asked. "Nothing weird happened with the accounts?"

"No," Lafayette said, "not that it's any of your business."

"But you said you thought something funny was going on," I insisted.

He rubbed a hand over his head. "Did I?"

"Yes," I said. "That's why you followed Johnson to the pier."

"*I* didn't say it. That other guy did, out in the hallway. I just overheard and started getting nervous. Why *are* you here?"

"Because someone killed both Cassius and Johnson," I said. "The killer has to be connected to that office somehow."

"And we'll figure it out later." Hyperion steered me toward the exit. "Enjoy your evening."

"Hold on," I said, digging my heels into the stalk-covered ground. "This is—"

"It was Carla," Lafayette blurted.

"What?" I said.

Hyperion let go of my elbow. "Are you sure?"

Lafayette's hands clenched and unclenched. "She knew he was cheating on her."

"How do you know?" Hyperion asked.

"I arrived early for my appointment one day. That receptionist was out of the office. So was Johnson. Cassius and his wife were arguing. I could hear them through the office door."

"What exactly did you hear?" I asked.

He shrugged. "She said she knew all about the others. She was angry. What else could that mean?"

"Thanks," Hyperion said and half-dragged me away.

I wrinkled my forehead, my insides twisting unpleasantly. "He looked terrible. Maybe we should stay with him."

"He'll get help when he's ready," he said. "You're not going to talk him into a cleaner life."

"But—"

"No. And this time I mean it."

I nodded. The path to a good life seemed so obvious to me—quit the drugs, do your work, focus on what counts. But when you're an addict, obvious isn't easy. We trudged on.

It took over an hour for us to find our way out of the maze. Finally, Hyperion promised the cat a can of tuna, and Bastet led us out. But when we reached the tearoom, full dark had fallen, and the staff had departed.

Glum, I studied the kitchen I'd promised to clean. I turned on my heels and marched into Hyperion's office.

He sat, his hands dangling, limp, over the arms of the high-backed chair. Bastet was back on the altar, striped tail curled around his paws. An empty can of tuna sat in front of him.

"So." I pulled out a chair and sat across from him. "Carla."

"Couldn't have hefted Tony into and out of his Jeep." Hyperion shot me a bored look.

And Carla had basically told me she'd known about the affairs, but I hadn't told Hyperion that yet. "But Lafayette is unstable. Who knows where his head's at? We can't count him out as a suspect."

He studied the ceiling. "Agreed. But it isn't exactly a smoking gun, is it?"

Bastet sneezed.

"No," I said, "but maybe we should be giving more consideration to the personalities involved." I sat at the table and picked up the Tarot deck.

"No more readings, please."

"Not a reading, I was thinking more of an evaluation." I pulled out the Tarot court cards: kings, queens, knights, and pages. "If Lafayette was a Tarot card, what do you think? He's impulsive. Out of control."

"Knight of Wands reversed," he said promptly. "But could someone impulsive and out of control have planned this set up? Because this frame is air tight."

"I don't know." I slid the Knight of Wands from the grouping and tapped its edge on the table. "The first time we met Lafayette, he seemed in control. Maybe he has more lucid periods. He has to have more lucid periods to run his business, but I don't know enough about how addiction works."

"Me neither. And I'd rather not have to find out."

"Speaking of drugs," I said, "has Tony gotten the test results back yet?"

"Not yet."

"But I thought—?" I shook my head. I pulled out the Queen of Cups and laid the card upside down on the crimson tablecloth. "Verena?"

He nodded.

"Everyone said she was in love with Johnson," I said. "But was it an obsession?"

"It had better not be since you invited her to the coffin race."

"Where we'll be able to keep an eye on her." I grimaced. "But she doesn't seem obsessed, just lovesick. So who's Carla? Queen of Swords?"

I drew the card, a queen holding an upright sword in one hand. I laid it on the table.

Hyperion lifted one shoulder, dropped it. "I see Carla more as the Empress."

"I thought the Queen of Swords reversed is a woman scorned."

"Have you been studying?" He arched a brow.

"You pick up a thing or two when you're surrounded by Tarot readers all day."

"Well, you're not entirely wrong about the Queen. But Carla's still got an Empress vibe to me."

Bastet dropped from the altar and padded to us.

I laid the Empress on the table. "Fine. She's the Empress. Reversed. What about Dr. Tarrach?"

The cat hopped onto the table beside me and released a tuna-fish belch.

Hyperion rubbed the back of his head. "I don't know. He's hard to get a read on."

"He may be a pillar of the community, but he's also got a girl on the side." I pushed the cat away.

"I suppose Cassius could have been blackmailing the dentist about the girlfriend. Blackmail's as good a motive for murder as any. But did Johnson know?"

"Maybe," I said. "But that would imply Johnson was a blackmailer too, looking to pick up where Cassius left off, right? I mean, sure, it's a motive. Tarrach is married, and California divorces aren't cheap. But what does that have to do with Tony?"

"Nothing." Hyperion stared, unseeing, at the cards.

Gathering the court cards together, I riffled them. I laid them face down in a four-by-four square. "Then pick a card that represents Tarrach."

Hyperion crossed his arms. "October, remember? I don't do readings."

"Pick a damn card," I snarled.

"Fine." He fanned the court cards on the table and drew one from the center, flipped it over. The King of Swords, reversed.

"So what does that mean?" I asked.

"You tell me," he said, waspish. "You seem to know more than you want to admit about Tarot."

"I'm not the expert."

The cat nudged a card with his paw.

Hyperion huffed a breath. "The King of Swords is someone smart, logical. But he can let his brain run wild with anxiety. He can turn nasty."

"That seems to fit Tarrach. But we've no evidence of him getting ugly."

He clawed both hands through his thick hair. "It could be any of these people or none of them. None of them have anything to do with Tony. He's got to come in somewhere, but how?"

"I don't know," I admitted. It was maddening. There *had* to be a connection. It couldn't be random. Could it?

"What's left?" he asked. "Razzzor even built an algorithm and we couldn't find the connection."

I leaned back in my chair and stared at the ceiling. "You know that saying about doing the same thing over and over and expecting a different result? How that's the definition of insanity?"

"Yeah."

"Then let's do something different." I straightened, meeting his gaze. "We've harassed our suspects to the point where I, who once *was* stalked, am starting to feel like a stalker. It's not good."

"You want to quit?"

"No. I want to go suspect adjacent."

The cat wailed, baleful.

CHAPTER 28

Hyperion and I sat at a sidewalk café, glasses of tap water in front of us. My partner was dressed like Sam Spade, fedora on his head and fake cigarette dangling from his lips. My sleazy moll costume was hanging on the back of the kitchen's door.

It was an unseasonably warm Wednesday, but sometimes that happened in Californian Octobers. The Pacific rumbled and crashed on the nearby beach. People jogged and biked and skated along the winding pavement.

Gino slowed as he approached our table. He looked like an Italian mobster in his gray suit. A *sexy* Italian mobster.

"Hey, Abigail." Gino removed his sunglasses, his gaze flicking to Hyperion. "I didn't know we'd have company. Again."

"You know my partner, Hyperion."

The two men shook hands.

Gino looked from me to Hyperion and back again. "Why do I feel like I'm being sandbagged?"

"Don't worry." Hyperion's eyes narrowed. "*Abigail* doesn't think you're a killer."

Gino closed his eyes for a long moment, sighed, and shook his head. He scraped back a chair and sat beside an enormous ceramic pot of multicolored impatiens. "Let me guess. You're getting nowhere in your investigation, so you thought you'd ask me more questions."

My partner cocked a brow. "Maybe *you* should read Tarot cards."

Gino set his dark glasses on the table. "Why—?"

A waitress appeared at his elbow. "Hi, have you had time to look over the menu?"

We ordered iced teas, and the waitress zoomed off.

"So what's going on?" the lawyer asked.

I pretended to study the menu. "We've decided to take a new tack."

"This doesn't feel new to me," Gino said.

"Are you ready for this?" Hyperion asked. "We're expanding our interviews outward, to not-so-obvious people who may have known the victims."

"Saying that like it's exciting doesn't make it exciting for me," Gino said.

"Really?" Hyperion canted his head. "That usually works."

"And you want to know… what?" Gino asked. "Are you looking for names? Contacts?"

"If you've got any," I said. "Do you know anyone else who was close to Johnson, Cassius, or Verena?"

Gino shook his head. "Our connection was strictly professional. And I'm not going to give out names of other professionals we worked with."

"Why not?" Hyperion asked.

He angled his head. "Because *I* want to keep working with them."

"I suppose that's fair," my partner said, grudging.

"Okay," I said, "what about—?"

The waitress appeared with a tray of drinks. She set our teas on the table. "Is there anything else I can get for you right now?"

"Sorry," I said. "We haven't even looked at the menu yet."

"I'll have the Reuben sandwich." Gino glanced at me. "I come here a lot."

"So do I," Hyperion said. "The fish tacos."

"I'll have the quiche," I said.

The waitress bustled away.

"What do you think of Verena?" Hyperion asked.

"She's pleasant," Gino said. "Well organized. I never had any problems with her."

"But?" Hyperion asked.

A kid whirred down the nearby sidewalk on a skateboard.

"Why do you think there's a but?" Gino asked.

"There's always a but," Hyperion said. "Nobody's perfect. Especially Abigail."

I shot him a look. He hadn't been there when I'd said that. Had someone told him?

"She was very *involved* in Johnson's work," Gino said.

"You mean she had a crush on him," Hyperion said.

Gino grimaced. "Maybe more than a crush."

"You think she was obsessed too?" I sipped my tea.

"Too?" Gino asked. "Other people have said that?"

"You're not the first," I said. "But why do you think so?"

He sighed and ruffled his curling hair. "I think she might have been… stalking Johnson."

Hyperion laced his fingers together, elbows on the white tablecloth. He propped his chin on his hands. "I'm loving it. Tell us more."

"I saw Johnson at lunch with that dentist—tall guy, dark hair, roman nose..."

"Dr. Tarrach?" I said.

He shrugged. "Maybe. Anyway, Verena was in the next booth, wearing big sunglasses and a scarf over her head. She looked like Audrey Hepburn playing PI. She was writing in a notepad."

"That sounds more like spying than stalking," I said.

"Is there a difference?" Gino asked.

"Absolutely," Hyperion said. "One is creepy, the other merely disturbing."

"There could have been an innocent explanation for her being there," I said.

The two men looked at me, their expressions twin studies in skepticism.

"What?" I said. "There could be. Maybe she just happened to show up at the same restaurant for lunch? Maybe she didn't want to interrupt their discussion."

"No," Gino said. "She was totally stalking him."

A seagull landed on the nearby railing.

I flapped my hand at it. "Go away."

It squawked and strutted along the rail.

No one listens to me.

*****

After lunch, I hurried back to the tearoom, because my absences were getting embarrassing.

Hyperion holed himself up in his office, and projected gloom through the twinkle-lit door. The waitresses stumbled about, dropping cups and spilling tea. One customer burst into tears during her Tarot reading and fled from the tearoom. And I burnt an entire batch of test scones in the new oven.

Sierra tore into the kitchen. "Is Hyperion here?"

"Yeah, he's in his office." I waved my oven mitt over the smoking scones.

She braced her fists on the hips of her jeans. "You've got to get him out of here. The curse is expanding. It's affecting the entire tearoom."

"There's no curse."

There was a wail from the tearoom, and we hurried from the kitchen. A customer wept over her cucumber sandwich. Her friend patted her shoulder helplessly. Women looked on in consternation.

"No curse, huh?" Sierra hissed. "That's two weepers in one day. Get him out of here."

I unknotted my apron. I do actually know a thing or two about curses. Most seem to be a result of the reverse placebo effect. Once people think they're cursed, they subconsciously act in ways that support the curse. Or they just see every little thing that goes wrong as evidence of a curse. By this point, even the customers knew about Hyperion's October curse. Maybe it really *was* expanding.

"I'll see what I can do." I hurried to the kitchen and made a phone call. Then I crossed the hall to his office, knocked twice, and walked inside.

Hyperion sagged in his chair and stared dully at his laptop.

"We've got to get you— We've got someone else to interview," I said.

"What? Who?"

I grabbed his hand, and he let me pull him from the chair. "I'll explain on the way," I said. "You can drive."

"I always drive."

We took his Jeep to the dental office, and Hyperion parked across the street.

Hyperion frowned. "Um, Abigail, doesn't Tarrach drive a BMW?"

"Yes. Why?" I slouched low in my seat and studied the front of the low building. My partner adjusted his fedora.

"Because there's no BMW in the lot."

"Maybe Tarrach's car is in back."

"But Tarrach has his own spot." Hyperion pointed at the blue signs in front of two spots. "It's empty."

"We're not here for the dentist," I said. "We're here for Esther, his receptionist. She's suspect adjacent. We've got an appointment at five-fifteen, after the office closes."

"So why are we here now?"

"Surveillance," I lied.

At five, Esther stepped from the office and locked the door behind her. She got into a Honda CRV and drove from the parking lot.

"Where's she going?" Hyperion pulled his Jeep from our spot on the street. "I thought you made an appointment. Because if this is going to turn into a car chase, I'm totally down for that."

"We do have an appointment, at the wine bar behind Beanblossom's."

He turned to glare. "Are you kidding me? We drove all the way over here so we can go back where we started?"

"Look, I had to get you out of the tearoom. The cur—the whole staff knows you're upset about Tony, and they like you and want to help, but they don't know how since you're locked in your office. And that makes them feel bad."

He raised an eyebrow. "So you tricked me and dragged me out of the tearoom *because you care*?"

No, that didn't sound believable to me either. "Um…"

He gripped my shoulder. "You're a good friend, Beanblossom."

I clamped my mouth shut and didn't look at him.

We returned to the Beanblossom's parking lot and walked into the wine bar.

Esther, in a light-orange blouse and black pants, sat at its black, granite bar and spoke to a waiter. The ends of bottles gleamed in the wine racks lining the wall behind him.

"Hi, Esther," I said. "Thanks for meeting us."

The plump redhead turned and grinned. "I'll do anything these days for an evening out."

"You remember my business partner, Hyperion?" I sat on the barstool beside her and hung my purse on the hook beneath the bar.

"Oh, yes." She shook his hand. "I've been reading all about the murder," she said. "I love true crime stories. They're saying a policeman did it."

"He didn't," Hyperion said sharply. He flicked his trench coat aside and dropped onto the stool beside mine.

"And maybe you can help us prove that," I said.

"Really?" she asked. "How can I help?"

A young waiter in a black t-shirt cleared his throat. "Can I get you anything?"

"I'll have a glass of that Zinfandel from Paso Robles," I said.

"Same." Hyperion rolled his fake cigarette between his fingers.

The bartender eyed him. "There's no smoking in this bar."

Hyperion frowned at the plastic cigarette. "It's not real. It's part of my costume."

"Still," the waiter said, "customers are going to go ballistic."

Hyperion huffed a sigh. "Fine." He tucked the fake cigarette behind his ear.

The bartender nodded and walked to the other end of the bar.

"I've already ordered," Esther said. "I hope that's okay, but I was starving."

"You do you," my partner said.

She braced her chin on her hands. "So why don't you think that detective they arrested is the killer? Is it the DNA evidence? It's amazing what they can do with DNA evidence these days. All those poor people, wrongly imprisoned, finally getting released."

"Because the detective was in jail when Johnson Warszowski was killed," I said. "And it doesn't seem possible that the murders of two business partners in tiny San Borromeo are unrelated."

"I'll admit, that does seem unlikely," she said. "But what does that have to do with Dr. Tarrach?"

"Dr. Tarrach has been very helpful," I said. "He's been an excellent witness. But witnesses are only as good as their character. We were hoping you could tell us a bit about him."

Behind her back, Hyperion rolled his eyes.

"Oh," she said, "Dr. Tarrach has an excellent character. He volunteers at the local homeless shelter, and he supports a kid's baseball team. And he's a wonderful dentist. The patients love him."

"Where's that drink?" Hyperion muttered and dropped his fedora on the bar.

"Do you have any suspects?" she asked.

"A few," I said vaguely. "But I can't talk about them. It might be libelous. After all, only one of them could have committed the crime." At least, I hoped that was true.

Esther nodded. "Of course. I understand. So tell me more about this detective. How did you get involved in the case?"

"He's a friend of a friend. How long have you been working for Dr. Tarrach?" I asked. So far, she'd been doing a better job pumping me for intel than the reverse.

"Oh, about—"

The waiter appeared with three glasses, three mini carafes, and two bottles of wine. He poured half the wine into the glasses, and the remainder into the carafes. "Is there anything else I can get you?"

"A menu," Hyperion said.

"No problem." The waiter pulled menus from beneath the counter and handed them to us. He moved off.

"So you were telling us about your work?" I asked, bouncing my heel on the brass rail.

"Oh, right. Let's see." She tilted her face toward the ceiling. "I've been with Dr. Tarrach nearly seven years now."

"That long?" I asked.

Hyperion slugged back his wine and refilled his glass from the mini carafe.

"You must really enjoy the work," I said.

Her hand fluttered to her neck. "It's a great location, and I love the patients."

Only the patients? "But... not everything about the job?"

"No job is perfect," she said, not meeting my gaze.

"How so?" I nudged Hyperion, and he grunted.

"The doctor is wonderful with his patients," she said.

"But not with you?" I asked.

"No, he's fine with me. It's just..." She licked her bottom lip. "He's got some anxiety issues." Her round face pinked.

Whoa. Hyperion had nailed it with the King of Swords. "Money problems?" I asked.

"I doubt it," the nurse said. "It just seems that sometimes, people have a lot of worries about things that *might* happen. But those things may never happen at all. And then they lose sleep over what's in their heads, instead of what's in front of them."

"And Dr. Tarrach is one of those people?" I asked.

"It's not that unusual," she said rapidly. "We're a high-anxiety society."

"What's your work schedule like?" I took a sip of my wine. It was a big fruity Zin, just what I liked.

"It's great," she said. "We close early on Fridays, but we have Saturday morning hours, so it gives us a bit of a break."

But if the office was closed Saturday afternoons, it might leave Tarrach without an alibi for the first murder.

Esther braced her head on her hands. "Do you think the doctor's in danger?"

"Probably not," I said.

"Are you in danger?"

Hyperion shot me a wary glance. "Why?"

She grinned. "Because I don't want to be nearby if someone tries to kill *you.*"

CHAPTER 29

"Anyway, please give me a call back," I said into the phone. "I'd love to get this gift certificate to—" There was a beep and the call went dead.

I screwed up my face and pressed the phone to my forehead. It had been a long Friday, and I'd talked too much. Sometimes I did that when I got nervous. But Hyperion and I were running out of suspect-adjacent witnesses. We needed Tara Dactyl to call back.

I set the phone on the tearoom kitchen's metal table and stared sourly at the bucket of cleaning supplies by my feet. Tara was probably screening her calls, and why not? I never picked up when I didn't know the number.

My phone buzzed in my hand, and I started, answering without checking the caller ID.

"Your coffin's done," Razzzor boomed.

"Thanks," I said. "I really appreciate it."

"Are you sure you don't want the flamethrower?"

"The State of California is quite definite on that point." I leaned against the long table. "And I wish you wouldn't call it *my* coffin. It's a loaner."

Razzzor laughed. "Right. Look, you can pick up your loaner coffin at Brik's."

"Oh, good." I winced. But Brik *had* volunteered to help with the racer. He must have known that would mean seeing more of me. "Thanks."

"No problemo. We added a holder for Hyperion's scythe. Are you *sure* you want to lose the flamethrower though? Because I can put that back."

"Even if it wasn't going to get me arrested, the coffin race is usually pretty crowded. A flaming coffin might not be the best idea."

He sighed doubtfully. "If you say so. Anyway, I'll be at the race tomorrow to cheer you on. And my staff is ready to push your coffin in the pre-parade. Victory party at Beanblossom's afterward?"

Or a drown-your-sorrows party. If we lost this race... I didn't want to think about it. "Yep, I'll host it," I said. "It's the least I can do for my sponsor."

"Cool. See you tomorrow." Razzzor hung up.

I tried Tara's number again.

"Hello?" a woman answered breathlessly.

I straightened away from the table. "Hi, this is Abigail Beanblossom, from Beanblossom's Tea and Tarot. Is this Tara Dactyl?"

"Yes. How can I help you?"

"Like I said in my message—" i.e. my big fat lie "—an anonymous guest bought you a gift certificate for the tearoom. I don't know how it happened, but they didn't leave the address to send it to. And since they paid by cash and were anonymous—"

"Was it a man?" she asked quickly.

"Come to think of it, *yes* it was."

"I think I know who bought it. Can you email it to me?"

I stilled. "Oh, it's on heavy paper. The certificate is part of the fun. What's your mailing address?" I crossed my fingers and hoped it wasn't a PO box.

She rattled off an address on Sunset. Hastily, I copied it onto an order pad. "You know, that's not far from Beanblossom's. Would you mind if I saved some stamps and just dropped it by?"

"I'm not home tonight, maybe tomorrow morning? I'd tell you to just put it in my mailbox, but you need a key."

"That's no problem. Like I said, you're close. I'll drop it by tomorrow."

"Thanks." She hung up.

Elated, I finished cleaning the kitchen and drove home.

I hesitated in my bungalow's driveway. Then, stomach fluttering, I crossed the yard to Brik's front door and knocked.

Brik opened the door. "Hey, Abigail. You here for your coffin?"

He looked good. *Really* good. And with a man like Brik, all that took were jeans and a white tee.

Brik and I were just neighbors, that was all. But my body hadn't seemed to have gotten the message. "Yes. I'm here for the coffin."

He nodded, scooping his mane of blond hair into a ponytail. "We made some improvements—"

I covered my face with my hands. "Oh, no."

"No, these are actual improvements. After your accident, you need redundancies." He leaned against the door frame. "Now the person in the back seat can brake and steer too."

"Won't that mess with the steering in front?"

"Not if you don't do it at the same time. The rear brakes and steering are only for emergencies. And we tightened up the— You need to test it out and see for yourself."

I turned and stared at the street. It was already dark. "I'll do it tomorrow."

"The race is tomorrow. Come on." Brik grabbed his keys from a hook by the door and ambled to his pickup. The coffin racer was in the bed. "No time like the present."

"For what?"

He opened the truck's passenger door. "To go for a test drive."

My heart leapt, and I clenched my fists. Brik wasn't sending me mixed messages. I was receiving the messages I *wanted* to receive. But I wasn't up for playing the just-friends role tonight. "I don't know. I'm kind of tired."

"The race is tomorrow. You want to lose?"

"No." I really didn't. But right now, all I could think of was crashing on my virtual command deck and killing zombie Nazis in space. But I needed to win that race, and driving that coffin unprepared wasn't going to do it.

"Well?" he asked.

"You're right. I need to practice. Let's go." *And get it over with.* Feet dragging, I climbed inside the pickup.

We drove in uneasy silence to an office park high on a hill. Black stretches of Pacific gloomed between the thick eucalyptus trees enclosing the parking lot. Only a few cars remained at this hour, and the lot had enough hills to make a San Franciscan proud.

"We've got plenty of space here." Brik stepped from the truck. "Not that you'll need it. This baby has real control."

I stepped out more slowly. The lights from a container ship glowed, lonely, on the distant ocean.

Brik opened the tailgate and slid two boards from it to the pavement, making a ramp. I hurried to his side and helped him back the coffin down the two-by-fours. We wheeled it to the top of the steepest slope.

A chill wind carrying the scent of eucalyptus tossed my hair, and I clawed strands from my face.

"We can start with a smaller hill, if you want," Brik said.

"Nah." The sooner we finished, the better. "Let's do this. I don't mind a little risk."

He gave me a long look. "Okay, you take the front seat, since you'll be driving during the race. On the count of three?"

I nodded. We braced our hands on the coffin.

"One. Two. Three!"

We shoved off and jumped into our seats. The coffin took off, the wheels near-silent on the pavement. My stomach made a roller coaster swoop.

We flashed past empty parking spaces. An island with Eucalyptus trees rose before us.

"Turn coming up," Brik shouted.

"I see it." I pulled back on one steering stick, and the racer swung in an easy arc. "Ha!"

We blasted down the hill. Whatever he and Razzzor had done, the coffin was definitely handling better. I laughed. I couldn't help it. We probably weren't going that fast, but it *felt* fast, and I laughed harder.

Another turn came into view, and I pulled the other stick. Again, the coffin reacted immediately, and we took the curve. We hit the upslope, and the coffin slowed, stopped.

I jumped from the racer, my arms in a *V*, and whooped. "That was amazing! What did you do to it?"

He beamed. "We tightened things up, replaced the wheels, that sort of thing. FYI, you might want to back off the cackling during the actual race." Brik hopped from the racer. "You might scare Hyperion."

I bounced on my toes. "Don't tell me I scared you?"

He grinned, chest heaving, hands on his hips. "Not a chance."

We stood there for a long moment, saying nothing. A thread of warmth seemed to twine between us.

"Brik—"

His expression closed. "We should get this back."

Heat crawled up my chest and neck. I looked away. "Yeah. Good race. Thanks."

We pushed the car to the top of the hill, and I was glad he couldn't see my face.

"Should we try again?" I asked lightly. "This time with you steering in the back?"

"No time," he said. "I need to get home."

"Oh," I said, disappointed. Earlier, he'd sounded like he had all sorts of time. "Okay."

We guided the coffin into the bed of his truck, and I watched Brik put away the boards, slam the tailgate shut.

I smiled tightly and climbed into the pickup. It would be easier dealing with Brik without all this ambiguity. Or maybe the ambiguity was all in my head. Maybe I just didn't want the certainty of a final rejection.

He started the ignition and pulled from the lot.

"Your grandfather told me about your dinner with Gino," he said carefully. "You're still helping Chase out?"

"That's not how dinner started, but, yeah."

"I see." He glanced at me. "I'm glad you're still getting out there, taking risks." He stared through the windshield. "Not all risks are worth it though."

Yeah. He'd already made his feelings clear on that score. But I wasn't sure if he was talking about the investigation or Gino being a risk. And I didn't ask.

CHAPTER 30

"Nope." Hyperion shook his head. "I like to watch." He grinned cheekily.

I sat in the coffin racer and braced one elbow on its side. "You're my co-pilot. We *have* to practice together."

It was Saturday, and we were at the office park. There were few cars in the parking lot, thick with fog. A seagull, invisible in the mist, squawked above us.

"Why?" he asked reasonably. "All I have to do is sit there."

"No, now the coffin has redundancies. You have access to the brake and steering too."

He peered inside. "I don't know..."

"Do *you* want to be up front? Is that the problem?"

"I'm loving your enthusiasm, Abigail. I really am." He raised his chin. "The problem is in spite of my superior driving skills—"

"That is *such* BS."

"I refuse to endanger our chances of winning because of my curse. Abigail, if I get in the coffin now, its wheels may fall off. The race is this afternoon. We won't have time to get it repaired."

"You'd rather the wheels fall off *during* the race?"

"Yes. We might still skid across the finish line."

I started to lift myself from the racer, then dropped back into it. "Okay, I'm going to give it one more run, and then we'll... do something else. Give me a push."

He gripped the rear of the coffin and ran, releasing me. "Tally ho!"

The racer flew down the hill, turning and braking with ease.

"You go girl," Hyperion shouted faintly behind me.

I grinned. Without Brik in the back, the coffin didn't seem to fly as fast. There *is* something to be said for ballast.

We gave it a half dozen more runs. I rolled the coffin back up the hill, and Hyperion and I loaded it onto the trailer he'd rented.

We got into his Jeep, and he started the car. "So," he said. "Tearoom?"

"Sure. Or you could come with me to talk to Tara Dactyl," I said casually. "I found her address."

"The famous dinosaur girlfriend? How'd you track her down?"

"I called her. I'm supposed to deliver a gift certificate to her this morning. We may as well go now."

"How much is the gift certificate for?" The Jeep crawled through the fog.

"One Royal Tea." I sighed. The things I do for murder investigations... Those teas weren't cheap.

He was silent for a long moment. "Well. Thank you. I know things are tight after that oven."

"The oven I shouldn't have bought. Hyperion—"

He waved a hand. "You can skip the apology tour. We're past that."

"Have you talked to Tony?" I asked, tentative.

His brows drew downward. "Yes. He's still not happy I wasn't entirely honest, and I guess I can't blame him."

"But you're talking. That's good."

His mouth compressed.

Oh, no. "Isn't it?" I asked.

"He's been... It's more than me once going out with Cassius. This—all of this—has been getting to him more than he's been letting on."

"Of course it would. He's been accused of murder, and he's one of the white hats."

"It's more than that," he said. "I think he feels... let down by his department. I'm not sure he'll be able to go back after this."

I pulled my purse closer in my lap. "You think he'll move? Switch departments?" I asked worriedly.

He shook his head. "It's too soon to tell. But his work is his life. He can't lose it."

Inexplicably, the fog lightened as we descended toward the Pacific. The trailer rattling and bumping behind us. We turned onto Beach Street. I glanced out the rear window to make sure the coffin was still strapped to the trailer.

"Tara's house is up ahead on Sunset," I said, "though I'm not sure exactly where." I looked for the curve where the road changed names.

Hyperion groaned. "Are you kidding? How am I supposed to park this thing? You know how crowded that street gets."

"You've got the parking gods on your side. Remember?"

"Not in October. I can't count on anything in October."

But despite the Saturday morning crowds, he did find two spots together on nearby Beach Street, and we parked.

I loaded both meters with quarters. We walked down the misty sidewalk, looking for the Sunset street sign. Hyperion studied Tony's building opposite and shook his head.

"If you want to ditch me afterward to see Tony—"

"No."

The numbers flipped. We'd reached Sunset. I stopped in front of a tall condominium complex and double-checked the address. "Here it is."

An elegant man with a fluffy orange dog opened the door. The tiny dog snarled at me, and the man yanked it back. "Sorry," the man said. "He's a rescue."

We walked inside the elegant foyer with a massive bouquet on a round, central table.

"A rescue," Hyperion scoffed. "It's like that guy expects extra credit."

A chandelier hung from the ceiling. A carpet with a Greco-Roman theme of columns covered the floor. Post boxes lined one wall.

"I think rescue dogs are great," I said.

"You wouldn't if it had ripped your leg off."

"And Tara's on the fifth floor."

"Ocean view? I guess that's some compensation for being named after a dinosaur," he muttered.

I pushed the elevator button, and the doors glided open.

"I don't know," Hyperion said, stepping inside. "Our quest is starting to seem a little desperate. This woman's got several degrees of separation from the murders."

"Are you kidding? Pestering Tara is a *lot* desperate." I pushed the button for the fifth floor. "But Razzzor's program couldn't come up with a connection between Tony and the murder victims. We're going to have to color outside the lines."

"Abigail," he said in a low voice.

I looked at him.

"Thank you," Hyperion said seriously. "I mean it. You've gone above and beyond, helping Tony, pulling me out of my funk—"

"You helped me plenty of times. It's only fair."

"No, what you've done is more than fair. And I know I've been hard to take this month, with the curse and all. I know it probably doesn't exist. But it just seems to keep coming at me. And this October has been the worst."

My heart compressed. "We'll get through it." I squeezed his arm.

The elevator pinged. Its doors opened, and we walked into a lushly carpeted hallway. After a false start, we went in the right direction and found Tara's door.

I rang the bell.

Something inside the condo *thunked*. After a moment, the door opened.

Tara was tall and gorgeous. She wore a sports bra and yoga pants, and her tanned shoulders glistened with sweat. She swung a towel over them. "Oh, hi. Are you Abigail?"

"Yes," I said, "Tara? And this is my business partner at the tearoom, Hyperion Night."

"Oh. My. God." He squealed. "Have you got an ocean view?"

I managed not to roll my eyes.

"Yeah," she said. "I do. Want to see?"

"Do I?" He swanned past her and clapped his hands together. "You have got a real eye for design."

The home was open plan, in sleek, ivory tones. But you didn't need color when you had enormous picture windows overlooking the ocean.

Even I paused to stare. The view was spectacular. A line of fog hung above the ocean, the Pacific unfolding in ever deepening shades of blue.

She flushed. "Thanks. But I actually hired a decorator."

"Hyperion's the Tarot side of the tearoom," I said.

Her eyes widened slightly. "Really? You read Tarot cards?"

"I *do*," he said.

"I don't suppose..." She bit her bottom lip. "Is there any chance I can get a reading? I know I could go to the tearoom for one, but since you're here..."

Hyperion stilled.

Uh, oh. "He didn't bring his cards," I said quickly.

He straightened. "Of course I did. I don't go anywhere without them. Is that table free?" He pointed to a glass and driftwood coffee table in front of the curving, cream-colored couch.

My muscles released, and I loosed a breath I hadn't realized I'd been holding.

"Absolutely it's free." She motioned to the arcing sofa. "Please, sit down."

He dropped onto the couch and pulled a deck of cards from the inside pocket of his blazer. "Abigail, would you mind giving us some privacy?"

"Sure," I said. "Um, may I use your bathroom?"

"It's right down the hall." Tara pointed.

"Thanks." I headed in that direction.

"Now," Hyperion murmured behind me, "is there anything in particular you're interested in...?"

I walked into the bathroom. It was as gleaming and spectacularly modern as the living area. I opened the medicine cabinet. It was filled with essential oils and natural remedies.

As there were no drugs or weapons beneath the sink, I flushed the toilet and tiptoed into the hallway. I peeked through an open door and hurried into a ginormous bedroom. In its center stood a round, white bed with a turquoise throw.

I never really understood round beds. Finding reasonably priced sheets that fit had to be tough. But with a condo by the ocean, I guessed Tara wasn't worried about affordability.

A framed photo of a smiling Tara and Dr. Tarrach stood on an end table. I scanned the room for clues and found none.

Weaving my hands through my hair, I tugged lightly, thwarted. But a breakthrough here had never been likely. Like Hyperion had said, Tara was several degrees removed from the murder.

I returned to the living area.

"Seven of Swords," Hyperion said. "Deceit."

"Do you mind if I check out your balcony?" I asked.

"Oh, go ahead," Tara said. "The morning started out awful, but it's turned into a beautiful day."

I pulled open a sliding glass door and strolled outside. The balcony had that tile that looks like pale wood. Two broad, gray-wood armchairs faced each other with a small table between them. A telescope stood by the railing.

I walked over and put my eye to its eyepiece, then jerked upright, heart thumping.

More slowly, I peered through the telescope again. It looked straight into Tony Chase's empty living room.

I straightened. Unthinking, I lowered the scope.

I shook my head and looked through it again. The view was now of an adobe-colored wall. I shifted the telescope and was staring into the coffeeshop beneath Tony's condo.

The tall detective sat at the window, drinking from a paper cup.

Good Lord. Tony's condo was on Beach Street. Tara's was on Sunset. But I hadn't made the connection right away, because the street names were different. It probably didn't mean anything. This was a small town, and random people lived near each other. But—

The balcony's door slid open, and I straightened again. Tara and Hyperion wandered onto the balcony.

"Isn't the view magnificent?" she asked.

"Especially of the condo across the street." I swallowed, mouth dry.

She laughed. "Guilty. But can you blame me? That guy's a hunk. And I don't mind having a cop as a neighbor either."

Hyperion blinked. "Cop?"

"I've got his routine memorized." She checked her watch. "He'll be in the coffeeshop downstairs now."

I swayed. We'd had everything wrong. Tony *wasn't* connected to the victims. "He was just a convenient patsy," I breathed. We had to get out of here. *Now.*

"What?" Tara asked.

"We have to go." I strode to the glass door and pulled it open.

"But what about my gift certificate?" she asked.

"Oh. Right. Sorry." I dug it from my purse and thrust it toward her. "Hope to see you again soon."

Hyperion bent to the telescope. He sucked in a breath.

"Hyperion?" I said.

He straightened. "Right. Right. Let's get some coffee."

"Great idea." We hustled through the ivory living area.

"What the hell?" Hyperion whispered.

"We've got him," I said in a low voice and reached for the front door. "This is it. This is the connection."

A key scraped in the lock, and the door opened.

Dr. Tarrach gaped at us. "What are you doing here?"

"You killed them all and you framed Tony," I blurted. "You knew he was a cop. You knew his routine. You framed him because he had a gun and you knew you could do it. You had access to that knockout drug too because you do surgeries. You can prescribe drugs. *You* killed all those people."

The dentist stepped backward and slammed the door in my face.

CHAPTER 31

"Move." Hyperion grabbed my shoulder, wrenching me aside, and yanked the door open. He raced past. I stumbled, one arm banging against the wall.

A framed black and white photo of the beach rattled.

"What's going on?" Tara asked.

"I'll explain later." Lightheaded, I burst into the carpeted hallway. A door slammed to my left. *The stairs.*

I raced to the metal fire door and heaved it open. Footsteps clattered beneath me on the metal steps.

"Hyperion!" I jogged down the steps more cautiously. My back still wasn't right after our tumble on the pier, and I kept one hand on the rail.

I pushed open another heavy door to the street.

Hyperion's dark head vanished into a throng of tourists.

I ran across the street and into the coffeeshop so fast I skidded on its polished wood floor.

Detective Chase put down his coffee mug and raised a brow. "To what do I—"

"Dr. Tarrach killed them and framed you." I panted, bracing my hands on my knees. "Hyperion's chasing him." I pointed in the direction he'd gone.

The detective bulleted from the café.

I straightened and laid my palm against my pounding heart. We'd done it. We were right. We were right, or Tarrach wouldn't have run. They'd have to let Tony off.

And I needed to get more aerobic exercise.

Curious, I checked what remained in Tony's mug. *Chai. Huh.* He really did like the spicy tea. I thought he'd been buying it from me out of guilt.

I returned to the condos across the street and pushed the button for Tara's unit.

"Yes?" she asked, her voice tinny.

"It's Abigail. Can I—"

The door buzzed, and I walked inside the lux foyer. I took the elevator.

She yanked her condo's door open before I could knock. "What the hell's going on?" Nose flaring, she braced her hands on the hips of her sleek yoga pants.

"Your boyfriend, Tarrach—"

"Yeah," she said. "I know he's my boyfriend. What's that got to do with you?"

"His two financial consultants were murdered. That cop you pointed out was framed for the first killing. He and Hyperion are chasing Tarrach now, and they know I'm here."

She blinked. "Wait. Know you're here? You think... What *do* you think? Because it sounds like you think I'm going to do something bad to you."

I didn't. I thought she was ignorant of what her boyfriend had been up to. But a little insurance didn't hurt. "How long have you lived here?"

"Nearly a year." She pursed her lips. "Why? I don't understand what's going on."

Then Verena hadn't lied about the time of purchase. The dentist had. "And when did you notice Detective Chase?"

"The cop across the street, you mean? Week one. That man's a tall drink of water, even if he is an idiot."

"Why do you think he's an idiot?" I asked.

"Well, it's not very smart, is it, keeping to the same routine? Sasha says cops don't believe they have to be security conscious; they *are* the security."

My pulse quickened. "So Dr. Tar—Sasha knew the detective's routine too?"

"We laughed about it." Her face pinched. "What does that have to do with your partner chasing him away?"

A door opened in the hallway and a well-dressed, gray-haired lady glared out. "Would you mind keeping it down?"

Tara waved the woman away, dismissive. "You'd better come inside," she said more quietly. I hesitated, then followed her into the living room.

She dropped onto the curving, bone-colored couch. Putting the coffee table between us, I sat in an uncomfortably stylish chair opposite.

"*What* is going on?" Her fingers dug into the arm of the couch.

"Okay," I said, "what has Sasha told you about his advisors?"

"That they're crooks." She tapped her foot in the air. "They've been mismanaging his funds."

I nodded. "Do you think that's true?"

She blinked. "I— Sasha can be a little tightly wound," she admitted. "But he's sure of it. And he's a doctor, well, a dentist, but they're doctors too. He's not the sort of person to make mistakes."

I nodded. But people—even doctors—did make mistakes. And just because someone believes something, doesn't mean it's true. And in the end, it didn't matter if it was true or not, only that the dentist believed.

I braced my elbow on the arm of the ivory chair. "Someone killed his adviser, Cassius Santori, in an apparent road rage accident. But the man blamed for killing him, your neighbor, Detective Chase, has no memory of the accident. He doesn't remember anything since leaving my tearoom that day."

Her eyes narrowed. "Or so he *says*."

"He's waiting for the test to come back to prove he was drugged. There'll be evidence one way or another. My partner and I have been trying to figure out who or what the connection is between Tony and Cassius. But we haven't been able to find a thing."

She folded her arms and slouched on the cloudlike couch. "Well, if it was road rage, you wouldn't, would you?"

"Did Dr. Tarrach tell you how he got that poison oak?"

"He said he was out hiking the other weekend."

Yeah, hiking away from the murder scene. Those hills were practically covered in poison oak.

"And then someone killed Santori's partner," I said, "Johnson Warszowski. Detective Chase couldn't have done that—he was in jail at the time."

"So," she said, "he's off the hook."

"He wasn't though. The police are treating the murders as separate cases. But what are the odds? These are two men who run a small business together in a small town. They have to be connected."

"And the detective?" she asked.

I leaned forward in my chair. "We thought whoever was framing Detective Chase, had to have a grudge against him. There had to be some connection there, too. I mean, you don't frame a random person for murder, right?"

She nodded. "Unless it wasn't a frame, and it was road rage."

"It wasn't road rage," I said more sharply than I'd intended, and I blew out my breath. "It was a frame. This condo is the connection. Chase wasn't framed because Tarrach had a grudge against him. Chase was framed because it was convenient. Tarrach knew his schedule, his habits."

And every Saturday afternoon, Chase stopped by the tearoom for a cup of chai and to see Hyperion. "Who better to frame for shooting someone than a man who always carries a gun?" I asked.

She jerked to standing. "That's crazy. It's..." She paced between the sofa and the glass coffee table.

"*Is* it crazy?" I asked.

Someone knocked on the door. Tara shot me a wary look.

I stood and followed her as she went to answer it.

Hyperion and Detective Chase stood in the hallway. Hyperion shook his head. "We lost him."

"Mind if I come in, Ms. Dactyl?" the detective drawled. "I'd like to ask you some questions."

*****

For some reason, Tony didn't want us hanging around while the cops came to question Tara. And I wasn't looking forward to encountering Detective Baranko either. So we left. After all, I had a tearoom, a parade, and a race to run.

We returned to Beanblossom's, and I did tearoom things until darkness fell. Hyperion shut himself up in his office. But no psychic emanations of doom drifted from his door. No customers burst into tears. No waitresses dropped teacups.

And when we left for the parade, Hyperion in his Death costume, my partner was actually smiling. In his skeletal makeup, his grin was terrifying.

Razzzor's team of zombies pushed our coffin into place. Rows of coffin cars lined up four abreast in front of and behind us. The fog hadn't returned, but the night air was chilly. Hyperion turned sharply, and I ducked beneath his scythe.

"Watch it," I said.

"Don't worry, it's too rusty to do any damage." He touched a long finger to the pointed end.

"Aside from tetanus," I grumped.

"What's the problem? We cracked a murder case. Tony's off the hook."

A uniformed patrolman paced along the edge of the sidewalk. He warned a couple who'd strayed into the road to get out of it.

"Sorry," I said. "We just need to win this race. I'm worried about that bet."

"Toot, toot, after today, I'll believe anything, even that we can beat the curse and win."

"You do?" I asked, hopeful. I mean, if he thought we could win—

"No way," he scoffed. "Are you kidding? We're days from Halloween. We're screwed." Hyperion pulled his midnight cloak tighter. "We may have saved Tony, but that doesn't mean the curse is done with us."

"I hate to say it, but Razzzor and Brik did a great job on the racer. We may have a real chance."

"I'm talking about Dr. Tarrach's madcap escape. I'm not saying I have a feeling of impending doom, but I feel like I *should* have a feeling of impending doom."

"They put a BOLO out on Tarrach. He may be on the run, but the police are on his trail."

"It's October, Abigail." He leaned on the scythe. "*Nothing* goes right in October. As much as I want to, we can't trust this good news. It would be just like October to fake us out only to pull the rug out from under us."

"So why are you smiling?"

"I'm not smiling."

"You're totally smiling under that face paint."

He cocked his head. "Abigail, that *is* the face paint."

"Oh. Nice job with the makeup."

The row of coffins moved forward, and we pushed our racer closer to the starting line. The race was timed, four coffins going at once, so the timer could log which coffin was fastest.

"Tarrach saw us," I said, "and he ran. That doesn't mean he's guilty, but it's a pretty good—"

The phone rang in the pocket of my pirate costume. I pulled it out and smiled. "It's Verena." I didn't have many female friends in San Borromeo, and Verena seemed cool.

Hyperion waved, dismissive. "Go ahead and answer."

I put the phone to my ear. "Hi, Verena. What's up?"

"Hi. I just wanted to tell you— They did an audit of Lafayette Grief and Dr. Tarrach's accounts."

"So soon?"

"I pushed for those two to go first," Verena said.

"What did they find?"

"Nothing. There's *nothing* wrong with those accounts."

I shifted my weight. "That's... what I figured. Thanks for letting me know."

"Have *you* heard anything?" she asked.

"Er, not yet. If I do, I'll let you know as soon as I can."

"Thanks." She exhaled heavily. "This is getting to me, you know? I'm starting to feel like *I've* got a target on my back. What if he blames me too?"

"Listen, the police are looking for Dr. Tarrach. If you see him, call nine-one-one."

"Tarrach? Is he the one?"

"It looks that way," I said.

"Then it's almost over. I hope they catch the bastard."

I hesitated. "Were you ever suspicious of Tarrach?"

"No," she said explosively. "I would have told the police if I had been. Why would you think that?"

"It's just... Someone saw you in a restaurant, sort of hiding behind a menu when Johnson and Tarrach were having lunch."

She laughed. "Yeah, I was hiding. I was supposed to be in the office taking calls. And then Johnson and Tarrach showed up for lunch at the same restaurant."

"That was all?" I asked, relieved.

"That was all." She cleared her throat. "I'm near the finish line. I'll be rooting for you."

"Thanks. Are we still on for drinks at Beanblossom's afterward?"

"Oh yeah. I'm *so* in the mood." She hung up.

"Well?" Hyperion slid his scythe into the holder Razzzor and Brik had installed.

The coffins moved forward, and we rolled ours up a coffin length.

"They completed the audit of Dr. Tarrach's account," I said. "There was no skullduggery."

"See? I told you. Tarrach's going to get away with it."

"No, I don't think so. He told his girlfriend that he thought Johnson and Cassius were cheating him. As long as he believed it, he's got motive."

"Abigail!" Razzzor shouted.

I scanned the crowd. Gramps and Tomas had managed to set up lawn chairs in the front row of the people thronging the sidewalk. They huddled under blankets and waved. Razzzor and Brik stood behind them.

Razzzor blew a vuvuzela horn. The crowd around him winced.

"They're not going to see the race," Hyperion said. "They're behind the starting line. See? October."

"They saw the parade with Razzzor's zombie team. And this way they get front row seats to see all the coffins again."

And I had to say, ours looked the most like a coffin, even if it was covered in stickers for Razzzor's new game. Most of the others just looked like go-carts.

The whistle shrieked, and the racers in front of us took off.

My stomach butterflied. It was only a coffin race. Just for fun. And if I ended up on the hook for a charitable donation I couldn't afford... I'd deal with that. We'd managed to track down Cassius and Johnson's killer. What was a massive bill compared to that?

We rolled our coffin into place. Gripping the sides of the car, I glanced at a man displaying the winning time: one minute and thirty-two seconds.

My mouth went dry. Less than two minutes seemed awfully fast.

The whistle blew.

Hyperion and I sprinted forward, pushing the coffin. We hit the jump line a little bit behind the other three coffins and hopped into our seats. Our racer took off down the hill.

"Ow!" Hyperion shouted behind me.

I glanced over my shoulder. He lifted one hip and extracted the mini pumpkin cannon.

"Are you crazy?" I yelled and pulled on the right turn stick. "You can't shoot that here."

We caught up to the lead coffin.

"Yes, I can. It's—"

"No, you can't!"

We swerved around the bend, past the children's theater. Our racer reclaimed front position.

I risked another look behind me. Hyperion's eyes were squeezed shut. He hugged the cannon to his chest. I relaxed. My partner wouldn't be shooting anything.

But he did need to pay attention in case he needed to steer or use the brakes. "Watch the road," I yelled.

We bumped over a manhole cover, and the coffin on our left nosed ahead.

The crowd roared.

"You watch the road," Hyperion screamed back. "You're driving."

We blasted around another bend, and my pirate hat flew off. But we gained on the lead coffin.

Our two racers were neck and neck. I leaned forward, as if that could give us an extra edge. But who beat whom didn't matter. What mattered was our time. And at this point, I had very little control over the outcome.

We zipped around the last bend to the left. Hyperion and I flew past the lead coffin.

"Ha! Eat graveyard dirt!" I laughed maniacally and leered at our competitors, falling behind.

I could see the finish line now. The ocean was a dark line on the horizon. Faces in the crowd flashed past. Dr. Tarrach moved through the crush.

I did a double take. The dentist vanished behind a family of four. I swore.

"What?" Hyperion yelled. "What? Did the wheels come off? Are they falling off?"

"Dr. Tarrach's here. Call Tony."

"I can't. I'm sitting on my phone."

"You were sitting on that stupid cannon and you got *that* out from under you."

"The cannon's bigger." He wriggled in his seat, and the coffin wobbled.

"Watch it," I said.

"Got the phone. I'm calling."

We flashed past the finish line and I hauled on the brake. Before the coffin stopped, I jumped free and ran toward the crowd.

"Wait! Wait!" Hyperion shouted.

I turned. He threw me the mini cannon, and the coffin racer glided forward. I caught the pumpkin cannon easily. Our coffin picked up speed.

"Hyperion, the brake," I shouted.

"Where is it?"

"It's..." But the coffin had rumbled past. I ran after it.

Verena waved at me from the crowd.

Dr. Tarrach, a determined expression on his face, walked toward the redhead.

Oh my God. Verena was right. She did have a target on her back. Tarrach was going for her as well.

I aimed the pumpkin cannon at him, and he moved behind a steampunk couple. But I knew where he was headed.

I raced down the road to Verena.

She hopped up and down at the edge of the sidewalk. Her foot hit the corner of the cement, and she stumbled into the street. "You—"

"Tarrach is here. I think he's looking for you."

The blood drained from her face. "What?"

"Hello, ladies," the dentist said. He wore sensible loafers and a neat blue sweater. And he held a scalpel in one hand.

I took a jerky step backward. *Scream.* But no one would hear in this chaos. The crowd wasn't paying attention to us, and if even they did...

Knives were bad news. Hyperion had studied some form of martial arts. More than once, I'd heard him and Tomas saying they'd rather confront a gun than a knife.

Especially when faced with someone who knew all the arteries that could bleed out so quickly. *Like someone with medical training.* And why did a dentist need a scalpel?

"Verena, Verena, Verena." He shook his head. "You've kept bad company."

"No," she said. "I didn't. You're crazy. Johnson and Cassius did nothing wrong. They were helping you."

"Helping destroy my business," he snarled.

I shook my head, trying to restart my breathing. There was no sense arguing with him. He'd seen what he'd wanted to see. He was like my parents in that sense, blind to all but his own personal reality.

And that had made this case harder to unravel. People generally do things for a good reason, or for what they think is a logical reason. But the dentist hadn't been working in the world of logic or reason at all.

"The police are onto you," I said shakily. "They're looking for you. You should get out of here."

"I'm not done yet." He pointed the scalpel at Verena.

"You told me you'd bought that condo a couple months ago," I said, stalling. "You implied that's why you'd been arguing with Cassius. But Verena told me you bought it last year. You lied. That wasn't what the argument was about at all. You thought they'd cheated you."

The muscles corded in his neck. "They *did* cheat me."

"And the lipstick in Johnson's office," I said. "You put it there to frame Verena, just like you tried to frame Tony."

"That *was* my lipstick. You took it out of my purse." She hissed an indrawn breath. "I thought the police were going to arrest me."

"Stop whining," he told her.

I aimed the cannon at him. "One more step, and I'll shoot."

"You'll shoot me with a t-shirt?" he asked.

"This cannon is loaded with mini pumpkins. And believe me, at this range, one'll take your head off."

There was a crash, further down the street, and my breathing stopped. *Hyperion.* The crowd groaned and shrieked. And I'd left Hyperion to—

My knees turned to water. But I couldn't think about Hyperion. I had to focus on the threat here and now. And how I was about to completely fail Verena. *No.* My hands tightened on the cannon. *No.* I would *not.*

"They conducted an audit of your account," Verena said. "There was nothing wrong with it."

"Liars," the dentist snarled. "You're all covering for each other. Of course no one will admit it."

"No one stole money from you," Verena said, pleading.

His eyes bulged. "They did. I could tell. I know. I'm not stupid. They were cheating me."

Verena pressed her hand to her neck and shook her head. "No. No, they weren't."

"And you!" Veins bulged in his forehead. "You're covering up for them too. You were all together in it. Laughing about what a sucker I was. They deserved to die."

He raised his knife arm.

"Wait!" I said. "I have one question. How did you get the drug into Tony Chase's tea?"

"I didn't," he said. "I injected him in the parking lot."

"Oh. Thanks." I aimed low and pulled the trigger.

An orange t-shirt shot from the cannon, hitting the dentist just above the groin.

He looked down. "That wasn't a mini pumpkin."

"Oh," I said. "Damn." I swung the butt of the cannon up and struck him in the face.

He staggered backward.

"Run," I shouted to Verena.

But she took a step forward instead and kicked a field goal. Tarrach doubled over. His knees folded inward, and he hit the sidewalk.

"Or you could do that," I said, shocked.

The uniformed officer I'd seen earlier strode toward us. "What's—"

"He's got a scalpel," I said. "There's a BOLO out on him."

The cop pulled his gun. "Drop the knife," he roared. "Lie on the ground!"

Dr. Tarrach dropped the knife. He laid on the ground.

CHAPTER 32

I set our second-place trophy and a bottle of champagne on Beanblossom's counter. Hyperion sprawled in a chair, an icepack on his elbow, and groaned.

Detective Chase patted his shoulder. "You'll survive."

"October," Hyperion said. "Let it *end*."

"I like October." Gramps settled on one of the barstools. "The weather's nice, and it's fun for the kids."

I pulled two more bottles from the mini fridge beneath the counter.

"You're just saying that because you won first place in the homeowner's decorating contest." Tomas sat down beside him. "You cheated. You had a ringer helping you." He motioned toward Brik.

The contractor sat silent, his expression shuttered.

My grandfather grinned. "That sounds like sour grapes."

"Bah." Tomas motioned him away.

I handed Razzzor a bottle of champagne. "You were the sponsor. Do you want to do the honors?"

Razzzor popped the cork. It narrowly missed a chandelier hung with paper bats. "I can't believe we didn't win first prize."

"Oh, shut up." Beatrice, dressed like a green dragon, slammed her third-place trophy beside mine. "No one's going to be talking about the winner anyway after your performance."

"Oh," I said modestly, "I don't know —"

"A dramatic crash? Taking down a killer with a t-shirt cannon? You disgust me," she said. But her emerald eyes twinkled.

Gino, looking like James Bond in a tux, winked. He'd made a last-minute decision to be Beatrice's racing partner after her receptionist had quit.

I have *no* idea why she'd quit, but it *might* have nothing to do with us.

"The crash *was* pretty spectacular." Hyperion tilted his head back and smiled.

Beatrice made a face. "Stop. It was the PR stunt of the year."

"It wasn't a stunt." Verena pulled out a chair and dropped into it. "That jerk tried to kill us."

"Is it enough?" Hyperion asked Tony in a low voice. "Is there evidence to get him for the other murders?"

"It doesn't look good for Tarrach," the detective said. "Especially since he pretty much confessed." He nodded to us.

"Pretty much?" Hyperion asked sharply.

"They've got a good case against Tarrach," Detective Chase said.

"They?" Hyperion said.

"I'm not a part of it," he said. "This is for Baranko to put together."

"And will he?" I poured the champagne into flutes.

Chase nodded. "He's an honest cop."

But what would become of Tony? I wanted to think that all was well that ended well. But his police department had treated him like a criminal. They'd even lost evidence that could have exculpated him.

I rubbed my thumb against the curve of my champagne flute and studied the rising bubbles. If I were in his shoes, I couldn't go back. I'd never trust them again. We weren't the same though. I didn't know what Tony would do. I just hoped it worked out for him and Hyperion.

There was a knock on the front door, and a little witch stepped hesitantly inside. "I saw your lights on," she said. "Are you open?"

"Sorry," Hyperion said. "Private party."

"Wait," I said quickly. "Were you here a few weeks ago? It would have been a Saturday afternoon."

"Oh, yes. Did you recognize my costume?" She fluffed her green hair.

"It's great," I said.

"I loved your cranberry-orange scones," she said. "Is there any chance I can get the recipe?"

"Come back tomorrow," I said. "I'll make a recipe card for you."

"Thanks!" She bobbed her head and swished out the door.

"What was that about?" Razzzor asked.

"Loose ends," I said. "She'd been in costume in the tearoom when Tony... Well. I wondered. Most of our guests don't come in costume, especially that early in the season."

"I still can't believe my algorithm didn't pick up the connection." Razzzor took a glass. "If Tarrach hadn't put the condo in his girlfriend's name, and if the street hadn't changed from Beach to Sunset *right* there, it would have."

"But you can see why Tarrach didn't put the condo in his own name," Tomas said.

"Yeah." Verena raised her champagne flute. "He was a scumbag."

"That, and he didn't want his wife to know about his love nest," Tomas said.

Gramps chuckled darkly. "She'll know now. And that's the least of his problems."

Razzzor handed Beatrice a glass of champagne.

The PR consultant glared. "Are you kidding me?" But she snatched it from his hand and gulped it down in one go.

"I'll take one," Gino said.

Razzzor passed him a glass. "Brik?"

"No. Thanks. I've got to drive home, and I should probably go now. Congratulations everyone." Brik walked out the front door. It shut behind him, the bell jingling with finality.

My heart sank. I'd taken a risk tonight, a big one, and Brik wasn't happy about that. And he wouldn't change. It was wrong for me to *want* Brik to change. I hoped—I believed—someday he could find his own way to move forward. But in the meantime, I'd move on.

Because I couldn't regret the risk I'd taken. The police had dropped the charges against Tony. Verena was alive. And I'd do it all over again for any of the people in this room—even for Beatrice.

I traced my finger across the little golden coffin. Plus, we'd won a cool trophy for the tearoom.

"Sometimes," I murmured, "the risk *is* worth it."

"What was that, Abigail?" Gramps asked.

I looked at the people around me, new friends, old friends, and frenemies, and my heart swelled.

I raised my glass. "To joy."

Note from Kirsten:

After I returned from overseas, I worked briefly as a financial planner. It's something I still believe in—planning for the future isn't hard, but it is important—but managing other people's money got too stressful. There is a lot of sales involved, and I hated that part, so I quit to become a writer. On reflection, the switch to writing was the looniest and the best decision of my life. Sometimes, you just have to take the leap.

I haven't started the next book in the *Tea & Tarot* series, but there will definitely be one! (I'm thinking Christmas in the tearoom. And murder.) In the meantime…

If you laughed at the antics of Hyperion and Abigail, you won't want to miss Alice Sommerland in my new Big Murder Mystery series.

The first ebook in the series, Big Shot, is on sale for the special pre-order price of .99. Be sure to pick up your copy today at: **https://www.kirstenweiss.com/a-big-murder-mystery/big-shot**

Recipes

Chocolate Peanut Butter Cup Scones

Ingredients:
3 ¾ C bread flour
¼ C sugar
3 T baking powder
¼ C cocoa powder
¼ tsp salt
8 T cold unsalted butter
1 ¼ C milk
1 bag Reese's® Baking Cups and Reese's® Pieces Candy (or you could create your own mix).

Heat oven to 375 degrees F.

Mix flour, cocoa powder, sugar, baking powder, and salt in a medium-sized bowl. Cut butter into cubes and mix into the flour mixture with your fingers, crushing the butter, until the mix is coarse and sandy.

Add milk and stir until almost combined. Add bag of Reese's and mix in. You may need to add extra milk, a tablespoon at a time, until the mix is incorporated.

Knead dough in the bowl. Roll out to 1" thick. Cut squares 2 ½ inches in diameter, or cut into triangular wedges 2 ½ inches at the base.

Bake on ungreased cookie sheet until light golden brown. Circles take approximately 15 minutes. Triangles will usually take 20-25 minutes.

* You can use all-purpose flour instead of bread flour, and it will give the scones a denser, more cookie-like texture. Bread flour will "lighten" up the scones, so they're a bit more like biscuits (but not—they're still scones).

Cranberry-Orange Scones

Ingredients:
3 ¾ C bread flour*
¼ C sugar
3 T baking powder
2 T grated orange rind
1 tsp cinnamon
¼ tsp salt
8 T cold unsalted butter
1 C dried cranberries
1 ¼ C milk

Heat oven to 375 degrees F.

Mix flour, sugar, baking powder, cinnamon, grated orange rind and salt in a medium-sized bowl. Cut butter into cubes and mix into the flour mixture with your fingers, crushing the butter, until the mix is coarse and sandy.

Add milk and stir until almost combined. Add dried cranberries and mix in. You may need to add extra milk, a tablespoon at a time, until the mix is incorporated.

Knead dough in the bowl. Roll out to 1" thick. Cut circles 2 ½ inches in diameter, or cut into triangular wedges 2 ½ inches at the base.

Bake on ungreased cookie sheet until light golden brown. Circles take approximately 15 minutes. Triangles will usually take 20-25 minutes.

* You can use all-purpose flour instead of bread flour, and it will give the scones a denser, more cookie-like texture. Bread flour will "lighten" up the scones, so they're a bit more like biscuits (but not — they're still scones).

Justice Tea

Because honeysuckle is an herb which corresponds to the Justice card in Tarot, Beanblossom's justice tea is a honeysuckle blend. They serve it in a glass teapot. It looks and tastes lovely, and it's simple!

2 parts dried honeysuckle
5 parts dried rose buds

Boil water. Let it sit for a minute or two. If it's too hot, it can scorch the honeysuckle and change the flavor. Steep 1-2 teaspoons of the tea for five minutes (preferably in filtered or spring water) and enjoy!

Book Club Discussion Sample Questions

- For the person who selected the book: What made you want to read *Never Say Chai?*
- What did you like about *Never Say Chai?*
- What didn't you like about the book?
- At what point in the book did you begin to piece together whodunit?
- What hidden clues did you find in the book?
- How important was the Halloween season to the book?
- How did *Never Say Chai* make you feel?
- What did you think about how the story was told? E.g., was it too fast? Too slow?
- Was there any line or passage that stood out to you?
- Have you read other books by Kirsten? How did they compare to this book?
- Which recurring themes did you notice throughout the book?
- Did Abigail and Hyperion feel real to you?
- How would this story change if it were told from Hyperion's perspective?
- Agatha Christie wrote she disliked mysteries having a romantic subplot. Do you agree or disagree with her views? Do you feel the romantic element here enhanced or detracted from the story?
- If you turned this book into a movie, what sections would you cut?
- What did you think about the ending?
- How does this book compare to other mystery novels you've read?

More Kirsten Weiss

The Perfectly Proper Paranormal Museum Mysteries

When highflying Maddie Kosloski is railroaded into managing her small-town's paranormal museum, she tells herself it's only temporary... until a corpse in the museum embroils her in murders past and present.

If you love quirky characters and cats with attitude, you'll love this laugh-out-loud cozy mystery series with a light paranormal twist. It's perfect for fans of Jana DeLeon, Laura Childs, and Juliet Blackwell. Start with book 1, *The Perfectly Proper Paranormal Museum*, and experience these charming wine-country whodunits today.

The Tea & Tarot Cozy Mysteries

Welcome to Beanblossom's Tea and Tarot, where each and every cozy mystery brews up hilarious trouble.

Abigail Beanblossom's dream of owning a tearoom is about to come true. She's got the lease, the start-up funds, and the recipes. But Abigail's out of a tearoom and into hot water when her realtor turns out to be a conman... and then turns up dead.

Take a whimsical journey with Abigail and her partner Hyperion through the seaside town of San Borromeo (patron saint of heartburn sufferers). And be sure to check out the easy tearoom recipes in the back of each book! Start the adventure with book 1, *Steeped in Murder*.

The Wits' End Cozy Mysteries

Cozy mysteries that are out of this world...

Running the best little UFO-themed B&B in the Sierras takes organization, breakfasting chops, and a talent for turning up trouble.

The truth is out there... Way out there in these hilarious whodunits. Start the series and beam up book 1, *At Wits' End*, today!

Pie Town Cozy Mysteries
When Val followed her fiancé to coastal San Nicholas, she had ambitions of starting a new life and a pie shop. One broken engagement later, at least her dream of opening a pie shop has come true…. Until one of her regulars keels over at the counter.

Welcome to Pie Town, where Val and pie-crust specialist Charlene are baking up hilarious trouble. Start this laugh-out-loud cozy mystery series with book 1, *The Quiche and the Dead*.

The Doyle Witch Mysteries
In a mountain town where magic lies hidden in its foundations and forests, three witchy sisters must master their powers and shatter a curse before it destroys them and the home they love.

This thrilling witch mystery series is perfect for fans of Annabel Chase, Adele Abbot, and Amanda Lee. If you love stories rich with packed with magic, mystery, and murder, you'll love the Witches of Doyle. Follow the magic with the Doyle Witch trilogy, starting with book 1, *Bound*.

The Riga Hayworth Paranormal Mysteries
Her gargoyle's got an attitude.
Her magic's on the blink.
Alchemy might be the cure… if Riga can survive long enough to puzzle out its mysteries.

All Riga wants is to solve her own personal mystery — how to rebuild her magical life. But her new talent for unearthing murder keeps getting in the way…

If you're looking for a magical page-turner with a complicated, 40-something heroine, read the paranormal mystery series that fans of Patricia Briggs and Ilona Andrews call AMAZING! Start your next adventure with book 1, *The*

Alchemical Detective.

Sensibility Grey Steampunk Suspense
California Territory, 1848.
Steam-powered technology is still in its infancy.
Gold has been discovered, emptying the village of San Francisco of its male population.
And newly arrived immigrant, Englishwoman Sensibility Grey, is alone.
The territory may hold more dangers than Sensibility can manage. Pursued by government agents and a secret society, Sensibility must decipher her father's clockwork secrets, before time runs out.
If you love over-the-top characters, twisty mysteries, and complicated heroines, you'll love the Sensibility Grey series of steampunk suspense. Start this steampunk adventure with book 1, *Steam and Sensibility.*

Get Kirsten's Mobile App

Keep up with the latest book news, and get free short stories, scone recipes, and more by downloading Kirsten's mobile app.

Or make sure you're on Kirsten's email list. You can do that here:

KirstenWeiss.com

Leave a Review!

If you enjoyed the book (and even if you didn't), please **leave a review!** Reviews help readers and authors find each other. Here's the link to the review page on Amazon: **https://amzn.to/3Cos2ge**
And thank you in advance!

And if you REALLY enjoy leaving reviews, you might want to sign up for my read-and-review team on Booksprout to review future books:
https://booksprout.co/author/8142/kirsten-weiss

About the Author

I write laugh-out-loud, page-turning mysteries for people who want to escape with real, complex, and flawed but likable characters. If there's magic in the story, it must work consistently within the world's rules and be based in history or the reality of current magical practices.

I'm best known for my cozy mystery and witch mystery novels, though I've written some steampunk mystery as well. So if you like funny, action-packed mysteries with complicated heroines, just turn the page…

Connect with Kirsten

You can download my free app here:
https://kirstenweissbooks.beezer.com

Or sign up for my newsletter and get a special digital prize pack for joining, including an exclusive Tea & Tarot novella, *Fortune Favors the Grave*.
https://kirstenweiss.com

Or maybe you'd like to chat with other whimsical mystery fans? Come join Kirsten's reader page on Facebook:
https://www.facebook.com/kirsten.weiss

Or... sign up for my read-and-review team on Booksprout:
https://booksprout.co/author/8142/kirsten-weiss

Made in United States
Cleveland, OH
20 February 2025